I0682315

Perhaps A Butterfly
My Brother and His Sister

Milton Deemer &

Catherine Jeppe

Reed-Deemer Art Studios
Las Vegas, NM

Perhaps A Butterfly
Published by Reed-Deemer Art Studios 2021

This is a work of fiction. However, the historical events throughout the book actually happened, and every effort has been made to be as accurate as possible.

The main characters are fictional, and while some minor characters are loosely based on actual historical figures, their portrayals are purely fictional.

Revised First Edition
© 2021 Milton Deemer
All rights reserved.

ISBN: 978-1-7365355-1-6

Cover Art: Butterfly Dancer by Kimberly Reed-Deemer
© 2020 Kimberly Reed-Deemer

To three ladies:
Kim, my love, compass, and best friend
Ardythe, my critic, and Buddha,
And to my teacher, the real Cora Loomis

In the past
I fell asleep and dreamt I was a butterfly,
Flitting from blossom to bloom, free of burden.
Then I awoke. Now I do not know,
Am I a man dreaming to be a butterfly,
Or a butterfly dreaming she is a man?
A metamorphosis.

Chuang-Tzu
(4th century BCE)

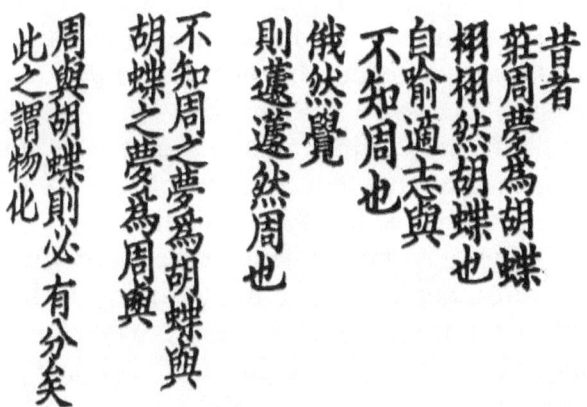

The Chinese script is quoted from "The Butterfly as
Companion" by Kuang-ming Wu, and reproduced here
with the kind permission of the State University of
New York Press, Albany, New York.

Chapter One

Our father lived in constant pain most of his life, and that affected both Sam and me in many ways.

His name was Frederick, and he was the third son of Karl and Gertrude Jeppe who owned a dairy farm near Racine, Wisconsin. One time Karl made a fife, and he gave it to Frederick. Father taught himself how to play it. One neighbor heard him and offered to teach Fredrick how to play the violin as well. Father played that the rest of his life.

As he grew up, Frederick discovered farming was not his cup of tea, but he did like wood carving, so he apprenticed himself to a cabinet maker in 1859. While splitting wood a splinter flew into his right eye damaging his sight. Nevertheless, when the Civil War began, he along with his brothers, joined the 2nd Wisconsin Volunteer Infantry Regiment. Because of his eyesight though, he was assigned ambulance duty. He was to drive a wagon filled with wounded soldiers from the battlefield to a dressing station well behind the battle line.

During the first major battle of the Civil War, Bull Run, the standardized uniform of Union blue had not taken effect. Wisconsin had issued gray uniforms to their troops, and there was great confusion because some of the Confederates likewise wore gray. As ordered, Frederick drove his wagon into the battle and retrieved those men he could. When he tried lifting a wounded and delirious Union officer into the ambulance, the man thought Father was a Southerner trying to take prisoners. The soldier drew a pistol and shot him.

At first the doctor thought the wound to Fredrick's abdomen was fatal. But the lead ball had missed the vital organs. However, it shattered a portion of his hip joint which never healed correctly. Thereafter he used a cane and was always in pain, especially when he walked. In those days people did not have the modern medicines we do today so they had to deal with discomfort in different ways. Frederick began using small amounts of alcohol to dull the pain.

After being released from the hospital, he returned to Wisconsin. His brothers ran the farm and while they were sympathetic toward Frederick and his injuries, they really didn't need his help. So, he left Racine and moved to Milwaukee in hopes of finding suitable work.

He found that a man who could not lift much and had trouble walking couldn't expect to find a good job. He tried being a night watchman, a worker in one of the many breweries, a driver on a horse trolley, and a bar tender. Nothing seemed to suit him. One day he saw a help wanted sign in the window of a small music shop. He immediately walked into "Diersdörfer's Instrument Sales and Repair." In a few minutes he had the job. The owner, Mendel Diersdörfer, was an older man who specialized in repairing stringed instruments. He also offered a selection of sheet music, musical accoutrements, and equipment for students and non-professionals.

Initially, Frederick's job was to tend the sales area leaving Mr. Diersdörfer free to concentrate on instrument repair. Frederick was well organized and easily handled the light customer traffic so there were times he had nothing to do.

Mr. Diersdörfer, being a good German businessman, noticed this idleness and assigned Frederick additional work, specifically, polishing and stringing instruments. This led to more and more work in the back room. Eventually Mr.

[2]

Diersdörfer hired another young man to handle the front and Frederick went to work as an assistant in the workshop where he learned the art of stringed instrument renovation.

***

One day a pretty, young lady, Miss Ada Kieffer, a music teacher in the public school came in the store. She brought a violin that had been knocked off a table by a rambunctious student. There was some damage, but the repairs were not difficult. Frederick was attracted to Miss Kieffer and so explained in great detail the repair process and she in return paid careful attention to him. Normally the repairs should only have taken a short time, however Frederick also replaced a cracked bridge and carefully polished out the scratches acquired through the use by beginning students, returning the instrument in excellent condition. Needless to say, Miss Kieffer was very impressed, while Mr. Diersdörfer was very amused.

A few weeks later Miss Kieffer returned with a viola that had certainly seen better days. It did not belong to the school, she explained, instead it had been given to her by a now deceased uncle. Frederick took on the project with great enthusiasm. He assured Miss Kieffer the cost would be minimal.

Mr. Diersdörfer was not amused at this. Frederick agreed with him to work on the viola during his lunch hour and Ada frequently stopped by to view the progress. She began to bring her lunch with her. Their mutual interest in music and in each other grew over the next few months. Their conversations spilled over to leisurely walks, eventually extending to lectures and concerts.

***

Let me tell you about our mother, Ada. She and her sisters were daughters of an upper middle-class couple. Her father was a banker, so the children were taught all the social

[3]

graces expected of young ladies in that day such as entertaining, dancing, music, reading, and writing.

Unfortunately, Grandpa Kieffer contracted cholera during the 1854 epidemic and died shortly thereafter. After an appropriate period of mourning, their mother, Sarah, remarried. While the man of the house was not unkind to his stepdaughters, he was overly strict and failed to show much affection toward them. So, it is not surprising that each girl moved from the home as quickly as their circumstances allowed.

Ada, being quite smart, and very independent, chose to move to Milwaukee where she lived with her Great Aunt Betty, and where she was hired to teach music in the public schools.

Single women in the 19th century had little personal freedom. They were to be protected from themselves and men supposedly seeking to take advantage of them. Thus, Aunt Betty was technically responsible for overseeing Ada's moral standing, but since she was in her early eighties, and one not caring much for tradition, Betty seemingly took little notice of Ada's activities. Actually, after meeting him the ever-smiling Aunt discreetly encouraged Ada's and Frederick's romance.

The school's principal was of greater concern because if he knew Ada was dating it would mean immediate dismissal. So, she strove to keep her relationship with Fredrick unimpeachable and undetected. After eight months Fredrick asked for her hand in marriage, and she accepted with the understanding the engagement would be kept secret till the end of the school year.

So, on a Saturday shortly after the end of school in 1866, Frederick and Ada had a simple wedding. A honeymoon was not financially possible, therefore on Sunday the newlyweds traveled to Chicago to visit Ada's mother and sisters. By Monday Frederick was back at work.

***

Of course, Ada knew of Frederick's physical disabilities and his medicinal use of alcohol. Although she did not imbibe herself, she was sensitive to his situation and felt neither his

[4]

disabilities nor the alcohol would interfere with family life. Besides Frederick didn't go to the bars to drink with the riffraff. Instead, at home, he would pour a glass of locally made Polish vodka and nurse it for hours. At work he kept a flask concealed in his coat. Mr. Diersdörfer knew he drank while working, but his work was excellent.

My parents found a three-room apartment above a store they could afford. When I was born in 1867 things were cramped, but when Samuel came along four years later, they were forced to move to an apartment house in a tenement district known as Kilbourn Town. The building was owned by a German and he made an effort to keep his investment in reasonable condition. Repairs were made as time allowed. Insects and rodents were kept to a minimum. As long as the rent was paid on time, he never bothered anyone.

Our home had two small bedrooms, a small sitting room, and a tiny kitchen in the back. The outhouses were located behind the building. A parent had to go with us when we needed to use them because they could be scary. At night and in very cold weather we used a chamber pot.

The apartment was on the east side of the second of three floors so in the morning the sitting room was often aglow with sunlight. Sam and I loved to play in there after warming up next to the kitchen wood stove. Aunt Betty had given Mother an oriental rug for a wedding present, and that filled much of the floor. Mother's platform rocking chair sat in one corner. It was off limits for Sam and me, but now and then we tempted fate and quietly sat in it. Next to the chair was a side table covered with a lace doily upon which sat the oil lamp and Mother's prize cut-glass vase, while the Bible was on the shelf below. A couple of small paintings given to her by one of her sisters decorated the wall behind the rocker. Taken together, the corner summoned an image of the fashionable Chicago home she had left.

It was agreed Mother could give violin lessons at home, and thus supplement Father's weekly pay. Therefore, opposite the rocker, two straight chairs and a wooden music stand stood waiting for a student. There was also a small bookcase that Father made. In it there were three shelves of marvelous books.

[5]

This room was our bastion from which we could survey the world's wonders by way of windows and books alike.

There were always five other families in the building. Across the hall, Mr. and Mrs. Schormuller had lived in their apartment a long time. Grandparent-like, they took a liking to Sam and me. I used to look forward to knocking on their door because they always had a spicy gingersnap in exchange for a recounting of our day's adventures. I still keep a box of those delicious cookies in the kitchen.

Other families in the building moved in and out, and often we barely knew their names. Some had children, others didn't. Some were nice, others were not. We used to play a game to see how quietly we could sneak by the apartments of those we didn't like so they wouldn't jump out and eat us.

For the most part, people lived peacefully. As the social graces required, adults would always stop to greet and chat with each other on the stairway during the day. However, during the night the darkness cast a spell of silence. People acknowledged one another but did not speak. Where they were going and what condition they were in was their business. Privacy was at a premium and it was respected by all. The walls were very thin, so residents usually tried to ignore everyday voices and sounds coming from other apartments, but it was hard to disregard arguments, crashes, and crying.

In our building all the women stayed home to care for children, keep house, and prepare the meals. Some, like Mother, did contribute money with side jobs such as sewing piecework, making artificial flowers, shelling nuts, or assembling small toys. One lady made quilts to sell at a dry goods store.

I used to wonder what the men did when they left their homes early in the morning and returned late in the evening. In reality most of them did whatever jobs they could find. A number worked in breweries or drove beer wagons. Another worked in a slaughterhouse. Still another worked on the docks. I remember a couple of men worked on the railroad. I was proud of Father because he did not come home dirty.

Because of the flow of families in and out of the apartment house, there were also a variety of languages spoken although German and broken English were the most common. This was no different than the rest of Kilbourn Town, and for that matter, much of Milwaukee. People also knew who could speak English well, so Mother often read legal documents and taught new immigrants basic words and phrases. In return, it wasn't long before I picked up German, French, Swedish, and Polish words and phrases and included them in conversations with my parents, much to their chagrin, but eventually it was a great benefit to me.

***

Sam developed asthma when he was young. I don't remember when because I was too small. I do remember all of us would occasionally go to a park, and Sam and I would run around chasing each other. If we played too long or too hard, he would have a hard time breathing, and he would have to sit for a while, sometimes the rest of the day. It was not much fun running by myself, so we just sat together and read, drew pictures or looked at things.

As we got older, he caught more colds than I did, and sometimes he would cough at night. He learned not to overtax himself and take frequent rests. He told me once he hated not being able to play sports with his friends, although he did play baseball. The other guys must have understood the problem because they made him permanent catcher, that way he wouldn't have to run much. He was pretty good too. No one tried to run past him when he had the ball because he would knock them down. He told me, "They have the whole field to run in, but home base is mine and they can't touch it."

Sam had a hard time in the winter weather though. He had to stay inside more than other children. During that time, he would either read or draw. When he did go out the cold made him wheeze, so he had to bundle up which aggravated him too. Other boys would wear a light jacket and hat, but he would have to have a heavy coat and muffler. Perhaps this was one reason he often chose to be by himself.

As we became adults, he rarely mentioned the asthma. Sometimes maybe he forgot about it, but probably he chose to

[7]

ignore it which was typical for Sam. Normally he didn't see things as barriers, they were just challenges. That approach to life worked to his advantage sometimes, but it caused real problems as you will see. Actually, I'm pretty much the same way. Possibly we both learned that from Father. I don't know.

***

The apartment was near Mr. Diersdörfer's shop, so six days a week Father could slowly walk to work except when it snowed, and he had to catch a horse-drawn streetcar. While the streets in our area were still dirt they had been graded and wooden sidewalks had been built not too long before so Sam and I could also walk down to the shop to visit every now and then.

Occasionally during warm weather Mother would let us take a special lunch to Father. She didn't worry about our safety because there were lots of people around, and then people looked after children more than they do today. Going to the shop was a reward the two of us always looked forward to because when you are young doing something on your own is very important. It is a sign to everyone you are responsible and growing up. Besides, if an adult accompanies a child the child knows they are like so much baggage. They go where the adult goes. They go at the adult's speed. They stop when the adult stops. But when you are alone, the trip is like visiting an entirely different world. You can go at your own speed, stop to look at anything you want, or listen to sounds an adult ignores. Time ceases to exist. There is only the moment. So it was for Sam and me.

Our apartment windows looked out upon a narrow side street which was usually rather quiet with only the occasional pedestrian or horse cart passing by. On the other hand, our trips took us to a main thoroughfare which was always busy. Everything on that street seemed to move to an unconscious rhythm. People hurrying from one place to another performed a waltz of courtesy. Wagons of every description carrying people, wood, iron, grain, and any other imaginable material supplied the percussive beat reinforced by hundreds of horses'

[8]

hooves on dry dirt. Even pigeons, in search of a morsel, moved between rolling wheels and peoples' boots with the grace of ballerinas. Added to that, church bells, clock chimes, train whistles, boat and factory whistles from both near and far helped create a symphony that had no beginning and no end, yet the composition was complete at any point. Blanketing everything were the odors of manure, cooking food, factory smoke, and the occasional whiff of women's perfume.

Amongst all this confusion were the many shop windows to peer through, signs to interpret, doors to consider, and spooky alleys to avoid. Some windows displayed common things such as clothes, food, or furniture. Some windows were curtained off which only added to their mystery. Some signs like "Shoes" were clear to us while others like "Drug Store" meant nothing to our young minds. Others were only names followed by letters such as M.D. or Atty.

***

Mr. Diersdörfer's shop door had a small bell that rang announcing a customer's entry or exit. Once inside, a customer found the sales area clean, well-stocked, well-organized and not very interesting, but if they were as fortunate as we and they got to go in the backroom they found a workshop that was a strange, cluttered wonderland.

There were rows of hanging violins, violas, cellos, and guitars. Sometimes a double base was propped in a dark corner. Wooden shelves were piled with all sorts of strange shapes, cat gut strings, cans, and boxes of odds and ends. The workbenches, each under its own small window, looked as if they had been there for a hundred years. Little hammers, knives, chisels, clamps, small planes, pieces of sandpaper, and a heated glue pot lay about in a jumble. Meager light allowed one to see cans of varnish, different polishes, brushes, and scraps of cloth on nearby shelves. Wood shavings, curls, and especially sawdust pervaded everything while a pungent odor of pipe smoke hung in the air.

On one side of the central wood stove sat Mr. Diersdörfer firmly positioned on a straight-backed chair, his

[9]

pipe swooping down in a gentle curve unlike father's straight stem. Beyond the warm, friendly greeting, "Hello *meine lieben Kinder*" he rarely spoke. He always wore a long blue denim apron covering a typical dark wool suit which showed distinct wear marks. He had a white shirt with frayed cuffs and collar, and a neat black bow tie. His wire-rimmed glasses along with his obligatory salt and pepper mustache, like his workbench, were always covered with a thin layer of wood dust.

Father's work bench was on the other side of the wood stove and duplicated Mr. Diersdörfer's, although it was a little neater. He too sat on a side chair, but a pillow cushioned its hard seat while his cane was always wedged between the workbench and a shelf.

Usually, the men seemed oblivious to one another and their surroundings, instead they were always engrossed in the minutia of their work. Occasionally the solitude would be broken when an instrument was finished, and it was auditioned. First it was tuned, and then reintroduced to the world with a fragment of Mozart, Beethoven or Brahms that brightened everything within earshot, even though it seemed totally out of place in the dusty workspace. Once, to my delight, they finished their respective projects at the same time and joined in a lively jig. I don't think it was the first nor the last time they did that.

Thinking back, the scene reminds me of two cloistered monks practicing their daily rituals within a monastery. While they were deep in their personal solitude, Sam and I were left alone to explore. We would begin by politely watching the men work or carefully examining an unused tool as if we were evaluating one of the violins. When we first started visiting the shop, both of us asked questions to which the masters inevitably responded with "watch and learn" so we stopped asking. Watching didn't always answer our questions, but it was good practice.

After tiring of watching instruments being repaired, we would wander among the instruments themselves. At first glance they seemed to be endlessly repeated copies differing only in subtle color and size. Upon closer examination though,

[10]

I discovered each instrument was unique. I realized a musical instrument assumed the characteristics of its owner. After extended use any instrument will show discolorations and wear spots caused by hands playing the same notes over and over again. If the musician was conscientious and respected the instrument, there was a soft glow from it, a smoothness to the touch, an almost undefinable warmth to it. But if the owner was uncaring and rough, the wood was dull, often scratched, dented, and stained. I tried to imagine people playing these wonderful instruments whether in a beautiful salon or a dirty third floor walk-up and I created stories to go with the instruments.

For me, the workshop and other buildings surrounding us were points of departure to worlds far beyond the limits of Milwaukee. They were a springboard to the world beyond my imagination.

***

Another pathway to the world beyond Milwaukee was through books. As far back as I can remember, Mother read to us as her mother had read to her. There were nursery rhymes at first, but soon she started reading serious literature. Sometimes the books were hers, sometimes they came from a nearby library. Each day after lunch, we would gather in the sitting room to hear the next chapter of a novel by Robert Lewis Stevenson, Louisa May Alcott, James Fenimore Cooper, Emily Bronte, or my favorite, Charles Dickens.

At times other children and their mothers would be invited to join us, then Mother had quite an audience. She was a born teacher, and I could tell when she was drawn into a story because she would change her voice for each character and then stop to explain a difficult passage.

We grew up knowing that not all people looked like us. But whether people wore togas or turbans, kilts or kimonos, and whether they were heroes or villains, whether they were fabulously rich or desperately poor, whether they might be someone who built their lives around a single idea, or sailed

[11]

the earth looking for adventure, we learned deep down, people are pretty much all the same.

***

Back then it was not unusual for people to keep a journal or diary for their own reference to past events or ideas. Often the mundane was entered such as the weather and daily activities. Other times deep thoughts were set to words. Our mother decided early on that her children were going to practice the art of writing and they were going to do so in their journals. With that decision made, we spent some time every day working on an entry. With our pencils and necessary erasers each would retreat to her or his private corner to remember and organize the adventures of the day, and the thoughts and ideas resulting from them. Mother would then carefully read each entry and make comments. When one was done well the writer would be rewarded with a small cookie or biscuit, but if the entry was found wanting there would be no reward and a failing effort resulted in erasure and the patient demand for another try. This might seem harsh, but her standards were high. She expected her children, and her students, to do the best they could do. Her approach was at times frustrating to me, but I learned to expect nothing less from myself.

Sam used most of his time describing things he saw while looking out the window or going around the neighborhood. He had exacting, dispassionate descriptions, almost scientific. He illustrated his entries with pencil drawings. For instance, his account of a disorderly horse would lead the reader step by step through the entire event from the first snort to the final commands of the owner, topped by a drawing of the horse. His style was perfect for an academic life, although he certainly would have been a fine reporter.

I, on the other hand, relished the chance to write fiction, and often spent several hours a day composing imaginary scenes based on a passage in the current novel. I almost always portrayed the heroine emerging victorious over severe

[12]

odds or rescuing an important man. I tried using language beyond my understanding which frequently brought a reprimand from my Mother. However, in the end, those writing exercises helped me harbor a life-long love affair with words which I have never regretted.

Chapter Two

Up to this point I haven't mentioned our brother Edward. He was born in 1876 when I was nine and Sam was five. As a young child Edward loved to laugh. He saw something funny in almost everything. He was quick to learn and got into everything causing our parents great aggravation at times. Since I was the eldest, I was assigned to watch him and Sam while Mother was fixing meals, doing laundry, or giving lessons. I didn't like this job as I had other things I would rather be doing, but I had to do it. While I was overseer, Sam might be self-absorbed in looking at a picture book or drawing a picture, or building something with the wooden shapes that Father made at the shop. Edward, on the other hand, would usually be climbing on the furniture or wanting to play hide-and-seek. I recall he sometimes made me angry for which I still feel guilt.

Edward was never very strong. Like Sam, he seemed to catch any bug that happened by, so he was frequently coughing or sneezing. When he was four one of the boys in the apartment house got the measles. It quickly spread. Both Sam and I got them. A few days later Edward came down with them too. With Sam and I the disease ran its course, and we felt fine after a short time. Edward did not recover quickly. His rash was worse than ours and covered much of his body. Then he started coughing and had chills and just shook. He had trouble breathing. Father moved Edward's bed next to the window in the front room so he could look out and he laid there coughing, or fitfully sleeping, or just looking out at the buildings across the street. Mother sat by the bed hour after hour wiping his forehead with a wet cloth. He no longer

[14]

laughed or even smiled but became very quiet. He complained that his chest hurt. A doctor came. However, at that time no one really knew how to treat many diseases. My parents did what they could. I remember they gave him garlic to eat; they made a steam tent to help his breathing and rubbed smelly turpentine on his chest. Nothing seemed to help. A short time later Edward died.

For both Sam and me, Edward's death was a strange event. We had not experienced a death before and didn't entirely understand it. We were both frightened and curious at the same time. The idea that he was gone forever was too hard for us to understand. In a way the impact of his death was swept aside by events following his funeral because for us it was our parents that truly shook our little world.

***

When we were young, neither Sam nor I ever paid much attention to Father's drinking, and so we didn't realize that he began drinking more after Edward's death. However, we did know that he was moody and argumentative. At times, his face was tense and angry. His mouth was pursed tightly, his eyes narrowed. There were times he refused to go to work, choosing instead to sit and look out the same window that Edward had. He no longer visited, instead he used one- or two-word answers to a question. More and more frequently, he ignored people altogether. It seemed as if he was somewhere else other than our apartment. This upset the two of us, and we thought we had done something to make him angry. We were afraid of him and tried to stay out of sight.

Mother too lost interest in things. I saw her just staring at the wall. She had a gaunt, scowling look that never changed. Was she angry at us too? I became angry at Edward because it was his fault they were like this, not ours.

Father wouldn't and Mother couldn't shoulder the entire weight of the family, so Sam and I pretty much had to fend for ourselves. Neither of us could handle the stress that had invaded our home, so often we would go out on the streets. I went window shopping, perhaps looking for a happier life.

[15]

Some shops sold things I wanted, others didn't. It didn't matter, I looked at everything. I remember asking Sam where he went, and he said that mostly he went to the vacant lot a block away where there were weeds, flowers, birds, and insects because they were fun to watch and be near without having people around. Neither Sam nor I kept up on our journals, but Mother didn't care. There was no music in the evening.

Finally, after a terrible argument about Father's drinking, Mother went to Chicago to visit her sister. She stayed away for what seemed like a long time although it was probably no more than ten days. Regardless, the result was that Sam's and my world completely fell apart. First our brother had died and now Mother was gone. I was truly frightened. I didn't know what was going to happen to me.

After Mother left, Sam became angry and fought with anyone who confronted him. He began to leave the apartment and disappear for a length of time. His absences became longer till he started missing meals. Father told Sam he was shirking his duties around the house or just being lazy. Sam shot back that Father had no room to talk because he was just a drunk. With that, Sam walked out and was gone till quite late at night.

I think the argument scared them both. Father stopped criticizing Sam so much, and Sam began taking more interest in the apartment. He started doing chores around the house as long as he had some time to return to his world of nature. As the older sister, I could have directed him, but I hesitated to say anything for fear of making him angry again, so we did our jobs silently. Because of all those events, Sam and I grew to respect each other. We treated each other as equals, and in doing that became good friends during that terrible time and remained so ever after. We learned to trust each other. We talked as friends, not brother and sister. Interestingly, he started making entries in his journal again.

***

During all this I had turned thirteen. I resented having the responsibilities of keeping house forced on me. I knew I

[16]

was old enough to take on those duties because many girls my age were working full time jobs in factories and breweries or employed as servants in wealthy homes. I certainly had the knowledge to do what was needed, but on the other hand, my own interests lay elsewhere. I wanted to be around lively people, to talk to them and be where there was excitement. I liked living in the city and felt cheated when I was made to be a *Hausfrau*.

Many times, I had seen the women of the building informally gather on the building's front steps in the afternoon even on cooler days, still I had never paid much attention. Now I wandered down too, standing in the background in self-imposed isolation, just listening. In addition to the usual chatter and gossip, I began hearing stories of happiness and tragedy, of hopes and misery, of treachery and deceit or, now and then, of success and rewards.

For instance, there was Lotte. She was a middle-aged woman, thin and drawn with tinges of gray mixed in her plain brown hair. Her hands and face were toughened by years of hot sun, hard work, and lye soap. Actually, she didn't look that much different from the other women sitting there. She was usually quiet, neither asking questions, nor contributing to the conversation. The previous few days her three older children all had the whooping cough, and the strain of long days and sleepless nights was showing in her usually unemotional face.

One of the women casually asked how her children were getting along. Lotte angrily turned saying, "They are not my children. They are the children by John and his second wife. He had two sons by his first wife before she died. He remarried, and he and his second wife had these three nice children. She died in a fire when they were small, bless her soul. John just wanted me to just live with him because he needed the help, but I would have none of that, so he married me. I had no way to support myself, so I had no other choice." After a pause she continued, "Sorry, I did not mean to speak sharply, I am tired."

One of the others said, "You are a good woman, Lotte James. You'll be rewarded in heaven."

[17]

Lotte shot back, "I tell ye, I hope so because I shan't be rewarded here. I hope I'll be the first to go over because when John passes, everything, I mean everything, will go to his eldest sons, those two rascals. They don't like me or these children, so we will end up on the street with only the clothes on our backs. It doesn't say much for a life, does it."

All were quiet, not in shock, but in sympathy. They all could be in her shoes.

The building's front steps offered never-ending stories that constantly evolved, and I began to look forward to hearing the next chapters. I began writing in my journal again I suppose partly as an escape, but now my entries were different. Before, I wrote about the imagined glamour and glitter of others, now I wrote down this and other stories shared by the women on the steps, things seemingly held in common by all women.

***

It would be nice to say Father realized he had been acting irresponsibly toward Mother, Sam, and me, but his was a harder row to hoe. He had grown dependent on alcohol long before, so it was natural to turn to it more often now. If alcohol masked his physical pain, it was easy to drink to mask the emotional pain of losing Edward. It was just a matter of pouring another glass.

Sam and I had different reactions when Mother returned. To Sam, her absence was no different than if she had gone to visit grandmother for a few days. She was back and things could now return to normal. On the other hand, to me, she was the link that held our family together, and I felt she had abandoned us, she had abandoned me. I wasn't old enough to realize even the strongest chain link can gradually weaken and snap, so I had a hard time forgiving her.

In any case, the time away had allowed her to regain her strength and equilibrium. Now she was more patient with Father, she quietly talked to him. Little by little he began to talk to her. One evening, they were sitting together in the front room while we were on the floor. All was quiet, then I noticed

[18]

tears running down his cheeks. He was taking deep breaths, each accented by a shudder. Mother was watching him as well. She motioned us to leave. Sam and I silently went to our bedroom. We held each other's hand and listened. It remained quiet for a few minutes, then he groaned as if he was mortally injured. The dam had burst. Father could not talk through his sobs, just the word "why?" repeatedly leaked out.

Sam and I were crying as well. We sat on our beds for what seemed like an eternity. We could hear low murmurings separated by periods of silence. Now and then Father or Mother cried again. It was plain to us that he had been in terrible pain and had been unable to let it show. After a while, Mother came into our room. Her tear-streaked face was calmer than I'd seen it since Edward became ill. Wordlessly she kissed us goodnight and left. The only thing I remember hearing the rest of the night was their bedroom door closing.

The two of us didn't know what to expect the next morning so we both tried to be even more helpful than usual. Strangely enough, there was very little talk. Everyone tried to avoid looking at the others. We were just intent on performing our roles as well as we could. Father and Mother hugged for a long time and talked quietly. Then he took his lunch box in one hand and cane in the other and left for work.

Like a body that has been severely injured, it took a long time for our family to recover. At first, talk dealt with the necessary, later the mundane, and then the trivial, but gradually emotions were displayed, and plans were made. Sam and I knew things were getting better when Mother asked to see our journals. She read them carefully, handed them back saying we had both done well, and she no longer needed to read them. This saddened me because I was proud of my writing, but at the same time, I felt more grown up. I don't think my parents ever completely recovered from Edward's death.

[19]

Chapter Three

Neither Sam nor I were very good students in school, but then the schools were pretty poor, so it balanced out. Having taught, Mother knew what schools were like. So not only did she drill us on arithmetic, writing and reading, she also taught us about current events, economics, government, and anything else she could think of.

We also taught ourselves each in her or his own way. I watched people on the street as they hurried from one place to another. Conversely, Sam preferred to be away from people. His favorite place to go was the previously mentioned vacant lot a few doors down the street.

The lot had been vacant a long time and to most people there was nothing much to see. To a burgeoning naturalist though, it was a land of adventure. A few small trees and a variety of weeds offered homes to birds. Insects appeared and disappeared according to the season and there were always clouds to watch. Sam was truly at home by himself.

One day he wrote in his journal, "I was at the lot this afternoon drawing a picture of some leaves when a lady with a satchel came up behind me and asked what I was doing. She scared me and I said I was sorry for going on her property. She laughed and said it wasn't her property, but she had seen me a number of times and wondered if I was making observations. I didn't know what she meant. She explained that is the term for watching something for a long time to chart any changes. I said then I guess I was making observations because I liked to see the plants grow. She asked to see my drawing and I showed it to her. I said it wasn't good, but she said, 'quite the contrary young man, it is very good, however you need to strengthen the lines representing the important characteristics.' Then she set down her satchel, took my pencil and did that. It looks much better now. She said it was a Hollyhock, genus Alcea."

She introduced herself as Miss Cora Loomis and she hoped Sam would continue observing and drawing. It wasn't long before he would arrange to be in the vacant lot each day about that time and she would stop, look at his work, and talk about the plants and animals around them.

***

It turned out that Miss Loomis was a scientist, a geologist to be exact. She was working on the new Museum of Natural History's rock collection trying to get it in order so it could be put on exhibit when the museum opened. Within a short time, Sam and Cora Loomis became good friends and she invited him to come with her to the museum. Mother was quite interested, although she was a little suspicious so on the appointed day, we all met Miss Loomis and accompanied her to the museum. On the way there she began telling us about herself.

Cora was formerly married to a wealthy gentleman geologist. That means he was a self-taught amateur. She learned to assist him in the classification of specimens in his collection and drew illustrations for his articles. He often went on extended collecting trips, leaving her at home. During his absences she read extensively and corresponded with other geologists and in time became very good at identifying rocks and minerals. In addition, she also taught herself chemistry, geometry and mineralogy, paleontology, and botany.

When her husband was killed, she rewrote their notes and published them under both their names. Experts in the field became acquainted with her and she was hired to organize collections. That's how she ended up at the Milwaukee Museum of Natural History. She had a small apartment a few blocks from the museum. On her travels to and from the

[21]

museum she saw Samuel, and became curious, so she stopped to visit.

***

Mother and Cora were visiting about apartments when the four of us reached the Milwaukee Industrial Exposition Building that was to be the home of the museum. The monstrous building took up an entire city block. The interior was cavernous with a huge area in the middle that was open to the roof three or four stories above us. The skylights helped the electric lights illuminate the space below where workers were setting up an agricultural exposition.

The museum's rock collection was in one of the basement storerooms. When Miss Loomis unlocked the door, I could see wooden boxes filled with rocks stored on sturdy bookshelves, although one bookcase really did hold books, and journals. Large tables covered with rocks, bottles of chemicals and other unknown things filled the central area. To one side a desk was decorated with a single oil lamp, papers, several books and a magnifying glass. A series of small windows high on one wall and a single electric bulb provided the only light so overall the room was rather dim.

Miss Loomis unpacked her ever present satchel which contained a sack lunch, and several more books. With little introduction Cora began ordering Sam to unpack this box, repack that box, find yet another box. I was drafted into action and was told and to get such and such book from the bookcase or "the library" and look up a certain type of mineral. She did not order Mother to do anything, so she was left to wandered around and look at things. While we were busy doing these things, Miss Loomis was examining rocks and making notes. All the while she talked about types of rocks and minerals. Sam wrote in his journal, "I don't know what she was saying most of the time and I had no chance to ask questions, so I tried following Father's rule, 'watch and learn.' I did learn a little, but it felt like I was drowning and still she talked." Mother said her good-byes at lunch which told me she was satisfied that all was as it should be. I was impressed with

[22]

Miss Loomis and her straightforward approach to things. Even so, I was happy to return to the world of living things having learned more about rocks than I ever wanted to know. When she was packing her satchel, she said this was a good day and could Sam come back tomorrow? Acting as the family's spokesman I told her I'd ask Mother, but I was sure he could if he wanted. She said, "I know there is a lot to learn, still Sam has a sharp mind and I think we will get along just fine."

***

Sam did return the next day and for many days following. When school began, he was restricted to an hour or so in the late afternoons and on Saturdays. The next summer he was at the museum five or six days a week. As his experience and knowledge grew so did his enthusiasm for the subject. Geology books started to appear at home accompanied by more complicated drawings, and what was more interesting Sam began paying more attention to his schoolwork. Mathematics, and history were given increased attention and even his writing improved because apparently Miss Loomis had said his spelling "was atrocious." Our parents were somewhat pleasantly surprised at the change in him, and they did what they could to encourage his efforts. For Christmas, he was given a rock hammer and it stayed with him for many years. Sadly, he stopped visiting the vacant lot. It was as if he had outgrown it and I suppose in a way he had.

Early in 1884 the collection was finished in time to be placed on exhibit. Sam was worried that Cora would leave, but the museum offered her the position of assistant curator which she happily accepted. Looking back, she should have been made curator, but since she was a woman, she was not considered. Eventually the big day arrived and the Jeppe family walked down together to the exposition building. The museum was impressive without a doubt.

"I helped pick out specimens for this exhibit," Sam stated with pride when we walked into the geology room.

[23]

"You certainly did," came a voice behind us. Miss Loomis joined us. Looking at our parents she continued, "He has been invaluable to me and to the museum".

Father spoke, "Miss Loomis, all this is certainly most wonderful." He seemed a little unsure of what to say, but added, "Thank you for letting him help. It sure has made a big difference in him. I think he's found himself."

"What a lucky person he is then," she replied, looking at Sam. "To find one's self at such a young age. Many of us search our whole lives and never manage to achieve that goal. If I had anything to do with it I am most pleased, but I'm sure my role was quite small. You and Ada have done a fine job of raising your children."

Embarrassed Sam looked at his feet and mumbled "I wish it wasn't all over."

"Whatever do you mean, young man," Miss Loomis looked at him sharply. "Our work has just begun. I'll need you as long as you care to come."

"Really?" a grin began to spread across his face.

"Really. Now we can do some real research and if we're lucky maybe a publication or two." She looked both at Sam and my parents to emphasize the honesty of her statement.

"Gosh," was his only reply.

***

Perhaps in response to Sam's success or maybe because it was just time, I began to think about what I wanted to do with my life. I decided that writing might be just the thing. I considered writing stories and publishing them, however I had no idea how to begin. The only other thing I could think of was newspaper reporting.

Women had been hired as reporters for a few years. Nellie Bly was the most famous, although there were others, one even in Milwaukee. A girl friend of mine suggested I take writing samples to the editor of a newspaper and ask to be hired. We decided the Milwaukee Journal would be the best bet since it was new.

[24]

I carefully copied three of my best pieces, feeling that should be enough to show how well I could write, but not so much they would discover I didn't know what I was doing. I wore my best outfit which made me look as mature as I could. Walking up to the receptionist's desk, and in a meek voice I asked for the editor.

"Which editor?"

"Hmm, THE Editor."

"Honey, there are lots of editors, the Managing Editor, the Editorial Editor, the City Editor, the State Editor, the Business Editor, the Layout Editor, which one?"

I almost turned and ran, but I leaned over and quietly said, "I...want to be a reporter."

"Oh, you should have said so. Honey, I think you should talk to Mr. Davies in the Home Department. He's probably the nicest of a bad bunch. Do you have a writing sample?"

I waved the sheets to show her.

"Let me see them," she said with authority. She quickly flipped through them and handed them back. "At least they're in ink, neatly written and the words appear to be spelled right. You'd be surprised how many girls come in with erasure marks, creases, misspellings – it's terrible the way schools turn out illiterates. Now, don't be discouraged if he throws you out. A lot of people come looking for jobs here because they think they are the next Nellie Bly."

I almost blushed.

She eyed me carefully. "Uh-huh, just remember what you want, a job, any job. Something that gets your foot in the door. Tomorrow you can think about bylines."

What's a byline?"

"Never mind, just make him want to hire you and the rest will take care of itself. Good luck. The Home Department is up the stairs and turn to your right. Ask for Mr. Davies in person."

I quickly climbed the stairs and on the door I read "Home Department". Again, I felt weak when I opened the door and faced yet another receptionist.

[25]

"I'd like to speak to Mr. Davies," I said in a somewhat stronger voice.

"He's not here. Can I help you?"

"I don't think so, I need to talk to Mr. Davies."

"Well, he's not here. You can either leave your writing samples with me or wait till he returns which should be tomorrow at the earliest."

"How did you know these are writing samples?"

"Just a good guess, besides Rebecca is on the front desk and she always sends girls in here. Let me take a look at your stuff and I can tell you if you stand a chance."

So, for the second time I handed my future to a total stranger.

After what seemed like an eternity, she handed them back. "Not bad, not bad. At least you spelled the words right, and you have a good concise writing style."

I shook my head knowingly.

"I'll tell you what, leave the samples with me and give me your address so we can contact you." I looked doubtful. "Don't worry, we'll get the samples back to you one way or another. By the way, do you speak German?"

"*Oh ja, ich sprechen sehr gut Deutsch*," I said very clearly.

"It's s*preche* not '*sprechen*', but it'll do."

I left my name and address with Miss Gunther and hurried out passing the receptionist, Rebecca.

"Any success?" she asked.

"I don't know. Mr. Davies wasn't there, at least the receptionist liked what I wrote."

"Honey, Davies is there, he just doesn't want to be interrupted. Besides Gertrude Gunther makes a lot of the hiring decisions in the department, and she wouldn't keep your samples if she didn't think you could do the job. Congratulations, you may be a reporter." I floated out.

***

I won't bore you with the details except to say I got the job and worked at the Journal for two years reporting on

[26]

German social and cultural events. Eventually I wanted to try writing real news stories. Since the City Department editor refused to consider a woman reporter I began looking elsewhere. I had always thought of Milwaukee as uncultured, and rough. Even though I'd never been there, my idea of the height of preeminence was New York City. Therefore, I had my heart set on going to there to be part of the glitter and glamour.

At that time, the thought of a young single girl from Milwaukee moving to New York City alone was ridiculous. I argued with my parents for weeks. I told them I was old enough to live on my own. I reminded them I was only two days away, I could write often, and there was always the telegraph. Eventually they relented after making arrangements for me to stay with a friend of Mother's who lived there. It probably didn't hurt that my mother had made such a move at my age.

Following a long train ride, and numerous application forms, I got a job with a weekly entertainment publication that tided me over till I found just the right job with the New York Herald, a sensationalist paper. Over time, I became a bit pushy and perhaps a bit loud, but people read what I wrote. I became a real newspaper reporter.

Chapter Four

About a year after I had moved to New York a catastrophic event changed our family forever. It began innocently enough with Mother's slight dry cough. She attributed it to a cold and ignored it. A few weeks later she developed chest pains. When that went away, it too was forgotten. A month later she did mention in one of her letters that she was having trouble sleeping. Shortly after that letter, Sam wrote:

> Mother has come down with a terrible cold. She
> coughs constantly, a deep cough that hurts to hear
> to it. When she is not coughing, she is constantly
> clearing her throat, so she does not get much rest.
> She does not eat very much. I can tell both she and
> Father are worried. He and I are fine.

After that, mother did not write as often, and I could see from her handwriting she was weak. Her reports though were always positive. Things were always getting better. I did notice she began to offer advice which she rarely had done before. She said, "I know we have not always seen eye to eye, but Catherine you are a very good writer, don't stop, don't be sidetracked. Don't be afraid of taking the rough road if it leads you to where you want to be." She also began reminiscing, "It has turned out much differently for me than I thought it would. There are things I have always wanted to do, but never had the chance. Still, I am very happy and would not have done differently." Something deep inside told me should go back

[28]

and see her, but I was busy and chose to believe Sam when he wrote:

> Mother said to tell you she is doing better and not to worry. I do think she is quite sick, but I am taking care of her and keeping house and doing the cooking. The ladies of the building are helping a lot. Father is holding up pretty well. He goes to work every day and then he does the shopping. In the evenings he sits by her bed and visits or plays the violin. He does not drink any more than usual.

After a couple of these reassuring, but distressing letters, I spoke about her to a physician who was a friend. As I described her condition he became very serious and quiet. He asked some additional questions and then said, "Without seeing her I cannot be sure, Catherine, but the symptoms you describe are similar to consumption." That was the name for tuberculosis back then. It was one of the most feared diseases because there was no cure like there is now. That night I began making arrangements to go to Milwaukee. The very next day I received a letter.

Father rarely wrote letters, so when I saw the envelope in his handwriting, I avoided opening it for several hours:

> *My Dear Catherine,*
> *I am sorry to tell you that Mother died last night. She fell asleep in the evening and just never awoke. Sam and I are alright. The funeral will be in two days so I do not know if you can come in time. You must do as you think best.*
> > *Love,*
> > *Father*

The letter was postmarked four days previous. My mother had died, and I had missed her funeral. I was devastated and angry at the same time. I fired off a telegram to Father accusing both of them of being thoughtless. I could have made it home in time, but deep down I knew it was not their fault.

If someone had asked me who I was angry at I couldn't have told them. In reality, I was angry at everyone. I was angry at Mother for dying. I was angry at Father for not telegraphing me when she died. I was angry at Sam for not being honest with me throughout the illness. But mostly I was angry at myself for ignoring the all the signs of her illness.

***

About a month later I felt calm enough to make the trip to Milwaukee and maintain my composure. Sam had written to say Father had not handled the situation very well. I was afraid Mother's death would drive him back to alcohol.

When I arrived and during the exchange of small talk, I watched Father. He hadn't shaved in some time, and he needed a change of clothes. The thing that struck me though was how much he had aged. I had always seen him as a thin-bodied, proud man with a slight limp. Now however, he was a straggly old man who shuffled across the room in search of his bottle of vodka. His hair was completely gray with streaks of white throughout. His vacant eyes no longer sparkled. Any pride had been diluted by alcohol and grief.

Samuel was coping as well as he could although I could see he was tired. His young face showed strain where none should be. The apartment was messy, but they had enough to eat although it was pretty plain fare. He was still going to school but missed classes frequently. He said he had only gone to the museum a few times to escape the situation at home.

Of great concern to Sam was their meager savings was just about gone and the rent was due. Most of Mother's things were still in place as if she had just stepped out. But unbeknownst to Father, Sam had sold a few small things at a secondhand shop for food money.

That evening after Father slipped into unconsciousness, Sam said, "I do not know what to do. Everything is hopeless. I never realized how Mother held the family together. You have to help me."

[30]

I was frustrated and replied sharply, "I don't know what to do either, do you think he can stop drinking?"

"There is no reason for him to stop, so I think he will just drink himself to death and at this point, I do not care," he said in anger. "You are gone, and I want to be gone, so there will be no one to care for him. He cannot be by himself."

"What about Mr. Diersdörfer?"

"Cate, he is an old man now. Besides, he was forced to send Father home till he sobered up and of course he never did. There is no one but the two of us." Tears were welling up in his eyes. "I just do not know what to do." I was crying too, and we held each other for a long time.

Eventually I said, "I'm so tired I can't think straight. I've got to get some sleep. Let's talk more in the morning." I laid down on my old bed but didn't really sleep much.

***

In the morning Father was sober enough to confront. I made sure Sam went to school, and after he left, I sat down next to the old man on the threadbare sofa. I recall searching for the right words to speak, but I lacked inspiration, so I just started.

"Father, we have to talk." He had been staring blankly out the window, but suddenly his eyes fluttered around the room as if searching for a path of escape.

"Sam and I love you and we are worried about you. You drink too much. I know what you've gone through and how much you miss Mother, but you can't make it better this way, you just can't. Alcohol won't make the pain go away now any more than it did when Edward died. You need someone to help you. I can't stay here and it's not fair to Samuel to expect him to take on the responsibility. You can't stay here by yourself and you're not in any condition to go to work. Father, we need help. Can you think of anyone you can live with for a while?" I reached out and held his hand.

He looked at me as he would a stranger who accused him of a crime. "I am perfectly alright. I am fine. There's nothing wrong that can't be fixed by time."

[31]

"No, you are not alright. You are turning into a drunk." If I had thought about what I was saying I could never had said it. "Besides, Sam said you are just about out of money. What's going to happen when it's all gone? How are you going to get more? The rent is due, and you don't have enough money to pay it. You'll end up on the street, Father," I said bluntly and more than a little angrily. "Is that how you want Sam and me to remember you, a drunk on the street? Please Father, I love you. Help me. Help Sam. What are we going to do?"

After what seemed like several minutes, he replied, "I don't know. Diersdörfer doesn't want me around anymore. There is no one. I think maybe I should just join your mother."

"Aren't there any relatives left?" I asked out of desperation.

"Na, just my brothers down in Racine, but I haven't heard from them in years. Maybe they sold the farm. Hell, I don't even know if they are still alive."

I was shocked, Father never swore. "Well damn it, I can find out. I'm a newspaper reporter. If I can find someone in New York City, I can certainly find someone in Racine, Wisconsin." He looked sharply at me, but he needed to be shocked. I was taking charge. Besides, I was beginning to see a ray of hope and was not about to let it go out. "I'll take the Chicago train down there today."

"Just write them a letter, I have no money for train tickets to Racine."

"I have money, but what I don't have is time. I can only stay till Friday, so we need to get things fixed by then."

"Well, before you go boxing me up and shipping me off to Racine don't you think you should ask me?"

I stood up sharply and glared at him. "Okay, what do you want to do? Stay here and drink yourself into a sorry grave next to Mother? She'd be a poor wife if she'd even have you lying next to her."

"Here, I'll not have you talking like that. It's bad enough that she is gone without her only daughter speaking those words."

[32]

"Then you have got to start behaving in a way that would make her proud again. Do you even know how proud of you she was? We all were - watching you walk out that door everyday knowing how much you hurt. I don't suppose you do know, but every day she stood at the window and watched you walk down the street. She was so proud of you then and she wants to be proud of you now. You didn't answer my question, what do you want to do?"

He walked over to the window and looked out for a few minutes. "Alright, but I don't even know if they are still there." I walked over behind him and wrapped my arms around his stooped shoulders.

"Leave that to me," I said softly. "If I'm not back by the time Sam gets home, tell him where I've gone and that I'll be back as soon as I can." He nodded. "And another thing. Promise me you'll not drink today."

"I won't have any more than my usual."

"No! Nothing. We need you to be clear-headed for the next few days. Mother would want it that way."

After a long pause he spoke more to himself than to me. "You work your whole life to make a home for your family. You make plans to buy a house where you can live the rest of your days. There isn't anything you would not do to make it happen, and just when things start going the right way, the world falls apart. You end up with less than you came to town with. Such a failure." Defeated, dejected, he sadly looked in my eyes, and he put his hand on my arm and squeezed, "I'll try."

***

The twenty-mile trip to Racine didn't take that long. On the way, I cried a little and stared out the window a lot. I wanted to be a little girl and climb in my mother's lap for a while. That couldn't be. I had to be a strong grown-up girl focused on getting the job done.

Once in Racine, I made a quick stop at the post office, and they told me how to get to Cyrus and Hiram Jeppes' farm. I found someone headed that way at a nearby feed store and hitched a ride. We visited along the way, and I learned the Jeppes were a quiet, God-fearing family who always went to church and always voted Republican, so I was encouraged by the time I hopped off the wagon and thanked the farmer.

Walking down the lane I tried to imagine Father working the fields alongside of his father and brothers. Somehow it didn't quite fit. Just as I walked into the barn yard, an older man came out of one barn crossing to another.

"Mr. Jeppe." I called.

He looked at me with some curiosity and replied, "Yep."

"Are you Cyrus or Hiram?"

"I am Hiram, Cyrus is tending a sick cow." He stared hard at me as if I was going to present him with a court summons. "How can I help you?"

"Well, Uncle Hiram, I am your brother Frederick's daughter, Catherine, and I've come to talk to both of you."

"Frederick! I figured he died years ago."

"No, he's still with us, but not for long if you and your brother don't help us."

He continued to stare at me, now curious but tentative. "How so?"

"Uncle Hiram, can I explain to both of you, I can do a better job."

"I told you, Cyrus is busy with a sick cow."

I had been down this road before, and I was not going to be dissuaded. "Well, can we go to him and talk?"

"I suppose so."

We set off for the white barn he just came from.

"What did you say your name was?" he asked.

"Catherine, and my brother is Sam. Do both you and Uncle Cyrus live here on the farm?"

"Yep. He lives with his wife and three children over there," pointing to an unremarkable two-story white frame house, "and I live over there," he nodded in the opposite direction where a small one-story house stood near the barn. "I never married," he guessed my thoughts.

"It's a very nice farm," I casually commented.

[34]

He looked at me, "mmm, run of the mill." With that we reached the barn door which he pulled open for me. I had never been in a barn before and was surprised at how dark it was.

"He is over here." Hiram motioned toward what I figured was a stall.

"Cyrus," he called, "have a minute?"

"I put a bread poultice on her eye, we'll see if that works. If it doesn't, she may lose it," came the reply. A second later a tall gray-haired man came out drying his hands on a towel.

Ignoring the diagnosis, Hiram introduced me. "Cyrus, this lady says she is Frederick's daughter which would make her our niece. Her name is Catherine." For a few seconds Cyrus stared at me.

"Well, I'll be. How do you do, Catherine. I'm Cyrus, your uncle."

"She knows that" inserted Hiram. "She says Frederick is in a bad way and needs our help."

"How so?" he responded with the same suspicious inflection as Hiram did.

Now it was my turn to speak. "You probably don't know, but my mother died of consumption about a month ago."

"No, we didn't. The Jeppes are not great letter writers," Cyrus replied. "We're very sorry to hear that but surely you didn't come all the way here to tell us."

"No, let me explain," I said using my New York assertiveness. "Father has had a hard time adjusting to her death and, well, he's taken to heavy drinking. I live in New York City and Sam can't handle him alone."

"Who's Sam?" Cyrus asked.

"Her brother." Hiram injected.

I continued without a pause. "We are sure he will not live till summer if someone doesn't help him stop his drinking. There isn't anyone else we know of except the two of you. Can he come here and live for a while till he gets straightened out? Please. You are really our last resort."

[35]

They looked at each other and conversed with their eyes. Cyrus scratched his head and Hiram stepped on an imaginary ant.

"Well," Cyrus said, "I'm not surprised at his predicament, he was a heavy drinker after he came back from the war. Papa said he might end up in the gutter. I don't know what we can do to help, Catherine."

"He needs to get some real earth beneath his feet, a reason for living, and people around him that care whether he lives or dies," I said using my best human interest story words.

After an extended pause, "He could stay with me. I have that spare room," said Hiram. With that I knew the hand was won.

"You can't deny your own brother, besides scripture says, 'forgive your brother's transgression,'" replied Cyrus looking at me seriously, "but we don't have a lot of time to hold his hand. He's got to pull his weight."

"If you give him a chance to dry out, I'm sure he will. You won't regret this," I said with tears again in my eyes.

"When can we expect him? Hiram asked.

"In just a few days. I've got to go back to New York at the end of this week."

"That so. Just what do you do there?" Cyrus perked up.

"I'm a newspaper reporter."

"I could have guessed that, you are pretty strong-willed and nosy for people around here," Hiram grinned for the first time.

"I must hurry back to catch the afternoon train so we can get him ready to make the trip. I'll send a telegram as to the exact time," I said.

"Never got one of those before, but there's no need. We'll be here and he knows the way," Cyrus replied.

"Thank you so much," I gave them both hugs. "I really must leave, can one of you give me a ride back to town?"

"No need, just go out to the road and walk toward town. Someone will be right along, and you can hitch a ride with them. We've got to get back to that cow. You be careful in that city, I hear it is dangerous there." Cyrus patted my hand, and then he and Hiram turned back to the stall and sick cow.

[36]

As they said, it was perhaps five or ten minutes, and someone did give me a ride right back to the train station.

***

I returned to the apartment in the early evening. Sam had dinner ready, and I was famished because I hadn't eaten all day. Over beans and boiled potatoes, I told them what had happened. Father seemed pleased but was clearly nervous. He paced the room and rubbed his hands together. Sam looked relaxed for the first time since I had come back to Milwaukee.

"That leaves only one big problem," I said. "What is going to happen with Sam."

"He will come with me of course. Cyrus and Hiram won't mind, and he can learn farming," Father pointed out as if it were a simple problem.

Sam looked at his father sharply. "I have got to stay here. There is school and the museum work too."

"You'll come with me and that is all there is to say."

"I am sorry Father, I cannot. I have responsibilities here and here is where I must stay." Father shuffled around the room, obviously angry.

"What if we can find someone that Sam can stay with?" I asked quickly.

"Who?"

"I don't know yet, but there must be someone."

"I can check with Cora tomorrow and see if she knows someone I can board with," Sam injected.

"You should come with me," Father stated wistfully.

"We'll see about that tomorrow. Tonight we need to start packing," I said sounding just like my mother.

The following day Sam skipped school in order to talk with Miss Loomis. As soon as he explained the situation and asked for her help in finding a suitable guardian she responded, "Samuel, you shall stay with me. I have been wanting to move to a larger apartment anyway. Your father is leaving his so I shall rent his. Perhaps I can buy some of the furniture and you won't have to move your things out. It's a nice apartment house and very close to the museum so that shan't be a problem.

[37]

We will each have plenty of space to call our own. Besides, that will give us more time to work on an article. Yes, that is exactly what we'll do."

Sam was thrilled at the prospect; however, he was also a little nervous. It was one thing to work together at the museum, it was a very different thing to greet one another in the early morning.

"Don't worry," she guessed at his hesitancy, "your room is your room, and my room will be my room, while the kitchen belongs to whom ever gets there first. Can you cook?"

"Only a little."

"Well, I'm a good cook so you can wash the dishes." With that the deal was struck.

The next few days were busy ones. Father was true to his word and didn't drink, at least not much. He was going to have to travel light, so he packed only his clothes, a few memorabilia, and his tools. Cora's offer to buy the furniture was a godsend which relieved us from toting all of it to the secondhand store. That left me the sad duty of packing my mother's things. Father objected when I suggested selling them, but I could see no alternative.

He went into the sitting room and picked up her carved glass vase. "She would want you to have this. It belonged to her grandmother. And I will not have you selling her clothes. Take things around to people in the neighborhood and give them away. Tell people the clothes are clean and not infected. The black shawl was her favorite, give it to Mrs. Schormuller next door. While you are at it, tell her about Miss Loomis and she will tell the others." He paused to look around the room, "This is very hard to do, Catherine. It will be like she never existed. I don't like it at all."

"I know Father, I know," is all the little girl inside me could say.

We settled the rent, and the landlord was happy to have an immediate tenant so by Thursday evening everything was set. I would accompany Father on the train and when he got off at Racine I would continue to Chicago and on to New York City. Sam would again skip school to be at the apartment to help Miss Loomis move in. After supper we gathered in the

[38]

sitting room and tried to make conversation. After several futile attempts we agreed to call it an early evening.

**

Friday morning was difficult for both Father and me. We hired a wagon to carry our belongings to the train station. There were goodbyes to the neighbors and a few last-minute directives to Sam. Then it was time to leave. Sam was excited at the prospect of being in charge of himself. It was good to see him happy again.

Our short trip to Racine passed quickly. Promises and tears were shared between long silent pauses. I helped him get his belongings off the train. Then the whistle blew, and I had to leave. As the train started to move, I watched the old man for as long as I could. He was standing alone on the platform looking somewhat lost, and perhaps a little afraid. Little did I realize that was the last time I'd see either Father or Samuel.

Chapter Five

During the next months, work was quite normal for me. Of course, there were cases of homicides, drownings, suicides, fires, and other gruesome incidents that fell to me to report on, but even events like these can become commonplace if they occur daily. I was becoming very calloused to the darker side of city life and while I didn't enjoy the blood and agony, it was challenging to create a story that would catch and hold the readers' attention without being morbid. I did that very well and as a result, I was becoming one of the most read reporters at the newspaper, much to the dismay of many of the male reporters.

In London, however, something truly sensational was happening. A number of women were victims of horrible murders, and it was making headlines all over the world. My editor, with the encouragement of the men in the department, assigned me to go over and cover the story from the "feminine perspective." I was given a second-class ticket on the steamship RMS Etruria along with the honorary title of "Special Correspondent," and was told not to spend much money, but make the stories exciting.

***

The Etruria was one of the largest and fastest steamships in the world. It took only six days to make the crossing. The first day out was fine. I walked around looking at the horizon and talking to the other passengers. We sampled the fare and enjoyed a glass of wine, congratulating each other on being such intrepid travelers.

[40]

That night a storm struck and followed us across the entire ocean. I don't know what the other passengers did, but I spent the remainder of the trip in my bed hoping beyond hope that we would sink and end the torture of seasickness. I suspect I was not the only passenger so afflicted because the people trudging down the gangplank looked nothing like those that had waltzed up it in New York.

***

The crimes in question involved the terrible killings and mutilations of lone women and were originally known as the Whitechapel murders. Later, another reporter invented the name Jack the Ripper and it stuck.

Most large newspapers were covering the story by exploiting the violence of the murders. Blood and gore always attract readers. I admit to some fascination with death but I can do without the gruesome results of violence. These murders were extreme. Many reporters focused on the murderer and accused different suspects on an almost daily basis. However, I didn't make any such accusations. Instead, I concentrated my stories on the victims. Each week I picked a different woman. I talked to associates, friends, neighbors, and if possible, the woman's family. I tried to make each victim as human as I could. I never forgot the women sitting on the steps of our apartment house in Milwaukee talking about their hopes, successes, and failures, and I knew each of the dead women had similar dreams. If my readers could see them as real living people, the pain of the crimes would be magnified.

New Yorkers couldn't get enough of the stories I sent back. My columns were the high point of the Wednesday edition resulting in increased sales. Because people were buying more papers, the publisher, James Bennett Jr., decided to make me the paper's permanent London Correspondent, of course with no increase in salary. I can still imagine the expressions of relief on the faces in the City Room.

The murders, while making great stories during the heat of the moment, really only lasted a few months. Soon the front-page stories became page two and three filler. The search for

[41]

the murderer went on, but a story that says there is nothing new to report won't sell papers, so I had to search for a new angle for my columns.

To a girl from Wisconsin, England was a whole new world. Everything was different, so I started writing about my personal adventures. It was just like writing in my journal again. My column no longer needed to be about crime, so if something happened anywhere in London, I was writing about it. I had good success too.

One week I might write about the newest avant-garde paintings. The next week I might be off to a steeple-chase horse race with Sir Somebody. The week following that I might interview a member of the women's suffrage movement. Then I would visit a baron and baroness at their castle complete with a tour of the dungeon. At first my editor complained about my expenses, but when my readership rose even higher than during the murders, he relented and even increased my expense allowance a little.

A side benefit to all this gallivanting was that I was becoming known in London. I think everyone, be they American, British, French or elsewhere, likes the idea of being written about. Many times, the better-known people become, the more attention they want, or need. The idea that theirs might become a household name in New York City was just too much to resist, so I got many invitations to events that would normally be off limits to most people. For instance, actors and actresses love to have the press nearby, so I attended several parties when the likes of the marvelous actress Ellen Terry, and Oscar Wilde. I recall meeting the playwright Wilde one evening. My hostess pulled me over to a slender, tall, young man saying, "I want to introduce you two. Oscar, it is my pleasure to introduce Miss Catherine Jeppe. Miss Jeppe is an American reporter who is here on assignment. Miss Jeppe, allow me to present you to Mr. Oscar Wilde."

He looked only at my eyes for several seconds without saying anything. Then he took a drink of his wine and seemingly tried to dismiss me by saying, "Did you have to come all the way here to find someone worth interviewing?"

[42]

"No," I replied. "I came to write stories about murders, have you seen any lately?"

"Many. Before meeting you tonight, I was being bored to death by everyone here." he responded. We both politely laughed, and had a short, but interesting conversation.

***

During the day I enjoyed my life as a London gadabout, but at night I realized I was unhappy. First, I was homesick. I missed my father, and Sam. Father almost never wrote, and letters from Sam came only occasionally. Strangely enough, I also missed Milwaukee. That was almost funny because when I lived there, I couldn't wait to leave. Another problem was the distance between us. In those days it might take two or three weeks to get to its destination, so a reply might be more than a month in coming.

While I lived in New York City I got a note from Father saying he was having a difficult time, but his brothers and Cyrus's wife were very patient. I found it worrisome, and I began to feel guilty about forcing him on them, but about six months after I got to Europe a letter reached me that surprising, but also comforting.

Father wrote to say he had found help for his drinking in the Bible." Now our family had never been much for religion, but when I remembered his brothers were quite religious, I could see how things developed, and if religion helped, I was very happy for him. He also said he had taken up furniture making again, so he was contributing to the family rather than being a drain which I'm sure was a concern of his. They had added a room on Hiram's small house for him, so he had some peace and quiet away from his nieces and nephew. It had an outside entrance as well as an inside door. That way he could go for long walks in the night and not bother Hiram. All in all, it seemed he was beginning to be happy again. When I finished reading the letter I suddenly wondered if I should go back to Wisconsin to be with him, but I decided I could not, not then anyway.

[43]

The second reason for my unhappiness was of more immediate concern. Back in Milwaukee I decided I wanted to write, and I thought newspaper reporting was the solution, but now I found myself becoming dissatisfied with the grind of churning out a column every week. I was always looking for subject matter, but never had the time to develop the story. There was always pressure to write a column that was more interesting, exciting, and colorful than the last one. I kept asking myself if I really wanted to do this for the next forty years. I kept thinking about writing a book. It was something I knew nothing about, but that had never stopped me before.

***

In between columns, I became acquainted with a number of socialites and well-to-do people, including the American A.P. Watt who later became the world's first literary agent, and who was instrumental in getting me published. I discovered he too was from Wisconsin, and we became good friends. He told me about his adventures in Paris, the people, and the wonderful places there.

In 1889 a number of us decided to take a short vacation and go to the Paris Exposition, the *"Exposition Universelle,"* which was going on there. When we arrived, we found a city experiencing a rebirth from the rubble of the Franco-Prussian War twenty years before. Big new buildings bordered wide tree-lined streets. Unlike London, Paris had no underground, so everyone walked the boulevards. Electric lights, *"fée électricité,"* shone brightly at many monuments, theaters, in public buildings, and some private homes as well, and of course at the exposition, so dark nights in the city were quickly becoming a thing of the past. There were still areas of decay and poverty where the poorest lived, but they could be avoided without too much difficulty. By the next day I found myself overwhelmed by the city. I thought someday I'd like to live there.

The question of my future residency remained undecided until the fourth day. That day we were supposed to go to Wild Bill Cody's Wild West Show, but I refused. I didn't

[44]

come halfway around the world to see some American cowboys. So, on a lark, a small group of us went to the strange world of Montmartre, the devil's nest.

This part of Paris was where good people went to ignore their protective morals, arousing the animal that resides in each of us. Members of our group relayed stories they had heard about alcohol-infested parties that sacrificed virgin beauties, or drug-laced pastries given to unsuspecting visitors who then were robbed and killed or ladies of the evening who offered their wares for little or nothing. It was all too much to resist. Once there, we toasted our way through famous cabarets: *Le Cabaret Artistique, Moulin Rouge, Folies Bergère.* We were waiting to be approached by Satan, but he must have been busy elsewhere.

As fun as the other stops were, it was not until we arrived at *La Chat Noir*, "The Black Cat," that I knew this was a very special place that I had to get to know. During the evening I saw or was introduced to Claude Debussey, Erik Satie, August Strindberg, and Henri de Toulouse-Lautrec. The *maitre de cabaret* apologized for such a small number of notables but encouraged me to come back another night when he was sure there would be many more. In that I was still a newspaper columnist of some note, my mouth watered at the thought of so many interviews.

***

The next day I again begged off the planned activity. Instead, I returned to Montmartre alone. While I justified my day as research for an article, I was actually exploring for myself. There were really two communities built around a steep hill, the highest in Paris. The one at the base in the Pigalle and Clinchy area was the loud, raucous district filled with cabarets and shops for visitors. Further up the hill though, there was the quiet part where people lived their private lives much like any other city in the world. It was the quiet part that attracted me. This section had narrow, twisting, brick and cobblestone roads bordered by old, enchanting, somewhat dirty stucco buildings almost always connected to each other, and

[45]

ranging from three to six stories in height creating a canyon-like feeling for those walking down the street. Even the tight alleys lacing the streets together had buildings on either side. Those avenues running up the hill were quite steep and offered a challenge to horses and humans alike. Staircases, both public and private, had been built in many places.

I could hear children's voices somewhere behind the buildings; a few women were tending small gardens; some pedestrians were on their way to the food markets, shops, restaurants, and other businesses closer to the hill's base, and a few carts were carrying supplies in that direction as well. I found myself relaxing, enjoying the atmosphere of people just going about their daily lives. There seemed to be no hurry, no yelling, no threats, no pretense, none of the things I had grown used to, but had also grown to dislike.

The shops of Montmartre were small and friendly. Many were brightly painted green, blue, or red. It almost seemed owners competed with each other to make theirs the most attractive. The fronts of the shops with their glass windows and ornamental woodwork reminded me of those in our Milwaukee neighborhood and also some in parts of London. They seemed to have anything a person might need, and everything was within walking distance.

Many buildings had apartments in the upper stories. I gathered some were quite small while others were almost palatial. I discovered I could afford a modest sized apartment if I budgeted my resources, and if I had a small, but steady income. To me, this was the fairyland I had dreamt of when I was young. By the end of that day, I decided that I really wanted to live in Montmartre.

I moved to Paris in 1890 and for the next 45 years I spoke French, ate French, dressed French, loved French. In other words, I was a dyed-in-the-wool *Parisienne*. At first, I wrote my columns as I had done in London, but now focused on Paris. They continued to be favorites with the paper's readers. However, the idea of a book continued to lurk in the back of my mind.

***

[46]

At the beginning of my adventure, my normal day began with shopping at the fresh food markets, and some housework which was followed by a walk in the sunshine to buy fresh flowers which was my only indulgence. The afternoon was given over to working on a column till about 5:00. The late evening was reserved for reading classics. Every now and then I would find a book that Mother had read to us when we were young and I read it again, visiting an old friend, and enjoying the experience as much as I had done the first time.

One morning, after living in the apartment for about a month or two, I walked down to my flower lady's stand to get my weekly bouquet. While looking at all the blossoms before deciding what color I wanted that day, another girl about my age stopped to make the same decision. We remarked to each other what a difficult choice we had. We talked about the colors, the blossom sizes, their cost, the temperature. In other words, we were sizing up each other. After making our selections, which were remarkably similar, we walked away in the same direction. Having no pressing obligations that morning, I boldly asked her if she would like to stop for *une tasse de thé,* a cup of tea.

"*Je pensais la même chose,* I was thinking the same thing," was her response. With that our friendship was sealed. As we shared our past experiences over tea, we found we had much in common, with enough differences to make our relationship interesting. At the time we met, Charlotte Lèvy was already an accomplished cellist playing in several ensembles throughout Paris. She was quiet and reserved with a wicked sense of humor.
Because of that she served as a perfect foil to my sometime brassy behavior. Yet we were strong willed women. Regardless of these minor differences, when our leases came due, we decided to combine forces and rent a larger apartment with a view.

We shared that apartment for years. We came to respect, trust, support, and depend on each other. For the next fifty-eight years Charlotte and I have shared *une tasse de thé*

[47]

almost every morning in spirit if not in person. We still seek each other's opinion. She persuaded me to write this book. To this day, I prefer her company to that of anyone else I know. I still enjoy listening to her play the cello. Its deep, flowing tones are so soothing to me. They sweep away any worries I might have created, and in their place is a more peaceful time of life. In fact, she is in her room playing as I write this.

Chapter Six

By the 1890s, the industrial revolution had won the economic war in the United States. Most urban people no longer thought of themselves as artisans who crafted products with pride. Rather, they had become hirelings, menials, as interchangeable as the parts of the machine they serviced. Workers, be they men, women, or children, were singularly focused on the wage they collected at the end of the week. What they did to earn that wage was of little importance.

So, I found it fascinating that both Sam and I were out of step with much of society. Our parents taught us that what we did was as important as what we earned. It was only fitting that they left us to decide what that should be. At the beginning of the decade, like me, Sam was searching for a vocation that fit his needs. The fragments of letters that follow reveals Sam's consternation regarding his future.

June 23, 1889
....Here, things wander rather aimlessly. High school graduation, which is an achievement that should be celebrated, was unimportant to me. Except for Miss Loomis, no one was here to share the event.

The next day I began looking for a job. There are a lot of brewery and factory jobs, but they are all dead-end positions. Finally, I finally found one that has possibilities. Not a great one, but it is a start. I am working for a man who owns several apartment buildings. He wants me to

[49]

collect money from renters and check to see if they have taken care of the apartments. It is part time so I can continue working at the museum. He only pays four dollars a week, but the work should not be that hard. Perhaps I can move up the ladder to be his partner, or maybe I can manage my own apartments someday....

September 8, 1889

....You asked about my work. My first impressions of the affair were wrong. I still do my job, but I do not like it. The work is not the problem, although I am nervous about carrying money around because of hoodlums. No, the problem begins with the filthy condition of the neighborhoods where the apartment buildings are located. The city does not seem concerned enough to send dump carts to pick up the refuse. As a result, it builds up. As you might expect, rats and mice are all over the place. The odor is overwhelming. It stays in my nostrils for hours after I go there.

The buildings themselves are very sleazy and shabby. The front doors no longer lock, if they ever did. There are no lights on the stairs, so residents are forced to carry candles when they move around at night. The odor of the tenements rivals that of the streets.

Most of the renters are immigrants who speak little English. Large families live in these small two- or three-room apartments consequently there is no way to keep things clean. From what I've seen many of the children are dirty and obviously undernourished. Families must be going without food in order to pay the rent.

The landlord, Mr. Bailey, is not interested in the condition of his buildings or his renters, only in the money I collect. The situation is distressing to say the least.

[50]

On another front, Miss Loomis and I were invited to the home of the museum's director, Carl Doerflinger, last Sunday. I was prepared for a boring afternoon, but he knew me or at least knew of me. He urged me to consider continuing my education at a college. "You can go very far with a degree, you know," he said. I was pretty embarrassed to say my family has no money to pay for a college.

"Pshaw." He really did say "pshaw." "There is money out there for such things. I know because I didn't have any funds either and I received a first-rate education."

Miss Loomis has said nothing about this idea, but I know what she wants me to do. Cate, I need you to give me your honest opinion as you always have. Do you think I might have the slimmest chance at succeeding in college? I keep thinking of what Mr. Doerflinger said to me, and going to college does sound exciting, but I am scared of the idea. I enjoy learning but the competition has me buffaloed. I consider myself only a mediocre student and I would be up against the top minds from hundreds of miles around. I cannot decide what to do, and I am anxious to hear your opinion.
Love,
Sam

The letters I sent to Sam were destroyed, including my reply to his question. However, I know what I would have written. I would have told him to go full steam ahead. I would have said he was one of the smartest persons I had ever met. I never went to college, but the competition he refers to is something he should seek out instead of avoiding because it will only make him stronger, and more confident.

November 7, 1889

Dear Cate,
        I received your letter, and I have thought
long and hard about what you said. My stomach
ties itself in knots when I think about what is ahead
if I try to go to college. Be that as it may, I asked
you what to do and you replied, "do it." So, I will
apply to a college. I only hope I will not be a
source of embarrassment to Mother's memory, to
Father, and to you.....
.....I received a note from Father last week. He
and Uncle Cyrus invited Miss Loomis and me to
Thanksgiving dinner. We both think it is a good
idea and I miss Father. I look forward to seeing
him. I will, of course, let you know our how things
go.
Love,
Sam

December 2, 1889
        ....We made the trip to Racine for
Thanksgiving. The day went well. True to his
word, Father has sworn off alcohol completely. He
still is in constant pain, so he takes laudanum in
place of the alcohol. His speech is good, as is his
memory. He seems to be in good humor.
        We went to his room, and it is very cozy.
A small wood stove, a table and chair, a commode
which he said he made, a bed and a small bedside
table supply all his needs. His few clothes hang on
pegs around the room.
        He gave me a small lap desk he made. It
even has my name carved around the ink well. It
really is a beautiful piece. I prize it highly and will
take it with me wherever I go.
        Upon returning to the house Father played
his violin for everyone and ohh, the memories
flowed back to me. I teared up thinking of how

[52]

Mother would have enjoyed the day. Too soon we had to catch the train back to Milwaukee. Everyone sends their love to you, and they hope you too can visit sometime.

In regard to college, after deciding to follow your suggestion I told Miss Loomis and I think she was so happy she almost cried. You and she seem to have much faith in me, and I cannot disappoint you two regardless of my apprehensions. I am partial to the University of Wisconsin. Miss Loomis is in agreement, and soon we will go over and visit one of the geology professors with whom she is acquainted.

To conclude this letter, I must tell you I quit my job. It was an embarrassment to take thirty pieces of silver from that snide....

February 20, 1890

....Miss Loomis and I have begun writing the paper I mentioned some time ago. It is called "Igneous Rocks of Wisconsin in the Milwaukee Museum of Natural History Collections." It may not replace Shakespeare's "Hamlet" as an outstanding piece of literature, but it will be comprehensive. Before starting I did not realize how many different varieties there are. I hope it will be published before I apply to the university in that it can only help my chance at a university.

June 16, 1890
Dear Cate,

Much of what was important to us as we grew up around here is vanishing. The town is growing and changing before my eyes. Even my vacant lot has a new building on it. Soon, all we will be left with will be our memories. I wish you would come back. It would be a little like it used to be.

[53]

Maybe it is me that is changing. I feel like a much different person than I was a year ago. When I graduated, I had no real plans, and no concerns beyond my next meal. Now I am looking down the path several years. Part of me likes the challenge, but another part finds possibilities very scary. At least I am no longer wandering in the wilderness.

The meeting with Dr. Salisbury, at the University of Wisconsin, was pleasant, but rather short. He said he was impressed with my credentials and the upcoming publication. He seemed to think I would be admitted to the university which was a great relief to me. However, he said he, along with the university president, was leaving the university. They are going to a new university that is not even built yet in Chicago. The University of Chicago is being created using the most modern teaching concepts, and it is gathering top faculty from all over the country. "While the University of Wisconsin is a fine school and I am sure you will get a good education here, I suggest you apply at the University of Chicago. I don't think you will ever regret it."

We had time enough to walk back to the train station. Miss Loomis was very quiet and deep in thought throughout the whole time. It wasn't till we were back on the train that she spoke.

"He's right. You should apply to the University of Chicago. There is no reason to think he is trying to mislead you. You will have the best teachers. This is a wonderful opportunity for you, and it will be a shame if you let it pass by." That was all she said the rest of the trip. So, she threw the whole scramble in my lap and was going to force me make the final decision, which as I think about it, was only right.

[54]

I spent most of the night sitting in the dark thinking. I knew she was right, but I was trying to think of reasons why I should not change my sights to the University of Chicago. I could not come up with any good ones. In the morning I told her, "I think he is right, too." I have burned my bridges.
Here I go,
  Sam

The University of Chicago was the brainchild of John D. Rockefeller who donated millions of dollars to it. It was designed to attract both the best instructors and the best students in the country. The university would have the most modern facilities and libraries and would operate on the most modern educational theories. It would eventually become one of the finest, most respected, educational institutions in the world.

July 22, 1890
....You asked about the starting date for the University of Chicago. They are planning to open in 1892. That sounds far off, but it will work to my advantage. The intervening time will give me a chance to work and save the money I will need for tuition, supplies, room, and board. It will also allow me to prepare for the entrance exams.
  Instead of competing with the best from Wisconsin, now I'm competing with the best from the whole country. I remember reading "The Charge of the Light Brigade." I know the hopeless feeling those men must have felt:
  Theirs not to reason why,
  Theirs but to do and die:
  Into the valley of Death,
  Rode the six hundred....
  I must tell you about my new job. It is much better than the previous one there is no comparison. I now work in a bookstore. The store specializes in antique and European books. Again,

[55]

it is only a part time job. Perhaps I can look for a second one. However, if I find a book I want to read I can sign it out and take it home. The owner will also take 20% off if I want to buy it. As with the previous job, I only get four dollars a week, but I'm hoping he will give me additional responsibilities and increase my wages.

September 30, 1890
....The article is done and it has been accepted for publication. Hooray! It will be in the "Wisconsin Geological and Natural History Survey" sometime next year. Miss Loomis now wants to start on another one.....
.....I did not know it when he hired me, but Mr. Bergström at the bookstore reads Greek. He has agreed to help me learn it because it is a very difficult language. Good things keep coming my way.....
.....I'm going down to Father's for Thanksgiving again.

December 5, 1890
          ....I must report Father, his brothers and Uncle Cyrus's family are all doing well. Miss Loomis did not accompany me this time in that she was invited to another dinner, which I will discuss in a future letter. Father is still taking laudanum for his pain. Everyone sends their love and hopes you can find your way back to Wisconsin sometime......

One of Sam's many concerns about college was the money he would need for his tuition and his room and board. He saved a lot of his pay from the book shop, but this was not going to be enough to get him through the first semester let alone four years of school. Bank loans required collateral, and he had none. Besides there was no way to assure them he would be able to pay them back.

[56]

Finally, he made an appointment with Mr. Doerflinger, the museum's director. When Sam and Miss Loomis had visited him, he told Sam money was available for promising students and now Sam needed to draw on those sources. Apparently, Mr. Doerflinger was encouraging. He knew people with resources who might be willing to help. To them $500 was not a large amount of money.

April 18, 1891
Dear Cate,
      It is a fine spring-like day here, and I'm playing hooky. I owe letters to both you and Father, so here I sit on the grass sunning myself and fulfilling my duties.
First, let me give you the good news. Mr. Doerflinger, true to his word, talked to two museum backers about helping with my financial woes. At first, they were uninterested until he suggested setting up a scholarship program sponsored by the museum and named after the donors. They enthusiastically supported that idea. The guidelines specify it be used for a student going into the sciences and who is in financial need. This year Mr. Doerflinger will make the decision. I am that choice. Next year a committee shall make the choice, but I will cross that bridge when I come to it. Each man gave two hundred dollars this year. That plus the money I will have saved comes very close to the amount I think I'll need. I feel about fifty pounds lighter.
      Speaking of savings, Mr. Bergström increased my hours at the bookstore, I think mostly so he can drill me on my Greek. I have to start keeping the accounts, but that is easy and takes only a few minutes a day. In addition, he has given me a $.50 a week raise, the second such raise I've gotten. He is only one of numerous people who have made me their project. I do not understand why. I am nothing unusual. If I do not

[57]

score well on the entrance examination, I will be only one of many who will be disappointed. The problem is that the fault will lay solely with me. I certainly have had the best and most enthusiastic tutors in all of Milwaukee.

Cora and I have begun working on another article. This time it is under the auspices of the museum. A bit of gossip, Cora has gone out for dinner several times with Charles Mutis, a botany instructor from Marquette College. This of course is none of my affair, it is just that she and I have become good friends and I am glad to see her do something other than work.

In closing, I received word that the exams will be held in Milwaukee on November 5. That gives me six months to finish my preparation. Cora believes I will do just fine. I hope she is right.
Take Care,
Sam

Over the next six months Sam's letters displayed concern to worry to panic and back again. I knew how important this had become to him. Still, there was little I could do to comfort him, so I wrote newsy pieces about Paris, my friends, and little trips I took. Shortly before November 5, I do recall writing a short note encouraging him to be confident, and that Father and I were very proud, and we loved him regardless of the outcome.

A telegram from Sam:

12/16/91
To: Catherine Jeppe
Paris
Accepted!
Sam

Charlotte and I had glasses of champagne that evening.

Chapter Seven

It wasn't until years later when I read Sam's journals that I discovered that while his preparation for college was going on, he was also involved in his first serious romantic relationship.

Courting back then was not the same as it is now. It was much more formal, and the man had better be able to profess strictly honorable intentions. If a man wanted to visit with a lady they would usually sit in her parents' parlor where they could be easily seen. If they were out in public, they would have someone else with them as a chaperon. Even the poorer families tried to present a proper image of their daughters. But Samuel was ignorant of such things, and he learned the hard way.

Journal Entries
1890

February 22

An Irish family has moved into our apartment house's top floor and their eldest daughter is quite attractive and friendly. We exchange greetings in the hallway and have discussed the weather. I must admit I am a little nervous having no real experience in such matters, and this is something I will not discuss with Miss Loomis.

I have greeted both her father and Miss Murphy in the hallway. Her name is Bridget. Did I say that she is very attractive and quite friendly, well, she is. She works in a cigar factory. Several times we have walked together in the general

[59]

direction of our respective employments thus we have had a chance to get to know each other without any serious effort or consequences. I think next week I will ask her if she would have an ice cream sundae with me.

February 26

I did ask Bridget if she would come to the ice cream parlor. She liked the idea, with the understanding that we do so in secret. I agreed without understanding the need for secrecy since we were not doing anything inappropriate. We met there and had a good time. I discovered that was the first time she tried ice cream. She liked it. She said, in her lovely Irish brogue, that their family, which includes seven children, is quite poor and cannot afford such luxuries. Like most working children, Bridget quit school after the eighth grade and has been making cigars since she was fourteen. She brought me one she made. Rather than telling her I didn't smoke, I lit it up. I am sure she immediately guessed I was new to the habit because I didn't prepare it before applying a match. We shared a good laugh, but I rather enjoyed the experience, and I will have another in the future. There is a band concert in the park next Saturday evening and we agreed to meet there. So far, I seem to be doing the right things.

March 2

What a time! I arrived at the band shell early and was waiting quietly for her when I was roughly pushed from behind. I almost fell but recovered and turned to confront the rude lout. In front of me was Bridget's father and Bridget, looking terrified. I assumed he had jokingly pushed me perhaps a little too hard, and I greeted him in a friendly way. In return he pushed me again and I could see he was angry.

"What'da you mean by sneakin' around with my daughter. D'you think she's a common whore that you can meet somewhere so you can sneak off and have your way with her," he shouted. He drew back his fist. The next thing I knew I was laying on the ground, and my jaw ached like blazes.

"Just because we're Irish don't mean you can treat us like animals. We can't afford readymade clothes and fancy

[60]

store-bought foods like you, but we still have our pride. Bridget ain't no trollop. How dare you," he shouted, staring down at me.

"Please, Mr. Murphy, my motives toward your daughter are only respectable," I cried. "Stop all this and we can talk."

"I don't want to talk to you. You're the lowest of the low. Ya belong in the pig sty. If I owned a gun, I would shoot ya. It is a good day for you that I don't."

"I am sorry," I whined. "I have not courted a lady before, and I did not know what to do." I was thinking as fast as I could to defuse the situation.

"All the worst. Is your family from the north lands? Didn't your father ever teach you anything? Have ya not the least amount of common sense?"

I could tell his volume was decreasing, I hoped his anger was as well. All this time Bridget was standing off to the side, her hands covering her face in embarrassment. As I glanced at her, she looked at me and I could see tears on her face.

Then a patrolman came along, not especially hurrying.

"What's going on here?" he demanded.

"This villain is try'n to seduce my daughter," Mr. Murphy said regaining his volume.

"Is this true?" said the officer looking down at me with obvious distrust.

"No, sir. Bridget and I were just going to listen to the concert."

"The cur didn't ask my permission and they had no one to accompany them," Mr. Murphy growled.

"Young man, don't you have any training in matters of the heart?" the constable said in a sarcastic tone.

"Apparently not," I replied. "I am sorry for my actions."

"Well, let the boy up, sir. You can't blame him for his poor upbringing," the policeman said stepping between Mr. Murphy and me.

"He deserves a good thrash'n anyhow," Mr. Murphy shot a look over the policeman's shoulder.

[61]

"That he does, but you are not the one to do it tonight. Now we'll just call this bout finished and you are the winner. Take your daughter and go home."

"Not until I get satisfaction," he growled. Bridget was pulling her father away before he got into a fight with the officer.

"Young man," the policeman, ignoring Mr. Murphy's comment and turning to me said, "It's not my job to teach you. I suggest you talk to an elder and find out the rules for courting before you get really hurt."

"I will sir," I mumbled, "and thank you."

"You go home too," he said to me.

"But we live in the same apartment house."

"Ha! You and the Irishman deserve each other. Take my word for it, if she was my daughter, I'd beat you too. Now take the long way back and hope he's not waiting for you."

The Murphys had moved off, but suddenly Mr. Murphy reappeared wanting one last word. "And don't ever speak to my daughter again, do ya understand? Not a word shall pass between you."

I stammered, "Yes sir, I understand. May I say sir that none of this is her fault." I lied, protecting her in doing so.

"Go, both of you, before I take you in," the officer said sternly.

I did as the officer suggested and took a very long way back to the apartment. I could see from the street the Murphy's windows were dark. I quietly opened the front door. I tried to quietly climb was the squeaky stairs imagining Mr. Murphy bursting out of his door, but nothing happened, and I quietly slunk to bed sore jaw, bruised ego and all.

March 14

Everything has been quiet since the ruckus. My jaw is still sore, but I have all my teeth. The discoloration has faded from my face and the swelling has gone down. However, it is still sore.

True to my word I have not spoken to Bridget, yet. However, I know she feels bad about the incident because each morning since that evening I have found a cigar next to the

[62]

apartment door. Yesterday we accidentally met in the hallway and smiled at each other. She pointed to my jaw and looked very apologetic, and I in turn shrugged my shoulders. I held up my daily cigar and mouthed "thank you." She smiled in return. With that we quickly went in opposite directions.

March 20

I know which way Bridget walks to and from work and about when she comes home, and I just happened to run into her. Up to now I had held to my promise that I wouldn't speak to her. However, a month is time enough for waters to settle.

Both of us are truly sorry for the disaster with Mr. Murphy, and we realize our mutual mistake. We talked about the possibility of me formally seeking Mr. Murphy's permission to visit Bridget. She isn't sure and is afraid such a meeting might stir him up again. I said I did not care and would be willing to take the chance. She felt the same and said she would approach her mother with the problem. We agreed to meet here in three days if the weather held. She left for home, and I wandered around the park for a while before heading back.

March 24

Bridget and I met in the park yesterday. Her mother agreed with Bridget that it is too soon for me to approach her father. While not giving her approval, she said if we continued to meet, do so in a less public spot such as the library. This was an excellent idea because Bridget said her father can't read.

April 10

Bridget and I have been meeting at the library for the past few weeks. We do not carry on much of a conversation because of library rules. We sit side by side and I go over notes for the article while she looks at magazines. We exchange notes and generally enjoy each other's company, and occasionally our shoes touch. Things are going along swimmingly.

[63]

April 22

Oh, how the worm has turned. Yesterday I spent the whole day at the museum. A small shipment of fossils came in from China on one of the lake steamers. Because I didn't have that much to do, I offered to accompany the museum's driver and retrieve it. We were going through the tavern district when I saw Mr. Murphy sauntering down the street arm-in-arm with a young lady. He did not see me. I wanted to leap out of the wagon and confront him as he had done to me, the cad. Bewilderment prevented me from doing anything, I just sat in the wagon.

I do not know what to do. Should I ignore the incident, or tell Bridget what I saw? If he had not made me look like a fool in front of Bridget, I would let it slide. My anger has not subsided, and I cannot forget what I saw.

April 24

Spent several days thinking about how to break the news to her. I know I do not have the words and the self-confidence to tell her outright. I have decided to write her a note and give it to her outside the library the next time we met there. That way I can describe the event with just the right way and yet I will be there to comfort her because I knew she will be crushed.

April 25

Today I spent a long time writing the note. At the appointed hour and armed with the note and my indignation I went to the library to wait outside. I could see from her expression that she wondered why I was standing outside instead of going in where it was warm. I said, "I think I had better give you this out here," and handed her the folded paper.

She read it while I watched her face for any reaction. When it came it was not the reaction I anticipated. Bridget threw her hands in the air, paced around, and cursed her father with every word I have ever heard and several that were new to me. "He promised us. He promised us. He said he would never do that again. He promised us. He told the priest he would be faithful from now on. He told us he would be

[64]

faithful. The bastard." She turned to me and looked straight into my face. "My father is a philanderer, a... womanizer, a..a..lecher. Every time we move to a new city, he grabs the first slut he sees, then when he is caught, he promises he will never do it again.

After a pause she continued, "I'm afraid to tell my mother. I think she will stick a knife in his black heart. I hope she does someday, then we'll be done with him.

"I thought when he said those things to you at the band concert he had changed, but he was being his usual lying self. I wish he would leave, then we would never see him again, but his is our only money besides my little bit," she said.

"Well, at least you can leave, you can get away from him," I replied, hopefully.

"I'd never leave my mother with that devil. I'm the only one she can turn to, I'm the one she talks to, and I need to help with my brothers and sisters. No. I am tied, and I cannot leave." She began to cry as the hopelessness of the situation sunk in. "I will be making those damn cigars till I die or till I join a convent." With that she turned and ran back the way she came. I went home too.

It has been several hours since our meeting and there has been a lot of yelling, swearing, and some scuffling from the Murphy's apartment. A short time ago heavy, angry boots went down the stairs and out the front door. I looked out the window and Mr. Murphy was headed down the street, his hands in his pockets, shoulders slumped, and it looked like he was talking to himself.

April 26
There was no cigar by the door this morning. I didn't see Bridget in the hall or going to work.

May 1 (May Day)
Today I spent the afternoon at the museum. Cora was meeting someone for dinner, so I came on alone. As I approached the apartment house, I saw a small wagon with boxes piled on it. Of course, that is a sure sign that someone is moving. As I climbed the stairs, I met Bridget carrying a box

[65]

down. She motioned with her head toward my apartment and continued down the stairs. I went in and left the door ajar.

In a moment Bridget came through and closed the door behind her. She spoke in a soft monotone, like a judge passing sentence, "We're leaving. My father knows someone in Chicago, and he can get a job on the docks, and I can get work in a cigar factory." She seemed drained of all emotion as if she had no fight left in her. I think she no longer cared what happened.

"Isn't there anything I can say that will convince you to move away from your family?"

"No, I'm the eldest and my mother needs me to help with the other children. He has promised to be faithful. I don't believe the bastard and neither does my mother, but what else can we do. We must follow him to a new town where he can start over."

She continued, "I will send you a note as soon as we find a new place and then at least we can exchange letters. It shouldn't be more than a week at most." She kissed me, we hugged, and she went out the door.

May 20

It has been over two weeks and I haven't received a letter from Bridget yet, but I am still hopeful. Perhaps it is for the better. I would not be able to write romantically. My letters to Bridget would be like shopping lists. What I feel and what I can write are two different things. Perhaps I could quote Shakespeare. What about, "A pair of star-crossed lovers," or "Tis better to have loved and lost than never to have loved at all." Did Shakespeare write that? I don't know. * Maybe I could get Cate to write some letters for me! She is good with words. It does not matter, because Bridget would have written by now. She is gone, and what am I stuck with – rocks. But at least they will not move away.

*Tennyson (a/n)

Chapter Eight

While Sam was being introduced to new ideas and new sensations in Milwaukee, I was having the same experiences in Paris. Eventually I decided to follow desires and try some serious writing. I wrote to the paper and told them I was taking some time off. They were unhappy, but there really wasn't anything they could do.

Life among Parisian artists of the 1890s was pretty heady stuff. A few great minds lead the way past the well-plowed fields of accepted styles and into the untilled land of the avant-garde. Some good artists, and many mediocre ones followed along in their tracks. Just being in that rarefied atmosphere, I felt I was part of something momentous regardless of where individual talents lay.

I was used to turning out a news story in an afternoon before tackling some other breaking event. Now, I wandered around my room trying to think of a word that subtly blended interest and color in an imaginary scene. This was harder than I had anticipated. After a while, I found writing late at night, when all was quiet, to be most productive. I kept the afternoons free to edit or destroy the previous night's work.

I chose to write short stories thinking they would be easier to do. The first was done in a couple of weeks. I was dissatisfied with the result which was melodramatic and sentimental. Rather than take the time to rework a good idea that was poorly executed, I put it away and started on the second. It was not much better than the first. I took the third story to a small publisher and was turned down flat. I was disappointed, but deep down I knew they were right.

***

I started to be concerned. I hated the idea of going back to the newspaper, and by this time, I had met Charlotte. I was becoming moody and argumentative until one day she demanded I take a twelve-hour recess from writing. It was a typical cold and wet November day in Paris. We visited the Louvre as we often did. We stopped in a bistro for refreshment. There were newspapers laying about and I had not seen one for a month or more. Newspapers were something that distracted me from my creative writing, so I avoided them. Since I was on recess though, I couldn't resist looking through them. A small article caught my eye. Oscar Wilde was staying in Paris. I remembered meeting him back in 1889 and while he wouldn't remember me, I wondered out loud if he, being an outstanding writer, might give me some help with my work.

"What have you got to lose? Send him a note and ask for a meeting," Charlotte answered. "He can only ignore you, and you'll be no worse off than you are now.".

"Do you think he'll be offended by a woman sending him a note?"

"No, this is Paris, and he is Oscar Wilde who cares nothing for rules."

That evening I composed a short note introducing myself and my desire to talk about writing. After sending it by messenger, I tried to focus on my current story. The following reply came the next day:

I will be most happy to meet with you tomorrow, Thursday, at 3:00. Have the concierge call my room.   OW

That evening I rehearsed what I was going to say and what questions to ask. His notoriety did not concern me. I had met too many famous people to be impressed by that. I just didn't want to appear to be an incompetent amateur. Rather I wanted to be one professional talking to another about a problem.

The next day, a few minutes after I arrived, we were sitting in the hotel lounge drinking hot chocolate. I began my

[68]

rehearsed introduction, but only got to, "I'm sure you don't remember me..."

"Of course, I remember you. Our hostess that night, who shall go unnamed, is a sweet dear, but she gives the most dreadfully dull parties. You were the only light spot for me the whole evening. Tell me, Miss Jeppe, how may I be of help to you?"

"I am attempting to become a serious author and I am here to ask your advice because I respect you and admire your work."

"Let me guess. You have written several pieces. None have measured up to your expectations, and you are discouraged. You have come looking for an easy solution to your problem."

"While your first assumption is amazingly accurate, the second is not. I expect to struggle to reach my goals, but there are many paths to take, I'm bewildered and do not know which is the best one to take."

"Alas, dear lady, there is nothing I can say that will be of much help, other than now you, as a writer, must choose the path that best fits your needs. Be aware however, many of the paths that may seem easy routes to success and fame are in fact dead ends designed by others to keep you within their artificial limitations, and those lead only to the mundane. Don't be afraid to pursue your own ideas regardless of what others may say. With that in mind, an idea that is not dangerous is no idea at all. Don't be obsessed with words, rather, concentrate on the idea and the words will come.

"One more thing, an agent would be most helpful to a person in your position. Now, Miss Jeppe, I must leave you to write to my publisher. I need to remind him that I am the one with the talent. It has been a pleasure meeting you again. We must do this every two years or so. Between then and now I hope to see your name in print. Goodbye."

He left without further acknowledgment. I sat somewhat startled at his sudden departure. To avoid any suggestion that I was being jilted, I slowly finished my chocolate while concentrating on what he said. Instead of

[69]

taking the horse tram back to Montmarte even though it was cold, I chose to walk so I could think.

**

The last thing Oscar Wilde said to me was, get an agent. I wasn't quite sure what an agent did, and the only one I knew was my friend back in London, A.P. Watt. I took an afternoon and wrote to him stating my interest in becoming a client. Twelve days later I received his reply.

A.P. Watt
Literary Agent
2 Paternoster Square
London, England

20 November,1892

Dear Cate,
What a pleasant surprise to hear from you. What has it been, almost a year I think, since we last talked. I hope you are enjoying Paris, it is one of my favorite spots.
I would be most happy to consider the prospects of you becoming a client of mine. If the stories you write are as good as your newspaper articles, my task will be quite easy.

I read and critique a work, determining whether publishers would even be interested in purchasing it. That may sound a bit unfair to you. However, I know their needs almost as well as they do. Rather than waste everyone's time, I shorten the process. If I think the piece will not sell, I will tell you exactly why. If I think it will sell, my job is to match you with a publisher.
My fee is ten percent of the author's profits. This may sound substantial, and it is, but for that amount I eliminate all the

[70]

scuffle for you thus freeing your time for more productive endeavors.

I have a large number of clients, and I seldom take on new authors, but we have been friends for quite some time, and I have great faith in your work. If you would like me to work for you, please forward a finished piece to me. In exchange I will send you the necessary papers to sign and we will get to work.
Sincerely yours,
A.P. Watt

I wrote back immediately that I would indeed use his services when I finished my current story. Upon reading for what seemed to be the fiftieth time I decided there were no more changes, additions, or deletions to make. It was done. I quickly mailed the story to A.P. Two weeks later I received the manuscript and a reply.

A.P. Watt
Literary Agent
2 Paternoster Square
London, England

22 December,1892

Dear Cate,
I read your manuscript over carefully, and I do not think it is salable in its present composition. Your descriptions are good, but the plot is weak, and the characters are hackneyed. You are asking the reader to care about these people, yet you give them no reason to do so. They do not seem real. While their story is tragic, it has no emotional impact on me. You need to write a story that cannot be summarily dismissed by the reader.

I know rejection is discouraging but try to take the long view. Even the most established writers are rejected. Most writers try numerous times before being accepted. Keep writing.
Sincerely yours,
A.P. Watt

I am by nature a problem solver. If someone has a problem, I can see solutions when others cannot. However, it's different though when I'm the one with the problem. Then I see no solutions, nothing but failure. I always end up relying on others to suggest answers. This time, Charlotte helped me see the obvious.

After I read the letter, I passed it to her. I sat, withdrawn, starring into empty space. She read it without comment and quietly watched me. She usually doesn't offer suggestions where my writing is concerned, but she could see I was very upset. After a while she poured two cups of tea and placed one next to my chair.

"May I say something?" she asked.

"What? I'm sorry. Of course."

"I read the story, and Mr. Watt is right, the characters do not seem like actual people."

"What do you mean?" I was irritable and feeling sorry for myself.

"Your news articles that I have read made people seem real. Why not write like that? You told me that when you were reporting, you interviewed a lot of people before you got a good picture of, say, a murder victim."

"Yes, I talked to anyone I could find who knew them. This is different. I am writing from my imagination. I can't interview someone who doesn't exist. How can I..."

"Write about someone who does exist then. Someone you can talk to. Someone you can get to know. The poor have just as many stories to tell as do the rich, and they are just as interesting, if not more. Paris has many people whose stories would be just as appealing as your imagined persons.

[72]

"I don't know, I guess I can't write fiction. Maybe I should just go back to writing newspaper articles. I was good at that..."

"Then do it," she interrupted, "report about real people, but write books, not articles. If you can make a corpse come alive, what can you do with a living person. Do what you like to do, what you are good at. Do what makes you happy.

I sat for a while. My thoughts were popping like champagne bubbles, and I was unable to focus on any of them.

Charlotte rose and started from the room. "Why don't you go for a walk, you always think better when you are walking."

Ten minutes later I called to her, "I'm going for a walk."

From the kitchen came her reply, "Good".

**

It was not difficult to find the poor in the Paris of the 1890s. The French economy, like that of most other Western countries, was unequally divided into a large slice for a small number of wealthy families, a modest portion for the *bourgeois*, and a small piece for a large number of poor people.

The poor were accustomed to either being ignored or exploited. They came to expect it, as a result, they were usually suspicious of strangers. You could see it in their faces and hear it in their voices. While they were proud individuals, they were also vulnerable, and they knew it. Thus, there were those who would not talk to me at all. Even so, it didn't take long to find people who, once they understood my motives, agreed to submit to my interviews. Some were actually quite eager to tell me their story.

One of them was Marie Gravois, my flower lady. We were used to visiting when I went to buy my flowers. So, over a period of months, we talked about many things. Usually I just asked her questions, and she went whatever direction she wanted. By doing so, she told her own story. I recorded what she said in my notebook using my own invented shorthand which I later transcribed at home. When finished, I had many

[73]

pages of direct quotes, observations, and background information, all of which gave me a good portrait of her. Here are some of the things she told me.

Early in our conversions I found out Marie was a foundling child. These children were given anonymously to a religious or state home by a parent who was too poor to take care of a baby.

Have you wondered about your parents? Who they were, where they lived, and why they left you at the home?

"Why, of course. Only a farm animal would forget its parents. When I lived at the Church's home all the children wondered about their mothers and fathers. We grew up looking at the front gate, waiting for the bell to ring signaling their arrival to take us home. When it did ring, I for one, always smoothed my dress as best I could and combed my hair with my fingers. Of course, it was never them, but I kept hoping. At some point though I did stop looking at the gate, however even today when I hear a bell there is a moment when I listen for my name.

Did you go to school?

"When I was eight or nine, I went to school at the home. I learned how to read and do numbers. That way I could read the catechism and maybe work in a store. The Sisters taught the boys how to write, but that was not important for girls. We didn't even learn to sign our name. Now as an adult, when no one is buying flowers, I read all sorts of things. I can't afford to buy books, but I have borrowed some from other people. I read a book by Victor Hugo called '*Les Misérables*'. It took me a long time, but I liked it. I wish I had lived back then. I read leaflets that I find, and newspapers people leave laying around. The papers may be a day or two old, but that does not matter to me. Just this morning I read a pamphlet about a group called Socialists. It was very interesting, and I want to know more about them."

[74]

Will you talk to me about your son? How old is he?

"He is seven. His name is Vincent. I named him after the patron saint of orphans. He is very smart. I met his father after I moved to Paris. We lived together very happily for several years. After I had Vincent, we argued about getting married, and he left. To earn money I tried cleaning, you know, scrubbing floors, polishing brass, washing windows, and such. I couldn't afford to pay someone to watch Vincent, so I took him with me. Masters and Mistresses always complained about him even though he never caused a problem. I never lasted very long in any one place.

"One day I watched a flower seller and thought, I can do that and keep Vincent with me. I love flowers. I know their names and when to plant them, how long they last. If you want to know anything about flowers, ask me. So, I talked to the lady. She was very nice. She agreed to help me as long as I went to some other part of the city which was fine. I found a basket to hold the flowers, went to the flower market on the *I'le de la Cité.* I bought some flowers and sold them for a profit. All of the money I got went to buy more flowers the next day. Eventually I bought this little cart and these pails. I am a good businesswoman."

"This corner is very good for business because men from upper Montmarte pass by on their way home from work in the city and they buy some flowers for their wives as an apology for being poor, while men visiting the cabarets on the *Boulevard de Clincy* below see me and come to buy flowers for their sweethearts because they feel guilty for lusting after the whores. Women, like you, come here too because they want a little color in their lives. This is my corner. Other flower ladies know that, and they stay away. I do well because I talk to people about the flowers. I tell them things about flowers they do not know, but I am friendly, not snobby. People like that and they come back. I may never be rich, but Vincent and I will not starve."

Where is Vincent now?

[75]

"He is in school. He is learning how to read, write, and do numbers. Then he can get a good job and not be a peddler. He will teach me how to write too."

A final word about Marie Gravois. Marie made enough money to buy a horse cart. With that she built a highly successful flower wholesale business and was known throughout the trade. She never married. She did learn to write and was active in training orphans to be successful businesspeople. Marie and I kept in close contact until I moved back to New York in 1938 and then we exchanged letters until her death in 1942.

Vincent did very well in school and eventually went to college. He was finishing his studies in French history at the University of Orléans when World War I broke out. He was killed in the Battle of Verdun in 1916.

***

When I finished Marie's chapter along with sixteen others, I mailed it to A.P. Then Charlotte and I took a short trip to the French Alps where I was able to hike every day to relax. When we returned, I found the letter I had been waiting for.

A.P. Watt
Literary Agent
2 Paternoster Square
London, England

14 July,1893

Dear Cate,
A most interesting approach you have taken. I don't think I will have any problem finding a publisher for you. Are you going to write more in this vein? You titled it "Women of Paris", but you just wrote about poor women. What about middle- and upper-class women? What about men? What about professional

[76]

people? I can see a whole series about people.
Congratulations.
Sincerely,
A.P.

I was a published author, well almost. I felt relieved. As a way of apologizing for my moodiness over the past months, I took Charlotte out to a nice dinner. Actually, I had to borrow a little money from her to pay the bill with the promise of paying her back with my first paycheck. We had a good laugh, and she still reminds me of it.

True to his word, A.P. did find a publisher. The book sold slowly at first, but some good reviews helped bring it to peoples' attention. By the end of the year, I was well into my second book and had sketched out a third.

Chapter Nine

For some, the move from Milwaukee to Chicago may not seem like a great transition. For Sam, it was the transformation from a caterpillar to a butterfly. The University of Chicago was a whole new world for him. And like any hatchling, he needed to move carefully to avoid ever-present threats and dangers.

October 15, 1892

Dear Cate,

My trip to Chicago was uneventful, but the university offices were closed by the time I arrived on campus. The next morning, I was standing in line when they opened. I was in for a shock. The university publication said the university had housing for its students. However, the men's dormitory is not finished being built, so they rented a nearby apartment building, but that filled quickly. The only remaining rooms are in the basements of two other unfinished buildings. The lady I talked to said those rooms are unheated, damp, and dark. She strongly suggested I find something on my own. Such is the price I pay for being miserly. If I had come a week earlier, I would be writing this from a university room.

After receiving this disastrous news, I wandered around picking up the pieces of my shattered plans. I was hungry and I remembered seeing a Chinese restaurant close to the train station, and I walked over to it. While I was paying

[78]

the bill, I noticed a sign in Chinese script prominently displayed on the counter. Out of curiosity I asked what it said, and the Chinese man said, "Room For Rent."

After walking several blocks, I began to seriously consider renting the room. Hopefully it was cheap, and it was near enough to the university I could walk most days. Maybe they would include board in the deal, certainly the food was good. I then returned to the restaurant and approached the waiter.

The Chinese man, a little shorter than me, but a few years older, wore a long apron not unlike that of Mr. Diersdörfer's. Beneath the apron he wore a loose tan tunic with floppy sleeves. His tan pants were also loose fitting and covered black cloth slippers. His close-cropped hair was covered by a boater's straw hat with a red and blue hat band.

I asked about the room. He looked at me with a wary expression. "The room is for Chinaman," he said firmly. I replied that I was a student at the university and needed a place to live because the university had run out of room. "The room is for Chinaman," he repeated.

"I am very quiet and will not cause any problems," I said.

"You would not be happy, we would not be happy. Now please, go away. The room is for Chinaman," he said a little louder. At that moment a woman came in from the back room. They heatedly talked in Chinese, she looked at me and they talked some more.

Finally, the man said grudgingly, "My wife says you can have the room if you pay for two months".

"How much per month?" I asked.

"$2.00 a week."

"Can I get food too?"

[79]

There was more conversation. "$4.00 a week for two meals a day. You eat what we eat." This was less than the university was going to charge me, and I asked to see the room. "When everyone is finished eating," he said. "Okay," I said and sat down at an empty table. I waited for twenty minutes or so until he leisurely cleared the now empty tables. He glanced at me several times to see if I would give up and leave. I did not. Finally, he motioned to me, and we went into the kitchen area where his wife and an old lady were cleaning, and then up some stairs.

Once upstairs, he showed me the room. The bedroom, if you could call it that, was small, very small. It was empty except for a chair and a low box about five feet long. I was about to thank him and leave when he said they had a trunk if I needed something to put clothes in, and they had an extra oil lamp.

"I need a bed too."

"There is bed," he said pointing to the box. "It is Chinese bed."

I figured the bed would not be too bad. I asked, "I would pay you $48 dollars for two month's rent and two meals a day, is that right?"

Doing some mental figuring in his head, he nodded. I looked around the spotless apartment. There was almost nothing on the walls, yet it felt like the people who lived there took pride in their home. In that respect it reminded me of our home. I did not think I would find anything better at the same price and I wanted to get settled. I reached to shake hands. Instead of shaking hands he bowed.

"When can I move in?"

"Two hours," was his reply.

"I will pay you $6 now and $42 when I return in two hours." He shrugged in agreement.

That is how I rented a room with a Chinese family. I have to admit I was nervous the first

[80]

couple of nights, and I moved the chair in front of the door, but I did not need to worry. The bed is very hard, but the people seem likable and trustworthy.
Love,
Sam

As trusting as Sam was, he was also quite naive. The Chinese population in the United States had been under attack for a number of years. The first Chinese were welcomed when they came in the 1840s and 50s. Later, Chinese laborers appeared, and began moving into gold mining operations which white Americans assumed were theirs. Soon wealthy Americans began complaining that the Chinese were becoming too powerful. Racists took up the line and started to physically attack them. Labor unions began to vilify them because they worked cheaper than union members. All this led to a series of national statutes referred to as the "Chinese Exclusionary" laws which intended to send all Chinese back to their homeland, though by now many had been born in the United States. While those Chinese who had businesses such as restaurants could stay for the time being, the writing was on the wall.

October 23, 1892

Dear Cate,
        Classes are going well. Geology is wonderful. Dr. Salisbury remembered me. Construction noise made it difficult to hear the lecture the first week, so he took us on a walking tour of the area.
        The students in the other classes set a fast pace which I am not used to. Everyone here is smart and frequently they seem to arrive at the answer before I figure out what the question is. I need to redouble my efforts. As I feared, mathematics is going to be my hardest subject. I am not alone in that several other students are

[81]

struggling as well. We have formed study groups for each subject to help each other. We have no time to waste because mid-term examinations are November 11.

If I am a respected member of the university family, I am just tolerated, and mostly excluded from the restaurant family. There are three people who own and run the restaurant, Lin Chung, his wife, Xue Mei and an old woman who's name I do not yet know. Chung's English is pretty good while Xue Mei has learned only a little. I do not think the old woman speaks at all. Together they run a very tight ship. Each has their appointed duties which are accomplished without command or encouragement. Each is an important part of a well-oiled machine.

The restaurant is small with only six tables, but its appearance is maintained with pride and care. The outside is painted a rich green with bright red trim, and a little gold paint around the door. Two windows each have red curtains framing a Chinese lantern hanging between. Inside, Chinese lanterns hang over each of the spotless tables. There is a beaded curtain between the kitchen and the customers.

The apartment is pretty typical. There is my bedroom and Chung and Xue Mei's bedroom. The old woman sleeps in a small kitchen. The remaining room is used for all the other activities. In the evening, Chung might be working on the restaurant records or reading the Chinese newspaper out loud, while Xue Mei is doing laundry, lots of laundry, while the old woman is sitting in the corner smoking her pipe. Xue Mei and Chung always carry on a lively conversation punctuated by laughter.

On my first evening I did not know if I should sit with them or retreat to my own room. I do not think they knew what to do with me either.

[82]

It was uncomfortable for everyone except the old woman. She sat by herself in the corner and took no part in the activities. Once during the evening Xue Mei brought her a cup of tea which she took without recognition.

The old woman is very quiet, never looking at anyone. She is expressionless. Deep wrinkles and what looks to be scars give her face a sculptured look. Her hands are gnarled. She is thin, very thin. Her hair, what there is of it, is white. She makes no effort to keep it combed, consequently she has a "wild" appearance.

After an hour, I asked Lin Chung if she is his mother to which he replied "No, we think her name is *Ah Kum* which means 'Good as Gold' in Cantonese, but that name may have been given to her once she arrived in America. We think she was born in 1841. When she was about eight, she was either sold or kidnapped and brought to San Francisco where she worked in a brothel for many years. Sometime about 1875 she strayed away. She no longer knows the difference between real and unreal.

I interrupted his story. "So, she had no relatives or friends?"

"No. After she left the brothel, she said she drifted from place to place. One day she wandered into our restaurant and asked for a bowl of rice in exchange for a day's labor. We had just opened and didn't really need any help because there was not much business, but we could afford a bowl of rice. We talked about it and decided she could stay till she found some place to go. She never left. She washes dishes and cleans because that is what she wants to do. She is at peace, and to a Buddhist, being at peace is happiness.

I was doing some arithmetic in my head. "You are saying she is only 52 years old?"

"You are surprised at her age? She is about that and yes, she looks much older because she has had a very hard life. She does not speak English, in fact she does not speak much at all. You must show her respect because she has survived much more than you can imagine, but still every morning she gets up and meets the day."

Such are my worlds of the university and the Chinese restaurant.

I have saved the best for last. I have a job, or at least I will have a job next quarter. It will be a wonderful job, better than any I could have imagined. The university has decided to employ students who have financial difficulties. Of course, I applied. In exchange for 15 hours of work a week they not only pay a small stipend, but they wave the tuition fees. Isn't that wonderful! In one day, I went from being a pauper to a student who has a slight surplus of funds. I feel rich. After I applied, Dr. Salisbury requested I be assigned to the Geology Department. He told me I will be working with the collections in the new Walker Museum. It is going to be just like the Milwaukee Museum, but with more responsibility, and I get paid!

Your Happy Brother,
Sam

***

Journal Entries
1892

September 15

I cannot stand the bed, too hard. I asked Chung about the laundry Xue Mei does in the evening. He said others pay her to wash and iron their shirts. Tomorrow I will ask if she will do my shirts too. I have never known anyone to work as

[84]

hard nor as long as Xue Mei. Chung works hard too but he will sit from time to time. She never stops.

September 22
     Xue Mei said she will wash and iron two shirts each week and launder my other things for $.65. What a deal! They don't seem to mind now if I sit with them for a while in the evening. They chatter while I study. We get along fine. Sometimes Chung asks me to help him with his English. Maybe he can teach me some Chinese.

September 28
     A bunch of us in geology celebrated the end of the fourth week of class. We went to an uptown restaurant. I like Chinese a lot, but it was nice to have a good German dinner. I discovered the boys think I am setting the pace in class. I asked them about Mildred Comstock, the sole girl in class. Got my share of teasing. No one knows much about her.

November 3
     We formed a geology study group. Mildred joined. Everyone seems to have a grasp of the basic ideas.
     A similar math study group is falling apart in that there is no one who knows what is going on. Another chap, Eli Redding, and I are going to study together. He is a friendly guy, a little quiet and unassuming. He seems to have a better grasp of math than I do.
     Complained to Chung about the bed. Told him I did not think I could learn to sleep on such a hard surface, but I cannot afford to buy a mattress. He thought a few minutes, then suggested I buy a hammock. Sailors on board ships use them. Good idea. I need to find a store that sells them.

November 5
     Eli and I were chatting, and I told him about my need for a hammock, and that I had no idea where to find one. He got a city directory from a secretary, and we looked up hammocks. A store on Wabash carries them. He offered to

[85]

make the trip with me since he is from Chicago and knows the area. Today we took the cable car to the downtown area. On the way I told him of my background, and he told me a little of his. Because his family lives on the north side, he rented a room to avoid having to make the trip twice a day. Got a nice hammock at a good price.

During the trip we worked on mathematics. We ate lunch at the restaurant. In the afternoon we continued working problems. Am starting to feel a little more confident.

Hung the hammock. I fell out the first time I laid down.

November 7

Success! Slept like a baby in a rocker. Just in time. I need all the rest I can get.

November 12

The exams are over. I think I did well in all except mathematics, I will be happy with a passing grade in that.

November 16

Got test scores back. Geology, 95; Latin, 89; English Lit, 86; Mathematics, 79! There is a God!

November 19

Eli invited me to Thanksgiving dinner at his parent's house. Surely! I wrote to Father and apologized for my absence from the family Thanksgiving feast.

November 20

Had a leisurely day. Wandered down to restaurant. I noticed eight Chinese men had pulled tables together and were engaged in loud talk and laughter, obviously enjoying themselves. Chung was kept busy refilling tea pots and bringing plates of food I had not seen before. One of the men pulled out what looked like dominoes and others began playing a game called *mah jong*. The talk and laughter got louder with some back slapping now and then. From time to time one or two of the men glanced over at me in curiosity, but the others seemingly took no notice. I eventually returned upstairs.

[86]

Chung usually closed the restaurant about 7:00 on Sunday, but today the crowd remained till 8:30.

After they left and everything was cleaned, Chung, Xue Mei, and the old woman came upstairs. They were tired, but in good spirits. They sat enjoying cups of tea. I asked Chung what that was all about.

He said the revelers were a group of laundry men who always gathered on Sunday afternoon and evening at area restaurants. It is their time off and they go out to enjoy themselves. It was a little bit of China for them. For Chung and Xue Mei it was an honor to be chosen as the gathering place. It meant the men recognized the high quality of food and the good service.

I could see they were tired, so I withdrew after congratulating them. Thinking about it later, I decided the gathering was not any different that of the group of students I accompanied to celebrate the end of the first month of classes. As unlike as people seem on the surface, they really are very much alike after all.

November 25

Went with Eli to his home for Thanksgiving. When we arrived, I was surprised by the size of the house – more like a mansion. Four stories with an ivy-covered brick wall surrounding it. There were a large number of people inside. They were all splendidly dressed, and I would have been embarrassed about my everyday suit had not Eli worn the same as me. It was obvious that these were all people with money, lots of money.

Eli took me to be introduced to his parents. His father was engaged in a conversation with two other men, he nodded to Eli, but kept talking. We stood waiting several minutes until the men departed. We then approached Mr. Redding. I was introduced. He was polite, although business-like.

Eli's mother was talking to some ladies in a room full of plants called a solarium. She came over to Eli when she saw us approach. I was made to feel right at home. Eli and I wandered around looking at things until the butler called for dinner.

[87]

Dinner was wonderful. Six courses or more, I lost count. Following Eli's lead, I ate in silence. I must say I felt a little out of place. The vast majority of people seemed not to have time for college students, although I saw Eli's mother smiling at him frequently from across the table.

Eli and I said our good-byes a while later and took the trolley back to the university. On the way back Eli said his father was an associate of Andrew Carnegie and made his money in steel. While he did not really want to, Eli was to assume a position in the Carnegie Steel Company when he finished his bachelor's in history. We have become good friends.

November 30

Eli and I studied math together today. After the session we were chatting, and I brought up a comment he had made on Thanksgiving Day while we returned to campus.

"You said you did not want to work in the Carnegie Steel Company but you had to. What do you want to do?"

Eli sat and looked at me with an astonished expression. "No one ever asked me what I wanted to do with my life." He sat in thought for a minute or two, "I have always wanted to be an architect. I love to watch big buildings being built and I want to design them. Just think about designing Eiffel's Tower or the Auditorium Building here in Chicago. Thousands of parts and they fit together perfectly. Architects are working on buildings that will touch the sky right now. What a wonderful chance.

I think he considered whether I should hear his private thoughts. "I wish I could see my name on a bronze plaque in the lobby of a great hotel. That's what I want to do."

Pausing to take a breath he said, "Instead, eventually I'll probably manage a steel mill like my father or supervise a railroad line that carries just iron ore and make lots of money. Who cares about that? I'd be forgotten the day after I retire." He was visibly upset, and he collected his things and left.

Brigit flashed in my mind. I guess it does not matter which end of the financial spectrum people are on, they all dream dreams that will never be realized.

[88]

I am not going to be kept from what I want to do. Except, I do not know what that is, yet.

November 30, 1892

Dear Cate,

I am sorry for not writing sooner, but things here are really busy. I have joined several university organizations.

I am a reporter for the student newspaper. Yes, I am following in your footsteps. I have joined the Prohibitionists' Political Club

The only female student in geology class, Mildred Comstock, and I are organizing a geology club. All the other subjects have clubs. As the two top students in geology, we felt it was our duty to do the same. We hold meetings every two weeks.

Finals are coming in a rush. Maybe I should study.

With Care,
Sam

Learning how to recover from a near disaster is as important as how to avoid it in the first place. I never went to college, but the same thing happened to me when I moved to New York, London, and Paris. The excitement of a new place, new sights, new activities, and new friends is difficult to ignore.

December 29, 1892

Dear Cate,

My dear sister, I wish you were here because I am in terrible trouble. I have not been dismissed from college, but I have been put on notice. To be honest with you, my grades plummeted during the second half of the quarter. After mid-term exams I had two firm A's, a solid B, and a high C. After finals I only managed a weak

[89]

B, and three mediocre C's. What has scared me the most is Dr. Salisbury is reconsidering my position in the museum. If I lose that, I also lose the tuition waiver, and that puts me in a serious financial predicament.

He called me in to his office and lectured me. He was quite adamant that my extracurricular activities must be cut back severely. He said, "you have forgotten why you came here. This is your job. It is no different than going to work in a factory or a shoe store. You have certain duties, and if you fail at those duties you will be released. Do you understand? You are not the only one in your situation. Twenty-seven of your classmates will not be returning next quarter. They have squandered a wonderful opportunity. Don't be number twenty-eight."

That day I resigned from the newspaper, and the Prohibitionist Club. I am maintaining my membership in the Geology Club, but I wrote a note to Mildred telling her I could not act as an officer. Study groups are an important part of classes so they will remain. However, I must study beyond them. I have been given a second chance. I have learned.
Sam

Chapter Ten

In the early months of 1893, there was great excitement in Chicago because the World's Fair, or the Columbian Exposition was going to open May 1. The University of Chicago had a special interest because the Fair was right next door. The project proved to the world how the city that had burned twenty-two years before could recreate itself.

Since I had been to the Paris Exposition a few years before, I thought I had a pretty good idea of what a world's fair was all about. I doubted Chicago could build anything that would top Eiffel's tower. I felt rather smug when Sam wrote about that city's preparations.

January 18, 1893
Dear Cate,

The new quarter has begun. My classes are mostly a continuation of last quarter, except I am taking a break from mathematics. In its place I am taking chemistry. Both Eli and I signed up for it since we work well together.

We wanted to sit together so we could rely on each other. Alas, such was not to be. Instead, a guy from England is to be my laboratory partner. He seems quite intelligent and eager to master chemistry, but his personality makes me wonder how stable he is. He seems to fancy himself a real Sherlock Holmes. He quotes the detective whenever possible while smoking an old meerschaum pipe. We were checking the reactions

[91]

of reagents on various metals, and he exclaimed "the plot thickens," or "this is a three-pipe problem" when there was no reaction. He is likable but his behavior makes me a little nervous.

Things worked out better in Geology Lab where Mildred and I are working together. It is both pleasurable and productive. She is friendly although she seems a bit formal. I can understand the latter since she is the only woman in the class and is trying to gain some respect. She still reminds me of Cora.

Life at the restaurant continues to go well. Last evening Chung told me a little about himself. He is from Macao and shipped on board a clipper ship as a replacement seaman and assistant cook. He went to Europe and then to the United States where he jumped ship. He met Xue Mei in New York several months after he left the ship. I will ask him to tell me more another evening.

January 21

Work continues on the Chicago World's Fair Exposition. There was a break in the weather. Eli and I walked over to see what was taking place.

There are two parts to the fair. The first, the Midway Plaisance, begins just outside the entrance to the university. It is about two blocks wide and extends all the way to the main grounds, maybe about a mile away. There will be all kinds of large exhibits put up by different countries.

One attraction will be a huge wheel that rotates in place. They are just now beginning its construction. In order to secure it, they are using dynamite to blast holes for its footings. These blasts constantly disturb our classes in Cobb Hall. I asked a workman how tall it will be. He said about 25 stories. That is much shorter than Eiffel's Tower, but this thing moves. I just hope it doesn't fall over.

[92]

At the end of the Midway, the visitors will enter the main fair grounds. There are fourteen huge buildings surrounding a large man-made lake. One of the structures is supposed to be the biggest building in the world and I believe it. In addition, there will be many other buildings built by each state and other countries.

I am thinking that once the fair opens, they will need lots of help. Perhaps I can get a job there. It will only last till October, but it won't interfere too much with classes.

Love,
Sam

Journal Entries
1893

January 7

A terrible cold snap. Yesterday, the thermometer outside the museum registered -2° at 3:00 in the afternoon. Today seems colder. Spent the day in the restaurant kitchen by the stove. The apartment, and my room especially, will not get warm. I may ask Chung if I can sleep in the restaurant kitchen tonight. Asthma is bothering.

January 12

The past few days not as cold. Still taking the cable car to school.

Eli and I have started a chemistry study group. We decided to invite Ambrose Arbuthnott, my lab partner, to join us. He still gets on my nerves a little, but he is okay.

Ambrose seems to pride himself on being a little off-center. I know from working on experiments with him, he knows quite a bit about chemistry, but is studying rhetoric. He is several inches taller than me, and very thin. He has long hair down to his shoulders which rarely sees a comb and combined with his long handlebar mustache and very thick glasses, he has a startling appearance, one might say almost laughable. I

[93]

found out a little about Ambrose. His parents are both actors from England. They are always on the road, usually in Europe, so he has a room near the university where he lives by himself.

January 15

Chung talked more about their backgrounds this afternoon. Xue Mei is actually half Chinese and half American. She was raised by her Chinese mother in a Chinese community and has no real contact with Americans except for me. He did not say anything more about it and I did not ask.

January 16

Still having problems identifying minerals. Mildred helps.

January 18

Midterm exams are on February 10. With that in mind the Geology Club is sponsoring a skating party on the University's lagoon on Saturday, January 28th. We will build a bonfire, have refreshments, and maybe some music if possible. Because there are not many club members, we have made it open to any student. I am in charge of feeding the fire since I do not know how to skate.

January 29

The party was a great success. But for me, the outing was a disappointment. I was hoping I would have some opportunity to visit with Mildred outside of class. Ha! How was I supposed to know she is a wonderful skater. She had partners for every skate. Even Eli got to skate with her. It was easy to see she thoroughly enjoyed herself. I fed the fire. I have got to learn how to skate.

February 4

Have concluded that Ambrose has assumed the persona of Sherlock Holmes because he finds that preferable to being rejected as Ambrose Arbuthnott.

[94]

February 11

Eli, Ambrose, and I met at Ambrose's room to talk about getting summer jobs at the fair. I had thought Ambrose just assumed the character of Sherlock Holmes as a public image, a sort of *nom de plume.* I couldn't have been more wrong. He has a bookcase was full of chemicals, test tubes and dishes. One corner of the room was curtained off with black material. When I asked about it, he casually said, "oh, that's my dark room. I'm a photographer, and I like to develop and print my own film." I believe Ambrose is the most unique person I have ever known.

In our discussion about work it quickly became apparent that I am most in need of the income. Ambrose is also wanting some additional resources even though he gets some support, while Eli really does not need the money but wants to avoid working in some office.

Word has it the best shot at a fair job is pushing wheelchairs. I cannot believe such a job will pay very well. Ambrose and Eli both think we will do all right.

February 14

Geology, 93 (minerals did me in, Mildred beat me again); Chemistry, 90 (Ambrose 96, Eli 88); Latin, 88; English Lit, 85 (could have done better).

February 15

Something is happening at the restaurant. Everything is being scrubbed and scrubbed again. Decorations are being hung both inside and out. A roll of red tissue paper has appeared in the sitting room. I, of course, asked Chung and he told me Friday was the beginning of the fifteen-day Chinese New Year celebration. At the beginning of the celebration, everyone gets to start over again. The Chinese gods are satisfied, and good fortune is enticed into the home.

February 19

On Friday, there were great festivities. Many Chinese stopped at the restaurant bringing small gifts and best-wishes

[95]

for Chung and Xue Mei. There were platters of cookies and sweets to be eaten.

On Saturday evening, Chung and Xue Mei presented me with several small gifts. I was embarrassed for I had nothing to give in return. Chung explained that it didn't matter, nor did the gift. The giving was the important thing for Chinese.

I noticed that except for receiving some small gifts, Au Kum played no role in the celebration. Chung said that was her decision. I felt she deserved a gift from me, and I am determined to get her one.

February21

On Monday, while we were waiting for class to begin, I asked Mildred if she knew a store close-by where I could get an inexpensive gift for an old lady. She thought a minute, then replied she had seen a ladies clothing store not far away. She saw my discomfort at the thought of going into such a place.

"Don't worry, husbands go there to buy gifts for their wives. If you want me to go with you, I can do so tomorrow afternoon."

"Thank you. I never bought anything for a woman before." She laughed, but this was very exciting. A chance to go shopping with Mildred alone. What luck.

While walking to the store the next day, Mildred said buying things for grandmothers was easy because they like anything you get them.

"She is not my grandmother, just a friend," I said.

"Oh, it's for her birthday?"

"No, it is a New Year's gift."

She looked at me sharply. "Aren't you a little late? This being February and all."

I laughed at forgetting which world I was in. It took me the rest of the trip to explain the situation.

Outside the doors of the store, Mildred looked at me. "Sam Jeppe, you are just full of surprises. I never would have guessed. You are so unassuming and quiet."

[96]

Inside, after looking at some of the prices, I whispered, "I do not have a lot of money to spend, so I hope we can find something in my range."

"I'm sure we can. How about a pair of gloves? Or a small broach? Bathing soap would work for grandmother, but not someone like…what's her name?"

"Ah Kum. It means 'Good As Gold.'"

"I've got it. Come over here. You should get her a gold shawl. It matches her name and will keep her warm."

I looked at the rack of shawls and saw the perfect one. "That is a great idea, but red is a symbol for good luck, so I think she would like this rose-colored one." I looked at the price, and while it was a bit more than I wanted to spend, I could afford it.

Mildred felt the material. "She will love it."

We chatted all the way back to the dormitory where I again thanked Mildred for all her help.

"It was a wonderful adventure, and I'm sure you will help me one of these days." She smiled as she turned to enter the building.

Back at the restaurant that evening, while we all were in the sitting room, I gave Chung and Xue Mei their gifts of fruit wrapped in red paper. They were surprised and touched. I then gave Ah Kum her shawl which I had also wrapped in red paper. For a minute she just looked at the package in her lap. I wondered if I had done something wrong. I looked at Chung and he was watching her too. Finally, she began unwrapping the paper. This was done with great care so as not to tear the paper for to her it was an important part of the gift. At last, she sat looking at the shawl. I think she would have sat there all evening stroking it if Xue Mei had not walked over, spread the shawl and placed it over Ah Kum's bony shoulders. You would think she had been crowned Empress of China. Her back straightened, her face took on a look of authority. Sitting straight in her chair with the red shawl covering her, she looked first at Xue Mei and then at Chung, and then at me, smiling all the while. That was the first time she had ever acknowledged my presence. Xue Mei got her the usual cup of

[97]

tea, which she accepted with a nod of her head, something she never did.

All the while, Chung had been watching first Ah Kum, then me. I glanced at him with a questioning look. He nodded his approval. I knew then I had done something right. Later, he said that was probably the first real gift she had ever been given, and that it was an act of great kindness. This was going to be a most lucky year for me.

February 28

The week following midterm exams, Eli, Ambrose, and I went to apply for wheelchair pushers. We found out later, men from many of the major colleges all over the country eventually applied for positions.

The pay is one dollar per day plus a percentage of the rental fee. The more we push, the more we are paid.

April 26, 1893

Dear Cate,

I am really enjoying my work at the museum. I have real responsibilities. Other students respect me and when they are using the collections, they seek out my permission to get specimens. I could see doing this for a living.

An interesting course this semester is paleontology. Mildred, as usual, is in the class. Sometimes I walk with her on the way home, at least to the point where our paths part, hers to her dormitory, mine to the restaurant. A couple of weeks after the quarter began, she said, "Something has been bothering me, Sam. I need to ask your opinion."

"Of course, my opinion is always free for the taking."

She smiled at me, "I've always known I wanted to be a geologist, and this semester I decided on specializing in paleontology. It is fascinating. I could spend every extra minute

[98]

learning about fossils. This is what I want to do with my life. The problem is that even with good grades I still don't have any experience. How can I compete for a job with someone like you? Do you know anywhere I can go to get some practical knowledge?

In a flash I answered, "I do. A woman I know works in the Milwaukee Public Museum's Geology Department. She is terribly smart, very nice, and can answer any question you have. I can put you in touch with her if you want."

"Oh, that would be wonderful. Would you please? What is her name?"

"Cora Loomis."

I had not written to Cora for a while. That evening I quickly composed a letter catching up with all the news I could think of, including that I was staying in Chicago to work at the exposition this summer. I then asked if Mildred could write to her. A week later Cora replied that she was sorry I was not returning to Milwaukee, but she certainly understood the need for a good job. She added she was most anxious to hear from Mildred. Her news was that she and Charles Mutis were engaged to be married in the fall.

Three weeks later Mildred stopped me outside geology class. She gave me one of her Mildred Comstock sweet smiles. "Sam, I got a letter from Cora Loomis and she has invited me to come to Milwaukee this summer and work with her at the museum. Isn't that wonderful." I felt a pang of regret because she was taking my spot at the museum.

Love,
Sam

***

[99]

The fair opened May 1 to a great hurrah. A number of university students gathered on the top floor of Cobb Hall where they could get a general idea of the activity even though it was a mile away. Far in the distance the President of the United States, Grover Cleveland, had come to open the fair. A few minutes after noon, he pressed a telegraph key and water fountains erupted a hundred feet in the air soaking many of the visitors. While Flags and banners unfurled, a cloth was dropped revealing a sixty-five-foot-tall figure of the "Statue of the Republic" whose gold leaf covering shown so brightly in the sun that people had to shade their eyes. The crowd, caught up in the euphoria of the moment, spontaneously began singing "My Country 'Tis Of Thee." Later, one of the most exciting events came after sundown when thousands of electric lights were turned on and the "White City" glowed as nothing else had ever done before.

Chapter Eleven

The Chicago Exposition offered the people of the United States a chance to travel the world without leaving Chicago. For Sam it was also a means of making money so he could continue his education. More than that though, it gave him a chance to deal with strangers on a daily basis, to be the expert to whom others look for direction, to be responsible for other people. I could see the change in his letters as he became more self-assured, and experienced.

May 27, 1893
Dear Cate,
....The Fair is a wonder. All over there are things to set the mind ablaze. In every direction you look there is something new or different. Are you sure you cannot come back, even for a visit?

We are officially pushers, but I am more of a gawker. However, I am still not sure if this is the best thing to do. We cannot work full-time yet and the visitors are few. A couple of weekends we have been lucky to get two customers apiece. I need to make money. Eli says he has a plan....

Journal Entries
1893

May 28
Eli called a meeting today. I hoped he would end this experiment, but no such luck.

[101]

He said he had watched what other pushers do when they get customers. He said, "They push, that's all. A mule could do more. Oh, some pass along a little information, but many know nothing about the exhibits at all.

"What if we learn all we can about the exhibits. We then lead the customer instead of just pushing them. We can suggest exhibits, create efficient routes, all sorts of things. In fact, why don't we work together. One can push while another talks, and the third runs errands."

Ambrose liked the idea but was not convinced we could make any money. Neither was I.

Eli was sure we would get referrals and word would get around. He thought we will have more customers than we can handle. We voted to try it.

June 10

We are ready to put our plan into action. Ambrose even got a haircut! I hope this works.

June 14

An older, well-dressed man walked over and sat down on our wheelchair. We explained he was our company's first customer and we wanted to make his experience a memorable one. Fortunately, he was a businessman and appreciated our efforts. So off we went. The other pushers stared after us with questioning looks.

After a few minutes of getting the hang of it, our customer, a Mr. Charles Burgess, retired owner of the Burgess Shoe & Boot Company of Omaha, Nebraska, began playing an active role. He offered suggestions, he asked difficult questions, and pretended to be cranky. Originally, he was only going to stay three hours, but ended up staying six. "Well boys, you have a fine idea and I hope you make a go of it. I have to go home tomorrow, but I will tell my friends to look you up." He left a very nice tip.

June 17

[102]

The Three Musketeer Chair Pusher Company is a success. We are making good money. Some other pushers have complained, but many have begun copying our style.

One last item. Last week Eli told Ambrose and me that his father had mandated that Eli work at the steel company during the summer. Eli argued that he was learning about business by working at the fair, but it did no good. As far as his father is concerned Eli's life was laid out for him, and there was nothing he could do to change it. "You guys will do just fine without me," he said sadly.

July 11

I took yesterday off, thank goodness. Once I entered the gates this morning, the smell of smoke was very heavy and even though the exposition had not opened to the public, there were a lot of people milling around. I went on to the wheelchair station where Ambrose was talking with another pusher, Jack Levstik.

I asked what had happened.

They said the Cold Storage Building had burned.

Stupidly, I said "There goes all our ice cubes. Ambrose was trying to gain my attention. Neither smiled at my flip attitude.

"Twelve or thirteen firemen and three or four workers died," Jack said quietly.

The seriousness of the moment struck me. "How did it happen?"

No one was quite sure. Jack gave some details. The building had a flat roof with a tower in the middle. When the firemen arrived some raced across the roof and climbed up the tower to fight the blaze. They didn't know it, but the fire spread underneath their feet. All of a sudden.... the roof exploded in flame. They were trapped in the tower and there was no way to save them.

Jack's voice was choking. I could see he was having a difficult time describing the scene, but he said, "After a while you could see them shaking hands and hugging each other.

[103]

Then they started....to jump off the tower.....into the fire below. It was horrible. I don't know how many jumped, but a lot. I watched it and I haven't slept since."

I stood frozen. Jack was visibly shaken, there were tears in his eyes, and he seemed to be unsure of what more to say. I put my hand on his shoulder.

After a moment, Ambrose added that thousands of visitors gathered to watch the firemen put out the fire. Some people were even eating their lunch when the explosion took place. All those people watched the firemen commit suicide. Jack could barely keep the tears back. I encouraged him to go home.

"I'd rather be here, around living people. Anyway, I have to keep my eyes open because when I close them all I see is people jumping into a fire. I am going to quit." He turned a walked away.

<u>July 23</u>

Wrote to Father and uncles to see if they were coming to the fair. They said it sounded like a grand idea, but they were too busy.

<u>August 8</u>

I got a note from Cora. She and Charles are getting married September 10 and plan on visiting the Chicago Exposition for their honeymoon. She is looking forward to seeing me. I will tell them to meet at the 59th St. entrance.

On September 12, Sam was standing by the gate as visitors poured in. When he did spot the newlyweds, he was surprised to see Cora on crutches as she and Charles approached the fair entrance. They were laughing as they made their way in the crowd.

"What happened to you?" he said as they approached.

She laughed and said, "it's a long story."

"No, it isn't," injected Charles. "She broke her foot to get out of going through the wedding ceremony, but it didn't work."

[104]

"I did not," she replied tartly. I was thinking of all I had to do, and I wasn't concentrating on what was in front of me. I was reshelving a sizable piece of granite, but somehow I didn't get it all the way on. It fell and landed on my foot. So, there. It's my own fault."

While Charles steadied her, she added, "we were hoping we could hire you to push me around the exposition."

"It will be my pleasure, and there is no charge. Step this way." Sam bowed and swept his arm in a grand gesture.

He introduced them to Ambrose and got Cora seated in the wheelchair. Then they set off down the Midway pleasance.

Many of the exhibits were reconstructed villages, and they made brief stops in "A Street in Cairo", the "Algerian & Tunisian Village", and the "Dahomey Village."

But Cora and Charles were fascinated by Ferris's huge contraption which dominated everything else. The slow, majestic motion of its steel frame and huge cars seemed to pull the viewer right out of the nineteenth century into the twentieth century. Charles insisted the boys accompany them and he paid the entrance fee. It was the first time either Sam or Ambrose had been on it.

Once inside the car, while it was stationary, Sam tried to be casual as if this were an everyday occurrence. But when the wheel began its rotation and the car began to ascend, it also began to gently rock. He grasped the railing in front of the glass window, his knuckles showing white. He had been in an elevator before, but not one that rocks.

> "I always laughed at stories about people going into shock when the wheel started up, but now I understood. Charles and Cora resorted to laughter and held tight to each other. Ambrose simply watched out the window, first looking up and then down."

The Ferris wheel cars were big enough to hold 60 people, so it was like a good-sized room in motion. Sam looked around at the other passengers and they too were being drawn into the totally unique experience. By the time they

[105]

reached the top, some 260 feet above the Midway, everyone had forgotten the movement of the car and were intently watching the expanding scene in front of them.

Few people stayed seated as the car neared the top, and Cora and Charles had moved over to the opposite side where they concentrated on the fairgrounds with its hundreds of buildings, walkways, lakes, and of course the thousands of people milling about. Ambrose was trying to identify the campus buildings while Sam walked back and forth trying not to miss anything.

After what seemed like a very short stay, the wheel began to move again. The ride down seemed more like gently floating down. After exiting Ferris's wheel, the four of them stood for a minute till they regained their land legs. Then they continued down the Midway, but it seemed to lose a bit of luster after Ferris's Wheel. Sam and Ambrose kept up their commentary.

It was not until the party reached the main part of the fairgrounds that the newlyweds had several requests. Cora wanted to see the Mary Cassatt mural in the Women's Building. She said Cassatt was one of her favorite painters, and she appreciated the nearly 60-foot-long work.

Next, they went to the Horticulture Building. Charles was particularly interested in the tropical plant display. Leaving there, they also looked in the green house.

After lunch, which Charles bought, they visited the Brazilian Building to which the Mutis's paid close attention.

The rest of the afternoon was taken up with stops at other buildings and exhibits. Cora was tiring and she said her foot was beginning to hurt. Charles suggested that instead of returning to the 59th Street entrance, they take one of the lake steamers to their hotel downtown. "Oh, how romantic," she said.

At the pier, Cora became solemn, "This has been a perfect day, and we owe it to both you and Ambrose. I have missed you, Sam. So often I wished you were back at the museum, but you have made the university and Chicago your home now. I can see that."

[106]

Sam had practiced a little parting speech, but when it came time to give it, he couldn't remember the words. All he could say was, "Cora, I owe you so much, and I can never repay all the things you have done for me."

She was a little teary and said they should part now before she cried. Hugs and handshakes were passed around. Cora said she could walk with her crutches to the boat. Sam and Ambrose took the wheelchair back to their station.

"On the way back, it seemed that, like a balloon, another part of my life had somehow separated from me and floated off. I no longer had any ties to it. Cora was right, I most certainly lived in Chicago now."

Chapter Twelve

8/22/93
        To: Catherine Jeppe
            Paris, France
Father died late yesterday. Letter to follow.
Sam

I sat in the apartment and reread the telegram. Then I looked around the room. Nothing seemed to have changed. The lilies I bought this morning were still blooming, I could still hear a delivery cart clattering down the cobblestone street outside, I could still smell the stew Charlotte was making for dinner tonight. And yet, my world had changed because my father was dead.

To be truthful it was not a complete shock. I had not been expecting the telegram, but he was an old man, and old men die. I knew someday I would get this telegram, but I was not expecting it that day.

It had been a nice day, warm with a hint of rain in the air. Charlotte and I had talked over tea about taking a boat ride on the Seine. Then the telegram came. I was shaken, momentarily confused, and saddened of course, but perhaps more than that I was suddenly very lonely.

For some reason I thought about his letters. Only a month ago I had gotten a short note from him. Even though I wrote to Father on a regular basis, he only replied three or four times a year, and even then, it was always just a short note.

The notes never contained anything about him. They were always about what was going on around him. The weather was always first. This is to be expected since he lived on a farm,

Been very dry since winter. The corn is small.

After that were little tidbits about the family,

Hiram wrenched his shoulder while scything.
Margaret won first place at the church bazaar with
her chocolate cake.

In my letters, I'd ask him how he was feeling, had he been well, what was he doing, did he want anything from Paris? I told him how much I missed him, how much I wanted to hear about him, but he never complied. I think he felt that what he did, what he thought, wasn't very important.

In one letter, I told him that he needed to talk about himself more. His next note contained one sentence about some furniture he was building for his room. After that note he didn't say any more about what he was doing.

Back in Milwaukee, I don't know if Father was embarrassed by what happened after Mother died. Perhaps he was, but he shouldn't have been. Some loads are just too heavy to bear. He told me he was a failure, and I said nothing. I was caught off guard. I was too busy being in charge. Besides, what do you say to your father when he says his life has been wasted? I've thought about that moment many times, and I have yet to come up with a good response. Still, that is one of those moments I wish I had back so I could say something, anything.

***

It was a couple of weeks before Sam's letter arrived, during which time I went through a spectrum of emotions. I took up the time with busy work since I found it hard to concentrate, not that I was looking forward to getting the letter containing details. I wished his telegram had been more informative. So, I waited.

[109]

To me, the letter served the same function as a funeral. A funeral acts as a period at the end of a sentence. It says, "This signals the end. From this day forward you can think of the deceased in terms of the past. You may resume your own life now." Sam's letter would take the place of the funeral I had missed.

June 20, 1893
Dear Cate,

I am sorry it has taken me so long to write this letter. I wanted to say a few things and it took me a while to get them right.

I am beginning to regain my bearings. It has helped to have the routine of work. However, at night I start thinking about things. Should I have done things differently? I miss him.

The first time I knew there was a problem was when I received a telegram from Uncle Hiram. That would have been August 8. He said Father was very sick and I should come as quickly as possible. I made arrangements with Ambrose to cover for me at the Fair and took the train to Racine as soon as I could.

As soon as I got there and found out how bad Father was, I began to feel guilty about not going to see him more often. That evening the family was sitting around after supper, and I started to cry. I told them how bad I felt. I told them you wished you could be here as well. Uncle Cyrus told me not to feel that way. He said parents expect their children to have lives of their own. If those lives take them far away, so be it.

He said our father was very happy at the farm. The more he recovered from the alcohol the more at peace he became. He always missed Mother, you, and me but now there were other things in his life for him to think about. He knew he made mistakes, but he learned to forgive himself. So, while he looked forward to seeing me

[110]

or getting a letter from you, his life did not revolve around us.

That was a great help to me. I was able to deal with the events of the next few days knowing I was not being judged. I thought you might be feeling guilty as well. I recall things you said to me when Mother died. I must tell you Father was very proud of you, and he knew you were doing something worthwhile. Every time I went to the farm, he said he wished you lived somewhere close by, but he knew you need to be in Paris to do what you are doing. I just thought you should know.

June 10

Uncle Hiram told me that last week Father was coming back from delivering a wagon part he made for a man when he was caught in a rainstorm. He came down with a chill and he took to his bed. The uncles went to town and asked a doctor to come out to the farm. He said it looked like pleuro-pneumonia. He told them to keep Father warm, and comfortable and hope for the best.

When I went in to see him, he was surprised I was there. He had a frequent cough, and said he had some chest pains. He was very weak. He had a fever during which he threw the covers off, but then had severe chills.

June 11

Father continued to decline, and I began to fear the worst. There were times he did not know me. During those times he wanted Mother, then sometimes he talked to someone invisible to me. His breathing was labored, and when he spoke, which was seldom, his words were slurred. He slept a lot. When he was awake, he often had hallucinations. He no longer ate anything, and only drank a little water.

[111]

Everyone here was very helpful. The minister came to pray over him. It was obvious to me that Father had become an important member of the family and community.

June 12

Father passed away late in the afternoon. His breathing became very shallow, and he just drifted into a deep sleep and then into the deepest sleep. At least he no longer hurt.

Uncle Cyrus wanted to bury him in the family cemetery on the farm and I said that was the right thing to do. The minister came the next day to perform the service. Uncle Hiram wanted to carve a wood headstone because Father loved wood, and that was fine with me as well. The service was short but was warm and caring.

Father didn't have many belongings and most of what he had was second hand, and I gave it all to the family. They can do with the things as they wish. I kept his violin and his papers. In that I do not play the instrument and my lodgings are somewhat lacking, I will send the violin to you.

I am back in Chicago. If you need to contact me, that is where I will be.

Love,
Sam

I always thought Sam would make a good reporter, but he was not very good at softening his descriptions. In any case, I appreciated his letter.

True to his word, Sam shipped Father's violin to me. It was a little dusty from lack of use and needed some minor repairs. I guessed Father had not played it much in the past few years. Charlotte recommended a good repair shop, and in due time they returned a fine instrument. Like Sam, I couldn't play it and I didn't want to pack it up and condemn it to permanent storage. Again, Charlotte saved the day. She knew of a young violinist who was very good, but also very poor.

[112]

She suggested loaning the instrument to him until he could afford one of his own. This I did. Later I placed the violin with a good teacher for him to loan it out to other young musicians who need a helping hand. Years later still, I gave it to a music school.

I wrote a lengthy letter to Uncle Hiram, and Uncle Cyrus and his family thanking them for all they had done to help Father during his last years. I told them that I had met people from all over the world, and the Jeppe family in Racine, Wisconsin were the most wonderful people I had ever known. They reached out and saved an old man from a slow, painful death on the streets of Milwaukee. Some might say they were obligated to do that because he was their kin, but there was more to it than that. The goodness that was deep in the soil, the buildings, and the people of that farm made it possible for my father to regain his character, and humanity. Whatever rewards they may reap will be justly deserved.

I tried to write a story about my parents. I worked on it for some time, but I found it impossible to find the necessary objectivity. I remembered the good times with great clarity, whereas the bad times were hazy and indistinct. I decided that is the way it should be, and I stopped. Eventually I did use some of it as the basis for the first few chapters of this book.

Chapter Thirteen

The Fair closed on October 30, and the city took a deep breath. Hundreds of thousands of people had gone through it. Most did not have the historical view that we do today. To them, it was an exciting, entertaining glimpse of a world many had never heard of, and other had only read about. The whole experience opened their eyes to the world outside their communities for the first time. The fair served as the calling card of the twentieth century.

Sam's Journal Entries
1893

October 2
　　Classes began today.

October 31
　　The fair closed yesterday. I was relieved, but a little sad too. It was a unique experience. Looking back, the things I first found fascinating soon became hum drum. Soon I was no longer overwhelmed by the rare or magical. That is too bad. I should strive to remain amazed by what I see, hear, or touch. The unique remains unique. It is me that changes.

November 10
　　In October, Eli came back from working with his father at the Carnegie Steel Company. He has avoided us most of the time since, and when we all have been together, he is

[114]

quiet, almost sullen. Both Ambrose and I know he was disappointed at not able to work the World's Fair with us. I also know, because he told me, he hates having his life planned out for him. But neither I nor Ambrose have done anything that should make him angry. We have need to talk to him and see if there is anything we can do for him.

November 16
Ambrose and I decided to make the 20th, my birthday even though, of course, it is not. Ambrose contacted Eli under the pretext of hosting a surprise dinner that evening. The restaurant down on 61st has a lake perch special that the three of us have had before. Eli, having no sound reason to refuse, accepted. He said he would meet us there.

At first the atmosphere was a little tense, and I hoped the plan was not a mistake. Ambrose ordered beer for himself and Eli. I, as usual, had tea. Those two managed to down two schooners before dinner came, and that eased the climate. Eli even laughed at little when we told him some tales of our adventures as chair pushers at the fair.

I have a new respect for Ambrose. I never realized how expertly he handles people. I have to wonder how many times he has manipulated me without my knowledge.

After a while, the topic of conversation drifted around to Eli. Ambrose pumped him about his summer adventures. Gradually it came out that his summer consisted of following his father around. He was not there to make suggestions or even ask many questions. Rather he was supposed to learn to imitate his father.

He began to open up saying it really was no different than the rest of his home life, or for that matter, for the lives of the rest of his family. His father rules with an iron hand. He will not allow anyone to display a hint of independence.

We just looked at him. What can you say?

He and Ambrose visited the men's room and ordered more beer. "I'm not finished with the story yet," he said when they returned.

In August his father announced that the family needed a bigger house. "You've been there, Sam," he said, looking at

[115]

me. "You know we have plenty of room and it's in good shape. But *he* wanted a new house because this one isn't big enough. He didn't ask anyone else's opinion, he just made the decision himself.

He found an architect and made Eli go with him so he could teach Eli "how to handle artisans." They met with a young man in his mid-twenties. His father described the type of house...the type of castle he wanted. It had to have turrets and everything. The architect listened and made notes until he finished.

Eli described what happened. "Then this architect began to talk. He said my father's ideas were out of style and a waste of time and money. He would design a house for my father, but it would look like it belonged in its setting, not something transplanted from Europe. It would have natural wood with quiet colors. Its surfaces would be clean and refreshing. The house's layout would be designed around our needs and not the ridiculous rooms found in most mansions.

"After a few minutes, my father's face began to get red, but he said nothing. Finally, when the architect finished, my father glared at the man and said, 'young man, you will either build the house I want, or I will go somewhere else.'

"The architect glared back and replied, 'I'm sorry we cannot do business.' My father stood up, 'Good evening, Mr. Wright,' and we left."

Since the restaurant was beginning to close for the evening, we finished our drinks.

"Let me pay the bill," Eli said. "This was a good idea even if Sam's birthday is in July." We all laughed.

While walking back to the campus, Eli continued, "As I sat there listening to the architect, I said to myself, I want to build houses like he is describing. Sam, I remember telling you I wanted to be an architect. Well, I've decided I want to design houses, not castles or skyscrapers." Eli's attitude brightened considerably, and you could hear his voice get more excited. "So, boys, that's what I'm going to do. I have talked to Mr. Frank Wright about what path to take. He suggested I learn drafting skills and construction techniques. When I finish those courses, I am to contact him for employment. I am

[116]

going to drop out of the university and sign up for classes at the Art Institute.

"When I told my father what I am going to do, we had a terrible fight and almost came to blows. He will not pay for any more of my education, and I have moved out. We haven't talked for the better part of a month. Paying for dinner was my last hurrah. I am now as poor as you. What do you think of that?"

I told him he could always get a meal at the Chinese restaurant as long as he had ten cents. "Seriously, you are quitting the university?"

"Exactly. I'll just be a short distance away, and we can still get together, but I am done with this place, my friends."

January 10

Ambrose and I helped Eli move his belongings to a small room nearer to the Art Institute. He will have a long walk to class, but like me, he can catch a trolley in bad weather. We promised to stay in touch. He said his mother is slipping him some money to help his cause, and he can get a part time job to make ends meet. He is excited to be doing what he wants to do, and not what his father wants him to do. But he is also afraid of failure because he could never face his father's scorn. The only way Eli can meet his father again is as two equally successful men.

That evening I thought about the difference between my father and Mr. Redding. Even with all his problems, my father stood head and shoulders above Eli's.

***

March 28, 1894
Dear Cate,

I got a letter from Cora yesterday. She said Charles has received a grant to research tropical plants in Brazil. It is going to be for a year, with a possible extension of another year. She is taking a leave of absence, so she can go with him.

[117]

That means her position at the museum will be open during the time she is gone. She asked me to fill in for a year or maybe two. I would have to stop taking classes for the duration. I asked Dr. Salisbury for his opinion. He said it has been his experience that students who take a year or more off rarely finish their degrees. In addition, he said he could not hold open my current job at the Walker Museum. So, he encouraged me to decline the offer.

That evening I wrote a letter to Cora thanking her for the offer, but I had to decline. I encouraged her to hire Mildred instead.

I think I made the right choice. I guess that is the thing about decisions. You do not know if you were correct until later, maybe you will never know.

Write soon,
Sam

Journal Entries
1894

April 10

Got another letter from Cora. I had to laugh because she said she was hoping I would refuse the offer. She felt obligated to offer the position to me before anyone else because I had worked there from the very beginning, and I was certainly qualified. Because Mildred had credits from another university, she would be graduating this year. Cora offered the position to her, and she accepted.

Last Monday Mildred came to the museum to thank me for helping her get the position at Milwaukee.

She said, "I owe it to you, Sam. The job in Milwaukee really belongs to you."

I told her, "I have to finish here, but thanks."

She gave me a quick hug and hurried from the room. We ran into each other between buildings the other day, but both of us were too busy to stop more than a second.

I wish we could have sat down and enjoyed the day, but all the girls I care about are busy going somewhere else.

***

During the summer of 1894, Sam worked as a stock boy in the same department store where he bought Ah Kum's shawl. It didn't pay all that well, but it wasn't very stressful either. While there, Sam was introduced to the art of bicycling.

April 28, 1894
....I do not know about Paris, but bicycles are all the rage here. Anyone who does not have one is just not up to date, and that unfortunately, includes me. But the other stock boy, Henry Mayner, is a wheelman. That is what members of men's bicycle clubs are called. He is teaching me how to ride and said he knows of a used cycle I can get for little or nothing, and he will help me put it in good shape....

After learning how to ride and fixing his bicycle, Sam often spent Saturdays riding around the city. Later he wrote,

....Yesterday I went for a ride along the lake front. I stopped to have a cup of hot tea in a wheelman's rest stop. I talked with three chaps who were just returning from a camping trip. They showed me their gear. It was quite simple and very compact. I am going to try camping when it gets a little warmer. That gives me all winter to collect my gear and figure out where to go....

Still later Sam decided on a destination,

[119]

....In my spare time I have been checking local maps and wheelmans' literature about bicycles and camping. I've settled on what could be a most exciting excursion. I'm going to go down the old Illinois and Michigan canal to the town of Morris. From there I'm going to go fossil collecting in the Mazon Creek area....

Sam didn't know it, but bicycling was very popular in Europe, especially in Paris. However, women were kept from using them because the early designs employed a large front wheel and a small rear wheel which made them impossible for women to ride if they were wearing the long dresses of the day. In the late 1880s a new design, the safety bicycle, was developed. It had two wheels the same size and the frame could be designed to allow women to mount it in complete modesty. While men saw the bicycle as a status symbol, a toy, women saw it as a means to liberation. Previously, if a woman wanted to leave her house alone, she had to walk, hitch up a horse, or rely on public transportation. Now she could ride a bicycle almost anywhere she wanted to go. It wasn't long before clothing manufacturers created new styles for women who rode bicycles. Bicycle bloomers, and shorter skirts replaced the floor length skirts that had been in use for hundreds of years. In France, a number of women began wearing culottes and regular pants which infuriated some men. But it was too late. Susan B. Anthony said bicycles had "done more to emancipate women than any one thing in the world."

I remember telling Sam I had been riding my bicycle for several years all around Paris, except the steepest parts of Montmarte. I'm sure I also needled him about being so fashionable.

***

Meanwhile, back at the restaurant, serious problems were brewing. They began one day at lunch hour. This time of day was usually busy even though most customers ordered chop suey of which several gallons were kept warm in a pot on

[120]

the back of the stove. People coming and going, always in a hurry, so Chung, Xue Mei, and Au Kum also had to hurry.

One day, six white men came and ordered expensive lunches. They ate all the food, but then complained about its quality. They refused to pay and stomped out turning over some chairs and a table in the process. They also insulted a Chinese couple, and another man who was also eating lunch. The next day they returned. When Chung refused to serve them, they started yelling and threatening him. Again, they messed up the place. This time they broke one of the Chinese lanterns that hung over the tables. This frightened Xue Mei, Au Kum, and Chung. They had run into anti-Chinese sentiment before, but they hoped they would not be attacked in Chicago because of the number of established Chinese already in the area. Sam wrote:

> ....I have noticed a change in Chung. He watches customers more carefully now. He is not as friendly toward them as he used to be, more businesslike. At night, he locks the doors as soon as the restaurant closes which he never did before....

The men didn't return, but everyone felt it was not just an isolated incident.

***

Late that fall, Sam had a real surprise. Chung told him Xue Mai was with child. There would be the normal stresses and worries connected with any birth, in this case however, there was an added concern.

> ....A problem arose a week ago and it gave me a lesson in our legal system. Chung asked me how someone becomes a citizen of the United States. He said neither he nor Xue Mei can become citizens, but he was told that if a child is born in the United States they are automatically a

[121]

citizen. I asked, "Why can't you be a citizen?" He said there is a law that says Chinese cannot be citizens. I had forgotten Congress passed such a law a few years ago....

Sam offered to talk to government officials and get the facts from the horse's mouth. He started with the U.S. Customs House. There he got the old run around. He was sent to the U.S. Circuit Court who sent him to the Cook County Court who told him to talk to a Judge Gresham back at the Circuit Court.

....The court clerk said, "Judge Gresham is in court and will probably leave shortly after adjournment. Besides, you need to talk to a lawyer, not a judge." I was getting angry. "I have a very simple question, and if he is any sort of a judge, he should be able to answer it very quickly.

A voice behind me boomed, "Most questions are simple until you look at the details. I've been a judge for twenty-six years and I can't recall a simple question in all that time. What's the problem, Edward?"

"I did not realize you had adjourned, Judge Gresham," replied a startled court clerk. I turned to see an older gray-haired, long bearded man, quite large and imposing.

"The trial hit a slow point and I was falling asleep. Who are you and what do you want," he said staring at me?

"My name is Sam Jeppe, sir. I am a student at the University of Chicago. I live with a Chinese family above their restaurant. They are going to have a baby and Chung, he is the father, wants to know if the baby will be a citizen of the United States when it is born."

"Walk with me, Mr. Jeppe, and we'll talk." After stopping by his office to get some papers, we walked down the hall. "This is not the simple question you thought it was. It is, in fact, one of

[122]

the most difficult questions the judiciary faces today. On one side of the argument, the Chinese Exclusion laws say a person of Chinese extraction is prohibited from ever becoming a citizen of the United States."

"I know, everyone has told me that."

"Good, you understand then there are no exceptions to that law. That's one side of the argument. The other side, however, points to the Fourteenth Amendment which says anyone born in the United States is automatically a citizen. So, the question is, can a person of Chinese heritage who is born here be considered a citizen? That question has yet to be answered, and when it is, there will be a lot of unhappy people on one side or the other. So, this judge cannot answer his question. Tell your friend not to get his hopes up because there are a lot of powerful people against him. Here's where we part, Mr. Jeppe. Also tell...what's his name?"

"Chung"

"Tell Mr. Chung he has a good friend. Be careful, Mr. Jeppe. It's a hard world out there." With that he walked through the doors leaving me standing in the way of others trying to get out.

That evening when I told him what Judge Grisham had said, Chung sat stone-faced. He quietly said, "Thank you," and left the room.

Somehow it does not seem fair to exclude one group of people while everyone else can come and go as they please. The small group of people who dictate such laws has too much power....

***

February 2, 1895
Dear Cate,

A very sad time here. I am fine, but my Chinese family has had a terrible scare.

[123]

It began last Friday when Chung walked to the market for fresh vegetables. This is something he does every other day so the food they serve is the best they can make. He always puts his purchases on account which he pays the last Friday of the month. Chung, of course, does not have a bank account, so he pays everything in cash.

The market is about five blocks from the restaurant. Frequently he cuts through an alley to shorten the trip. I am sure you have guessed what happened. He was waylaid by two men and robbed. What's more, they hit him several times and kicked him when he had fallen. The thieves then made their escape, leaving him lying in the mud almost unconscious. At some point someone saw him and called the police. Two officers came, but they would not seek any medical help because he is Chinese, and the Chinese Exclusion Act says Chinese cannot be treated at a hospital. They did get him sitting on a crate and gave him some water. To make matters worse, they demanded to see his identification papers.

Chinese are supposed to carry these papers with them at all times or else face immediate deportation. Because he rarely leaves the restaurant, Chung keeps them in a drawer rather than risk getting them stained by grease and dirt. He explained his papers were back at the restaurant and if the officers accompanied him, he would get them. Apparently one of the policemen cannot tolerate Chinese, and he was all set to turn Chung over to the courts for deportation, but the other officer had eaten at the restaurant several times and recognized Chung. He vouched for Chung's honesty and offered to walk back with Chung to get his papers. This would not do for the first officer, and they had an argument. Meanwhile, Chung sat on a dirty crate, bloodied and bruised.

[124]

Eventually they agreed to go to the restaurant with Chung and get his papers, but in their report, they would point out he had no papers on his person. One officer wanted to give Chung a ride to the restaurant in the police wagon, but Chung refused. He thought it was a trick and they would take him to jail. So, Chung and the second officer walked back to the restaurant while the first officer went with the wagon.

Chung showed them his papers which were in the cash drawer. The first policeman wanted to search the building for illegal Chinese but was talked out of it by the second officer. This was fortunate because Au Kum was upstairs.

Finally, they got around to the assailants and the robbery. Chung gave them descriptions of the men and how much money they had taken. The police told him not to expect the return of the money because they had little hope of catching the robbers. This is probably because they would not pursue the case, he being Chinese and all.

By the time I got home, Chung was stiff and sore from the beating. He was doing his best to take orders and serve food but was slowly wearing down. They were close to running out of some vegetables and Xue Mei was becoming frantic about the situation. I quickly took some money and went to the grocery store. There, I explained what had happened, got enough supplies to get through a couple of days, and paid some of the bill. I promised Chung would be in to settle up as soon as he was able.

Back at the restaurant, I demanded Chung sit in the back where Xue Mei could keep an eye on him. Then I took orders and served the food. I got lots of strange looks from both White and Chinese customers. Chung and Xue Mei do not have a large menu, and I memorized it long ago. In addition, I have watched Chung serve food

[125]

hundreds of times, so I had no problems during the evening. When the restaurant closed, we helped Chung upstairs and put him in bed. Xue Mei, Au Kum, and I went back downstairs and cleaned up.

Saturday, Chung said he felt better, but his face was badly bruised, and we all agreed customers would leave the first time they took a look at him. Being Saturday, I had no obligations, so I went back to waiting tables. Many of our regular customers expressed their horror when I explained what had happened. A couple of Chinese volunteered to help the family. There are worse jobs than waiting tables, but when it got busy, I must admit I got a bit ragged.

Today, Chung is up and slowly moving around. Xue Mei has been using some Chinese herbs on his face and while it is still swollen, it looks better. He sat and handled the cash drawer while I again waited tables.

It is easy to see both Chung and Xue Mei are depressed about what has happened. I think the worst of it is the way he was treated by the police. Instead of being the victim, he was treated as if he was the villain. Added to their disappointment regarding citizenship, I can imagine they are asking themselves what is the point of all their efforts. Still, they remain friendly toward me. They expressed their gratitude for my help, and Au Kum even smiled at me. The latter is a wonderful complement.

I am getting angry and frustrated at stupid people who hurt others because they look different. I am not sure of what I can do, but I feel something must be done. This sort of thing has gone on long enough.
Love,
Sam

***

[126]

April 12, 1895

….I've got to catch you up on events here.

First, I must tell you that things have been quiet at the restaurant since Chung's run-in with the robbers and the police. Of course, the former have never been caught. Chung has recovered fully. He lost some money, but he seems to have lost some heart too. He is more cautious now. He does not laugh much anymore. He frequently seems to be deep in thought.

Xue Mei is doing quite well, I think. She is not only carrying a child, but she is carrying the family as well. She continues to cook every day in the restaurant and wash clothes every night. Her enthusiasm is remarkable. Au Kum is...Au Kum. Nothing seems to bother her. She lives each day without complaint. It is as if she has forgotten her previous step and will not worry about her next step. The only thing that matters is the step she is taking. Maybe almost anything is better than her former life, or maybe she no longer cares about much. I do not know, but I have come to respect her for the way she sees life.

My bicycle trip is scheduled for next week. However, I am not sure I should go because of all the problems here at the restaurant. I asked Chung, and he said they would be fine. He appreciated the thought though….

***

June 8, 1895
Dear Cate,

My bicycle trip was a huge success. I left the Friday following the return of the field school. Packing was an ordeal because not only did I have food, clothing, and camping gear, but also bicycle repair equipment and geology equipment. My

[127]

bedroll was securely wrapped in an oil cloth and then lashed to the handlebars. It took a little getting used to carrying twenty pounds on my back while trying to control the bicycle.

The north end of the canal is about 30 miles from home. The roads are asphalt or graded dirt, and that part was not too bad.

The canal is abandoned, but overall, it is still in decent condition. The canal is about fifty to sixty feet wide which allowed for canal boats to pass each other. When it was operating, mules pulled the boats from one end to the other. They walked on towpaths on either side of the canal. Now the towpaths make perfect roads for bicycles.

Because I was anxious to try out my new camping gear, I stopped a little early to set up camp. Except for mosquitoes the night was fine.

At dawn's early light I was up and ready to go. My second day's pedaling took me to where the canal meets the Illinois River. From there it was only sixteen miles to Morris. There are some islands in the river nearby, and I found a clearing across from one where I decided to stay for the night so I could start my explorations fresh in the morning.

I sat for a while reading a dime novel I had brought along. Eventually though, I set up camp not that it takes very long since I had no tent, but I did have to collect some driftwood for my campfire. As I was sitting on a log eating my hardtack, dried beef, and bubbly water, a young bare-foot lady in a faded dress came walking down the river's edge carrying a fishing pole and a string of fish. Her dirty hair and unkempt look made it apparent she was probably a member of one of the hardscrabble tenant farmers located along the river. We greeted each other and I observed that fishing must be pretty good.

[128]

"'nuf for the family's dinner tonight. Doesn't look like ya did very well."

"Oh, I'm just camping here for the night. I'm on a bicycle camping trip.

"Good night." She shifted her line of fish and pole while walking off upstream.

"Good night to you." She did not reply nor look back. Make a note, bring fishing equipment next time.

I was bothered all night by sand flies and mosquitoes. Sometime during the night I heard large animals splashing in the river water. The moon was up so I looked to see who they were. A number of deer were crossing from the mainland to the islands. I guess island leaves are more tender to eat. I watched the scenery and slapped mosquitoes for a while then fell asleep.

In the morning, I boiled some tea water, had my last apple and prepared for the next chapter of my adventure. Normally I would still be hungry after just an apple, but the excitement of my expedition must have satisfied the need for sustenance. Shortly after sunrise, I pedaled to a nearby bridge that took me to Mazon Creek.

The fossils I wanted to find were encased in chunks of siderite also known as ironstone. Originally, these nodules would occasionally wash out of the riverbank and residents collected them. But starting in the 1850s, coal was mined in the area. The spoil or refuse from the mines contained many more of these concretions....

Sam's letter continues describing in general what he found at Mazon Creek, but I'm going to switch to his journal entries for those three days. I don't know what he was talking about much of the time, however, it shows how far he had come in a few short years. He really had changed from a timid teenage boy to a young professional man. I only wish Mother and Father could have read what he wrote.

[129]

Journal Entries
1895

<u>May 29</u>

Arrived at the mouth of Mazon Creek early in the morning. The sky was overcast and threatening. Found a thicket shielded with brambles where I locked the bicycle to a sapling and did my best to cover it with leaves. Changed to wading boots. Rucksack, canteen, and bedroll make for a bulky load.

The creek water level was low, and I had no problem crossing from one side to the other even though the stream was quite wide. This part of the creek was mostly straight with low banks no more than three or four feet high. Water line usually muddy. When the stream did change direction there were the usual cut banks and opposing cut bars. Here the hunting was much better. Any areas between the side of the bank and the water's edge were covered with small to medium sized rocks.

My prey, my objectives, were nestled in those rocks. The nodules ranged from walnut size to a little bigger than my hand. Generally, they tended to be roughly ovoid, medium brown to a reddish-brown, and pretty smooth. At first, I had a difficult time finding specimens, but soon I learned what to look for and they fairly jumped out of the piles of rubble. The creek was muddy by nature, and it was almost impossible to see nodules in the stream bed. It occurred to me to walk in midstream rather than on the bank. That way I could see both sides.

Had seen a number of nodules already halved either by natural causes or previous human effort. None of these had any fossil impressions. Along the way I collected half a dozen specimens.

Found a clearing and stopped to see what I had collected. Gently tapping my nodules did little more than mar the surface. I hit one harder with no particular result. Rotated it and gave it a meaningful whack at its apex. The nodule split in two nearly identical halves but revealed no fossil. Moved to

[130]

the second and the third with similar results. The fourth nodule, the first one I found, split nicely and rewarded me with a fossil print, part of a compound leaf. Called it Specimen #1.

By lunch time, had found seven additional nodules with fossils. I noted the times I found them. This way I had approximate locations for each even though I found it impossible to estimate the distance I had come because of the many stops I had made along the way.

It drizzled a little after lunch. Even so, was determined to go another four hours. During that time found nine more fossils. One of them yielded part of a feather-shaped leaf, and another had several bi-valves.

That evening was miserable. Because all the wood was wet had no fire to stay warm. I ate a cold meal and drank water. I covered the bedroll with the oil cloth and slept in wet clothes sitting against a tree.

May 30

About midnight, it stopped raining. In the morning I lit two candles and heated a small tin cup of tea for breakfast. The sun came out for a while, and I sat in it to dry off a little. While doing that I added to my field notes and tried to identify the fossils I found yesterday. #1 was a fragment of a leaf of a *Pecopteris* tree fern. #4 was a fragment of the seed fern *Neuropteris*. I was not sure what #7 was but I thought it was a series of *Heteroconchia* bivalves. Figured I should be able to identify most of the rest when I returned to the university.

The stretch of Mazon Creek that I passed through today meandered thus creating cut banks. They yielded a greater number of nodules. However, did not find an appreciable increase in fossils since other fossil hunters before me also discovered this to be a good hunting ground. Where I would have expected to find numerous nodules, there were only numerous broken ones.

Found another *Pecopteris* specimen and an unidentified bark fossil. I also recovered a worm trail. Finally, I found something that looked like a fossil but it had no discernible form, and marked it as unidentified.

[131]

The evening was a little more bearable since there was no rain. Found some wood under a fallen tree that was not too wet, so I had a comfortable fire. Mosquitoes tolerable.

May 31
The Creek continued to meander for a while, but soon straightened itself out. With the current slower than downstream there was little erosion and few nodules. I quickly walked the final distance and made it to a farm road by noon. From a map of the area, I figured the total distance walked over the past three days as being somewhere around thirteen miles. Caught a ride with a farmer who was headed to Morris. He dropped me off at the Illinois River where I retrieved my bicycle. The return trip was uneventful except for some rain.

Chapter Fourteen

On July 29, Xue Mei had a baby girl. Needless to say, having a baby in the household would be a new experience for Sam.

August 1, 1895
....It is a girl! Chung and Xue Mei had a girl July 29. She is very cute, but I guess all babies are. Mother and daughter are doing well. Xue Mei is up and around as if nothing in particular had happened. She wanted to open the restaurant as usual, but Chung insisted they close it for a day. They argued, but the restaurant is closed for a day. Au Kum is doing the laundry for two days. I asked Chung if there is anything I can do. Smiling, he told me to basically stay out of the way....

August 9

Journal Entries
1895

September2
August 31 was Mae's one month birthday. This is special and her coming out celebration. Friends stopped by to wish her well, and were given little red cakes and eggs dyed red. The cakes had the impression of two oranges on top to

[133]

signify she is a girl. Chung seemed as happy as I have seen him for a long time.

September 25

Chung and Xue Mei continue to be harassed. Most of the time it is little things, thank goodness. Last Friday someone put garbage on in front of the restaurant. Chung cleaned it up as soon as he discovered it, but you can tell he is getting tense again as if he is waiting for some real damage.

October 20

Late Friday, someone threw another brick through a window. This time they rolled it in paper upon which they wrote the most disgusting note. Basically it said, "get out of Chicago." The family is very upset. Xue Mei cried which is very rare.

Yesterday evening I noticed the family was unusually quiet. There was none of the usual banter as Xue Mei did her daily laundry of shirts. Chung just sat and quietly looked at the paper. Later, I was studying in my room when Chung knocked and asked to come into my room. I think that was the first time he had come in there since I moved in, so I knew something was wrong. He did not hesitate, but quickly said, "We have decided to close the restaurant. It is too dangerous to stay here. Xue Mei, Mae Lin and I will move back to New York City. Xue Mei still has family there, and we can start again."

I had feared something like this might happen, but I did not expect it so soon, and sat in silence. I could not think of anything to say. Finally, I muttered, "I am sorry."

"We have some things to do, and we will stay for next month, but we will close the restaurant on the 23rd. You are welcomed to stay till we leave."

"Thank you, I will. Isn't Au Kum going with you?"

"We want her to come, but we must take the train back to New York City. When we get on they will ask to see our papers. She has no papers, and she will be arrested. So, she must find a place to stay in Chinatown. She will be safe there, but it is very sad."

[134]

I stood up and faced him. "All this is wrong. You should be protected from vandals, and you should not have to carry identification papers. It is just wrong."

He shrugged his shoulders and left.

I could not study anymore. I just went for a walk.

The more I walked the angrier I got. These people were being bullied for no reason. They have never hurt anyone. They just wanted to live quietly and run their restaurant.

When I returned Chung was still sitting in the main room while Xue Mei finished up ironing some shirts. Au Kum was seated in her usual chair and Mae Lin was laying on a blanket.

"You cannot just leave," I exploded. "You have not done anything wrong. You must stand your ground."

Xue Mei stopped ironing and watched me. Chung sat quietly, listening to my harangue. He thought for a moment and then said, "Sam, we do not even know who our enemy is. We do not know how many there are. We do not know how strong they are. No, we will let them have this building. We will return to New York City where we can live in peace. By doing so, we will win in the long run."

Later, I laid in my hammock trying to think of something I could do. I kept coming back to Au Kum. I could not stop the family from leaving, but there must be a way to keep her with them.

She needs identification papers. The only feasible idea I could come up with was to get some counterfeit papers for her. But getting them, that is the rub. This requires stealth, smarts, and cunning. It requires Eli and Ambrose.

October 26

Tuesday, I found Ambrose at the library where he usually studied, and he readily volunteered to contact Eli. We agreed to meet over lake perch dinners Friday evening. I explained the situation to them while we enjoyed the usual hot tea and schooners of beer. Finally, I got to the counterfeit papers, and Ambrose calmly said, "Naturally. What took you so long to get to the obvious. First we need to find a dishonest printer".

[135]

I pointed out, "This is likely going to be an expensive undertaking. I am not sure where I will get a lot of money."

"That won't be a problem," Eli said. "Daddy dear will be happy to pay however much the cost will be. Of course, he won't know he's paying, but my mother will get the money from him, she will give it to me, I will give it to you, and you will give it to the counterfeiter. Simple. Besides who better to pay for such a stupid law than one who supports it."

November 1

For the better part of a week after our dinner no one had any luck finding a dishonest printer. Eli saw the obvious first, "What about a Chinese printer?"

"Maybe so," I agreed, "but we still do not know how to contact one."

"We don't, but Chung may know of one," Ambrose replied.

"I do not want to bring him into the plan until it is solid."

Ambrose nodded sagely, "You have no choice, my friend." I thought for a minute and had to agree.

The next day I explained to Chung what we proposed to do and our need for a printer. He smiled, "I thought of the same thing. I know a man who has a real paper. But we cannot get a photograph and the paper will cost $100, and I gave up," he said.

I laughed. "You know someone! Wonderful. Ambrose can take a photo, and Eli can get the money."

"A hundred dollars is a lot of money, where can this Eli get that much?"

I lied. "His father is very rich and very willing to support such an undertaking." Chung thought a few seconds. "This is very good news. We can go to Chinatown tomorrow."

"Eli will have to talk to his father and get the money so I do not think we can do it that soon."

"I understand. Tell me when you have the money, and we will go."

The next day I sent a telegram to Eli. A short time later I got a telegram back saying he would have the money in two

[136]

days. I found Ambrose in his usual study spot and let him know. He said he could photograph her tomorrow and have the picture ready in three days.

The next day Ambrose came with his camera, and we took Au Kum outside to photograph her. She was very nervous. She did not know what to do. He took several shots.

The next evening, I met Eli and got the money. He said his mother got a real chuckle when he told her what the money was for.

November 17

Ambrose brought the best photo to the restaurant. Somehow, he made it look yellow and it looked old. We avoided showing it to anyone in the Chinese family so they could remain innocent.

November 19

Monday, Chung and I went to Chinatown. On the way Chung told me how to act and what to say. Even though this was a business deal, it had to be done properly.

This was the first time I had been to Chinatown. The street we started down was pretty narrow and had only rough wooden walkways and a few oil lamps to light the way at night. The vast majority of people were Chinese dressed in their traditional garb. Some stores had display windows to show off their expensive objects such as fancy clothing. Most stores though were open to the street like booths with the proprietor standing in front hawking his wares.

We walked down the street to a side street to an ally to another alley. I was totally lost. By now little shacks had replaced the formal stores.

Eventually we came to a small building, a little nicer than its surrounding neighbors but still pretty basic. There was a small paper sign in the window with Chinese characters. Chung knocked lightly on the door and waited patiently till an older man opened it. He looked first at Chung and then sharply at me. The man formally bowed and stepped aside, and we entered. Only the light from a small window lighted the room.

[137]

Once inside, Chung spoke, "Mr. Shan, this is my friend, Sam Jeppe. He would ask your advice on a matter of great importance to him."

Mr. Shan replied in Chinese starting a lengthy and somewhat animated conversation. After a moment, Mr. Shan addressed me, "I was not trying to hide something from you Mr. Sam, but my English is not as good as it should be. I thought I might understand better if Chung told me about you in my own language. Please forgive me."

"That is perfectly alright," I replied. "May I explain my problem?"

"First, it is customary to have a cup of tea. Then we can talk."

"Thank you." We sat in the dark room and silently drank our tea. When we finished the tea, I told Mr. Shan I had a Chinese friend who had lost her identification papers in a fire. Chung had suggested I talk to him because he is very wise and might know of someone who had a blank copy of an identification paper and might be willing to sell it for $50. Mr. Shan shook his head, no there were no blank identification paper that he knew of for $50. "It is unfortunate that I cannot help your friend," he said. "How old is this person?" I replied I did not really know, but she looked old. He paused for a moment and then continued, "I heard there is an old man whose wife died. Her paper was lost for a while, but recently he found it. I think he might be willing to sell it, but not for $50."

"How much do you think he would be willing to sell it for," I asked?

"Not less than $150."

I paused. "That is unfortunate. I only have $75."

"Well, I might be able to get him to sell for $125, but not $75."

I paused again. "If I was able to get $100 would he sell it?"

"Perhaps. I would have to ask him."

"I would be grateful if you would ask him."

"It would be my pleasure." He got up and walked into the back room.

[138]

A minute later he reappeared with a paper in his hand. "My friend agrees to the price of $100."

"May I look at the paper?"

"Certainly."

It was too dark to see it clearly and I moved to the window. It was worn but legible. I thought the photo could be removed without damaging the paper. "I am satisfied." I handed Mr. Shan ten ten-dollar bills which he counted carefully twice.

"Mr. Shan, you have been a great help. Your reputation as a fair and wise man holds true. May you prosper."

Mr. Shan rose and moved toward the door. Chung, who had been silent the whole time, rose and followed him. Mr. Shan bowed to both of us, and I returned the act. Once outside and away from the door, I asked Chung how I did.

"You did everything right. Are you sure you do not have a little Chinese in your blood? Now put the paper in your pocket. I may be stopped and searched after leaving Chinatown, but they will not search you." The trip back was uneventful, thank goodness.

Ambrose removed the old photo, dirtied up the new one and glued it in the assigned spot. Au Kum's new name was Xiu Ying, which I found out means "Beautiful Flower." Her birth date was in 1833 which would make her 62 years old. Ambrose and I presented the paper to Chung on Thursday. He put it carefully away with his.

November 24

Yesterday, they kept the restaurant open as usual until the evening. About 6:00 they ceremoniously placed the closed sign in the window. A few friends come by with some special dishes. People tried to make it a gay event, but everyone knew Chung and Xue Mei were being forced to close. So, it became a rather solemn event. About 8:00 Chung called Au Kum out from the kitchen. Xue Mei placed the red shawl over her shoulders. Chung showed her the identification paper we had prepared. He explained that now she could come to New York City with them, and it was because of Eli, Ambrose and me.

[139]

She looked at the paper carefully. Chung explained the name on the paper was Xiu Ying and during the trip she must answer to that name, not Au Kum. She whispered to Xue Mei that she liked it better than Au Kum and would keep it. Then she pointed to the photo and asked who that was. When Xue Mei said it was a photo of her she laughed and tried to brush her hair. Then Au Kum did something totally unexpected. She walked over and stood in front of each of the three musketeers and bowed deeply to each of us. I almost cried. In return, I stood and bowed to her. The other two did likewise. That simple gesture more than paid for all the work we had put in.

***

December 1, 1895
Dear Cate,

I almost forgot I had to find a new place to live. Ambrose reminded me and at the same time suggested a solution. He invited me to move in with him till June graduation. I accepted quickly before he had time to reconsider. We will share the rent.

I considered staying with the family till the last possible minute, but I decided they needed their privacy. I helped dismantle the restaurant and helped take the things to the second-hand store a few doors away. It was very sad to walk into the empty room that once had been the dining area. So many warm times, and of course so many wonderful meals. I shall treasure the memories.

It took me two trips to Ambrose's to get my things moved. When I got ready to take my load of books with me, I told Chung I would meet them at the train station when they left. This way I delayed the good-byes a little while longer. I also thought if a White person was there to see them off, there would be less chance of them being questioned by the train security. I got the time and station and with no fanfare I walked down the

[140]

stairs and out the door. It would probably be the last time I would be in that neighborhood. I looked around. Frankly, I was glad to be leaving it. I did not care for some of the people that lived nearby.

I had not been to visit Ambrose in his room for some time. I assumed living there would be a cramped experience because of all the chemicals, costumes, photographic equipment, papers and books he had. So, I was pleasantly surprised even a little shocked when he opened the door to a spacious, clean, well-organized abode.

"I hope I did not force you to pack up all your instruments and things just to accommodate me," I said once I stepped inside.

"No, I hadn't used most of that stuff for a while and your moving here provided a good reason for packing it away. As you can see, I've kept the photography darkroom since it is an invaluable aide. Besides, it's time to move on to other personas."

"Ambrose, you are a constant source of amazement for me."

"I'm happy to be entertaining. My parents will be proud. I thought you might take that corner by the window. I remember you said your former room had no window. Of course, it is a little cooler during the winter, but it's not unbearable."

"Thanks, that will be fine. I am used to frigid temperatures and I will enjoy being able to look out at the world."

After sorting out the furniture, hanging the hammock and a rope for my hanging clothes, I began to feel right at home.

December 2

On the 30th I went to meet Chung and his family at the railroad station. Ambrose came along for support. I think he wanted to see if Au Kum's identification paper passed muster. The train was

[141]

not due to leave until 10:30, but we arrived at 9:30. The family was standing on the platform waiting patiently. After all the perfunctory greetings and questions, we lapsed into an uncomfortable period of silence. I wondered if we should have stayed away and let them get on their way, but I did want to make sure they had no trouble leaving. Xue Mei let me hold Mae Lin for a while. Au Kum, or rather Xiu Yang, wearing her red shawl, stood a little apart from the group, clearly nervous. This was to be her first train ride, and she did not know what to expect. Chung checked the tickets several times and watched the station clock.

The train arrived, on time. We approached the appointed car where the conductor was ready to take the tickets. I wished them all good luck in New York and thanked them for letting me stay with them. I tried to be unemotional, but I did not have much luck. Chung came over and offered his hand. It was the first time I had ever shaken hands with him. He said quietly, "We owe you a great deal."

"No more than I owe you."
He smiled, "When we have a son, we will name him Sam." Tears welled up in my eyes. Quickly he turned and presented the tickets and identification papers to the conductor who checked the papers and returned them, punched the tickets, and motioned the group on board. All of a sudden, it was over. My Chinese family was gone. I could see them walking down the aisle to their seats, but they were just shadows among other shadows. Ambrose and I decided to wait till the train left so we stood there saying nothing. A face appeared at a window. Au Kum had a window seat. We looked at each other as the train's whistle blew and it started to move. I bowed and she raised her hand as they left the station.
Love,

[142]

Sam

I am very proud of Sam and his friends for their actions. What they did was a small act of rebellion against unethical, unconstitutional laws. It was also courageous because had they been caught, it would have meant immediate dismissal from the university and probably legal charges. In 1898, the Supreme Court heard the case anticipated by Judge Grisham. Their verdict was in favor of the Chinese. That meant any person of Chinese heritage born in the United States was a citizen.

Looking back on the Chinese Exclusionary acts, they are sad examples of what happens when greed and fear overpower unbiased reasoning. Unfortunately, it took until 1943 for the government to repeal all of the acts.

An additional footnote. Sometime after I returned to New York City in 1938, just out of curiosity, I looked up the names Mae Lin and Sam Lin. I did find a Samuel Lin listed as a physician in Chinatown. I don't know what relation, if any, he had to Lin Chung and Xue Mei, but I like to think he is their son.

Chapter Fifteen

Sam had lost his second family. For a young man who was used to plowing the field by himself, this was distressing. He found the comfort of being surrounded by others was something he needed. Sam was lonely.

December 22, 1895
Dear Cate,
　　Happy Christmas from snowy Chicago. The semester is over. Not as bad as I expected, but not as good as it should have been. Things are going well with Ambrose and me. Right now, his parents are starring in a play which has traveled to New York City for the holidays. After final exams were over, he took the train to meet them. He will stay there until the Winter Quarter begins. I will meet Eli for Christmas dinner and that will be my celebration. I have a small gift for him. It is lonely here without my Chinese family or you. I have not heard anything from them, but I really did not expect anything.
　　The geology museum is closed so I cannot go and work. It is as much a home now as I have. Dr. Salisbury has left on a short field trip. The geology club once again sponsored a skate, but I did not go. Instead, I found a fireplace in the library and caught up on my reading. I have adopted Ambrose's habit of studying there rather than the room. It is warm and it is nice to have

other people around me even though I may not know them. When I tire of reading, I watch other students. It will close the day before Christmas and not open again until January. So, this means I will be spending a lot of time reading in our cold room or looking out the window.

I have been spoiled by living above a restaurant. I am used to having wonderful meals without having to do more than walk down the stairs and sit down. Now there is not even a pantry. We go to a market down the street and buy food that can be stored at room temperature and will not draw bugs. This limits our menu to fruit, raw vegetables, small amounts of baked goods, crackers, and a little cheese.

I eat out more often than I have in the past. Sadly, the nearest Chinese restaurant is several blocks away. Its food is not as good as what I am used to, but there is a good German restaurant nearby.

Love,
Sam

Journal Entries
1895

December 29

Eli and I had our Christmas dinner and exchanged our gifts. He gave me a rendering he made of the Walker Museum. It is quite good. We chatted a while, but he was meeting his mother and he could not make an afternoon of it. My asthma is bothering me with this cold weather.

Saturday I just did not feel like studying. I was trying to think of something to do when I realized I had not been to the Field Columbian Museum since it opened a year ago. Since it was located in the old Palace of Fine Arts of the World's Fair, it was not too far away. Saturday and Sunday are free days. So off I went.

[145]

I found the museum open, but quiet which was fine with me. Most of the things on display came from the World's Fair and I recognized some of them. I wondered through the geology exhibit rather quickly since I am quite familiar with most of the things they exhibit. The overall exhibit was good, but our exhibit in Milwaukee was better. After wandering through the zoological and botanical exhibits, I finally visited the anthropology exhibits.

Late in the day I came to the American Indian exhibit. The Woodland artifacts were similar to Milwaukee's collection. But I found myself captivated by the Southwest Indian pottery. There had been three or four displays of Southwest pottery at the world's fair, but I never took the time to look at them carefully then. At first glance, the Pueblo pottery seemed simple in shape, bowls, and jars and such, but they were beautifully made. However, the painted patterns on them are outstanding. Some are figurative, but many others have very complicated geometric patterns. Apparently, there were many different variations depending on the time frame and makers' locations.

December 30

Over the last few days, I have done little more than sit in the parlor to keep warm. I am one of the few boarders in residence, and I have the stove to myself most of the time. I have several books to keep me company, although my mind has kept returning to the Pueblo pottery I saw in the museum. I wonder about the people who made them, and why the pottery is intricately decorated. I have no way to find out since the library is closed and the faculty is gone. I have made up hypothetical solutions which I will test with facts when the new quarter begins.

***

January 14, 1896

Dear Cate,
        Happy New Year.

[146]

Here, the Winter Quarter has started. I signed up for a course in archaeology, a basic course in organic chemistry, and an advanced course in Geographic Geology. Only three courses this semester, but they will be tough classes and I will need extra time to keep up. I thought Ambrose was going to take the chemistry class with me, but at the last moment he backed out.

While he has not said anything about it to me, I think Ambrose has made a decision about his future. I am sure one of these days he will broach the subject. As demonstrative as he is in public, when it comes to his private being, he is quite secretive. I keep thinking about the Southwest pottery. I stopped at the Field Museum again. I was told to talk to a Mr. Holmes who is the curator. He was not there. I wrote him a short note explaining my interest and asked for an opportunity to talk with him. Shortly I received a note saying he would be happy to talk with me, but it had to be soon because he was leaving on an expedition to Mexico in about a month and needed time to prepare.

I found William Holmes to be a thin man with a salt and pepper handlebar mustache and a trimmed goatee. He struck me as being a little reserved and precise with his statements.

"Well, tell me Mr. Jeppe, what can I do for you."

I explained I was searching for a direction in which to proceed after graduation. Originally my intention was to work with a geologic collection in a large museum, however having done so for almost twelve years I felt the need to get out in the field. I told him I was not interested in working in the petroleum industry, and I doubted I could ever teach geology at a university. Finally, I saw the Southwest pottery exhibit in this museum. I was requesting his opinion regarding

[147]

my moving toward specializing in Southwest geology and cultures.

He replied, "A lot of people are buying pottery from the pueblos out there for themselves or museums, but only a few are trying to tie present day pottery to ancient pottery. The surface decoration may be the most obvious characteristic of interest in the identification and differentiation of a pot, but some men think the clay and the shape of the piece are of equal importance. There is some work being done, but it is pretty wide open. Of course, this is just one example of where geology is very important to archaeology, and geologists are much sought after when a site is being dug."

My smile gave away my excitement.

"However, Mr. Jeppe, keep in mind there are very few wealthy geologists, and those that are well-off are all in the petroleum or mining fields. A geologist specializing in archaeology can't depend on a steady income coming from excavations. They all teach in some institution, or, like me, hold a position in a museum. So, I would suggest you look for a museum position first, and then pursue the field of archaeology."

He smiled and said, "Unfortunately I must excuse myself. I need to prepare for the Mexican expedition. You don't speak Spanish do you?"

"No."

"That's unfortunate. We need another Spanish speaking person in the group. If you are serious about doing research in the Southwest, I suggest you learn some Spanish. It will be very helpful. By the way, if you are looking for a contact in that area of the country, I suggest you contact Adolph Bandelier in Santa Fe, New Mexico. I haven't heard from him in several years, but I think he's still there. He is a bit prickly,

[148]

however he is one of the leading authorities in the field.

I thanked him and made my exit.

I will not rush to a decision right away, but at this point I have to admit this is a very interesting scenario.

Perhaps Your Suntanned Brother,

Sam

***

February 24, 1896

....I am sorry I have not written in a while. I had a bout of asthma earlier this month, and it put me behind in my schoolwork. I am feeling better now. We had a warm spell last week, and that helped. Dr. Salisbury told me to go home and get well before coming back to work. For five days I sat by the wood stove in the sitting room and wheezed. I tried asthma cigarettes, and they helped a little. I also drank honey and hot water instead of my tea.

I spent the time by the wood stove thinking about pottery. I am getting excited. I must admit too, the idea of living in a warm climate is most appealing. So, I wrote to Adolph Bandelier. We shall see what comes of it....

***

March 30, 1896

Dear Cate,

I held off writing in hopes of receiving a reply from Adolph Bandelier. I am somewhat depressed over his lack of response. A letter in the negative would be helpful. Then at least I can begin searching for other options of employment, but now I do not know what to do. I should have explored the opportunities at the Field Columbian

[149]

Museum while Mr. Holmes was here, but now he is gone to Mexico so I will have to wait till he returns. There are some possibilities in the lead mines around Galena, Illinois. I continue to daydream.

Classes went well this quarter. Now I am moving into my last quarter. Can you believe that? I am taking a course in mining just in case I am forced into that field.

Dr. Salisbury has told me he is hiring another student in addition to myself at the museum. My task is to train him to be my replacement. That is an excellent example of planning ahead, and I am happy to oblige. Dr. Salisbury has started taking a group of students on a summer field school somewhere in the country. This year he is planning to go to the Black Hills in South Dakota. It sounds like an interesting trip, and I wish I were going. I am feeling like I am being gently shown the door. I guess that is why I came here four years ago, but still...

The Three Musketeers had their periodic lake perch dinner a week ago. I shall miss these little chin-wags, but I shall not miss the fish. Too many bones.

During the festivities Ambrose announced he was leaving the United States after graduation. He is returning to England to study law. "I am going to become a barrister and argue law cases in court. Once I am situated, I may run for Parliament, but that is a few years down the road," he said.

"A courtroom is a kind of stage, on which the lawyers, accused, and plaintiff play their roles before the audience or jury while the director or judge maintains discipline. Parliament is even a bigger stage. There are more actors, but there doesn't seem to be any director. So, I should do fine in both."

[150]

Eli and I both agreed it is the natural direction for him to take. "Only if you get to smoke that cursed meerschaum pipe," I commented.

"That will be my trademark, my friend."

"Well, if ever I go to England and design a building that falls down, I know who to call upon," said Eli, laughing.

"If I haven't been retained by its residents. Then you need to watch out." Ambrose and Eli toasted each other.

After thinking about it later that evening, I found it a little disconcerting that the three of us, who have been close, are going in such diverse directions. The firm friendships of these past four years are, in fact, very temporary.

Ambrose's decision leaves only me lacking a steady wind behind my sails. I certainly hope to hear soon, one way or the other.

Yours,
Sam

***

April 16, 1896

Dear Cate,

I received a response from Adolph Bandelier. I am shocked by it, but grateful that I did not invest any more effort in perusing a position with him. I will include the entire note for your reaction.

April 21, 1896
Callao, Peru

Mr. Jeppe,
Why are you writing to me? If you will take the time to look at the heading of this letter you

[151]

will see I am in Peru. My research in the Southwest is complete, and if I was working in the region, why would I hire a geologist who has no experience.

I barely know Holmes. I'm not sure why he is sending you to me. If you are in dire need of a job, I suggest you contact the new University of New Mexico and see if they need someone who has your qualifications. If they are filled, then try mining. Just stop bothering me.

Adolph Bandelier

Mr. Holmes said he was a bit prickly, but I think he is more like poison ivy. I am used to firm, but polite conversation not this boorish attitude. I, for one, hope he remains in Peru. However, I will follow up on his left-handed suggestion and contact the University of New Mexico either a teaching position or a museum position.

May 1

I received a promising letter from the University of New Mexico's Vice President. They intended to create a museum from the very beginning, but nothing has been done to date. They want it to be situated on the first floor near the modest library room in the only building yet built. People have given the university rock collections, animal mounts, antiques, and a botanical collection. I replied to him that I am interested in organizing the museum, something I have experience doing.

If I am offered the directorship, it will be a challenge. New Mexico Territory is poor, and they have meager funds with which to work. The university does not have a John D. Rockefeller to foot the bills, just the legislature's annual appropriation. My salary will be small, and my

[152]

museum budget will be about non-existent. A few days ago, I received a note from Vice President Hadley asking me to send a résumé. Dr. Salisbury helped me compose one which I sent off yesterday.
Hopefully,
Sam

***

May 27, 1896

....There were only four weeks left before I would be forced to join the ranks of the unemployed when the letter for New Mexico came. I admit I had sweaty palms as I opened it. Based on my résumé and a kind letter of support from Dr. Salisbury, the University of New Mexico has given me a one-year renewable contract to organize and run their museum! I am saved.

I am due to begin July 6 which gives me a very short time to graduate, pack and take the train to Albuquerque, but I will do it. I am excited by the challenge even if it is not dealing with archaeology. Perhaps once I am established, I can hook up with an excavation. If not, I still have a museum to run, and that is a big responsibility. I will make this a very short letter because I must write to Cora and Mildred....

***

June 15, 1896

Dear Cate,

This will be my last, quick letter from Chicago. I am going to take one day and go to see Uncle Hiram and Uncle Cyrus. It will be a sad goodbye because they are getting along in years, and I may never see them again. Eli, Ambrose, and I will have one last dinner together.

[153]

I must mention the museum. A few letters back I think I mentioned I am training my replacement. Surprise of surprises, my replacement is a young lady. She is very capable, and I am sure she will do a fine job.

Final exams are coming up next week. I am not too concerned because I have kept up with all my classes.

Graduation is on Sunday, the twenty-eighth. I do not expect anyone I know to be in the audience. I wish Mother, Father, and you could be here. Not because of my accomplishments, but because they, and you, deserve so much of the credit. Instead, the ceremony will be just for me, but I will be thinking of you three while I march down the aisle.

I will write while I am on the train. There will be plenty of time in that it is a two-day trip, and I will have nothing to study.

Your little brother is finally going on an adventure.

Love,
Sam

Chapter Sixteen

Sam said he was going on an adventure. The word adventure is defined as an exciting experience, so one need not necessarily go anywhere new to have an adventure. Sometimes an adventure begins in the most mundane way.

In 1896 Charlotte was invited to participate in an ensemble which was going to play some Impressionist works. Such music was quite avant-garde at that time, and she was excited to be included. One of the pieces, an early piano concerto by Scriabin, featured a Russian pianist, Chayim Galinski.

Because of the piano placement on stage, while he paused during the ensemble's part, Galinski noticed Charlotte in the cello section. Chayim was a young, somewhat vain, self-confident virtuoso, and he assumed that Charlotte would certainly respond to any advances of his. So, he made an effort to strike up a conversation with her after the rehearsals.

By nature, Charlotte has a tendency to be shy around strangers. Consequently, he received little satisfaction at first, but Chayim was persistent, and she eventually agreed to have a cup of tea with him. While tea was not his preferred beverage for the occasion, it served his purpose.

They first talked about the concerto, then music in general, then all things in general. Much to her surprise, Charlotte found Chayim to be personable and knowledgeable in a number of areas. Even though he was Russian by birth, his French was impeccable. However, Charlotte knew it was time to leave when Chayim casually said, "Tell me about your family." She had no desire to become involved with anyone who was in town for just a couple of days.

After the concert Chayim left Paris for England where he was going to stay for six months, and she gave him no further thought. Two months later she was surprised when she received a letter from him, especially since she had not given him her address.

He said he found where she lived from the organization that sponsored the concert. He explained that his English engagement had been cut short due to a conflict of personalities. Instead, he was returning to Paris where he was going to study with Camille Saint-Saëns. He then asked to visit with her once he got settled.

This was a busy time for Charlotte, and she conveniently forgot to reply to Chayim's letter. Chayim however, did not forget her. Once he was established in his apartment, he again wrote to her. In that it would have been impolite to ignore this note, she agreed to have dinner with him, intending to clarify that she was not interested in being pursued.

Charlotte and I shared numerous things over the years including many mutual friends, but we also had acquaintances of our own. So, we felt no need to notify the other of any social appointment as long as it did not interfere with a joint activity. Nor was it necessary for her to discuss her dilemma with me. In fact, on the evening Chayim came by to escort Charlotte to dinner, I was out with some of my friends.

A while later Charlotte told me the evening was very nice, and she was quite impressed with Mr. Chayim Galinski. He was very knowledgeable about French cuisine, the latest scientific discoveries, art history, and current political events in Europe. The assertive, brash young man had been replaced by a warm, considerate gentleman. In spite of herself, Charlotte was becoming attracted to him.

Over the next few months, they had numerous meetings, both public and private. One evening Charlotte and Chayim were discussing the clash of French attitudes that had led the country to an explosive division among its citizens. Chayim said, "it is not the Catholic Church, or the Free Masons, or the military, or the anti-Jews. It is the way society is structured that is the problem. Everything is based on hierarchical rulers.

[156]

By the time you get to the citizens, all the decisions have been made. There is no room for individual choice and responsibility, only lockstep conformity. If you do away with governments, churches, unions, armies, and such, then you can tell people 'you alone are responsible for your actions.'"

Charlotte looked at him in surprise. "Why then you would have chaos."

"No, not chaos, you would have anarchy."

"It's the same thing."

"Oh no. They are very different. Chaos is when no one is in charge. Anarchy is when everyone is in charge. Imagine how people would act if, for once, they were in charge. No laws telling them what to do, no self-appointed leaders telling them who to hate, no companies, churches, or unions telling them what to do. They would be free to make their own decisions. People would think, perhaps for the first time in their lives, about the impact of their actions."

"But people will always be selfish. Without rules, they will take as much as they can. So, you need police, and you need someone to watch the police, and so on. Besides, people would get hurt by the actions of others."

"People are getting hurt by others this very night. What's the difference? You probably will have a few individuals who cannot or will not be considerate of others. In reaction, the majority might shun the narcissist, isolate them so their behavior can't hurt others because most Anarchists are non-violent. But that would have to be an individual's decision.

"It sounds like you have thought about this a lot."

"Me and many others.

"Are you a communist?"

"No, I'm not a communist. I don't see any difference between communism and capitalism. Their goals are the same, to control the individual. One tells you what you can do, the other tells you what you can't do."

Finishing her glass of wine, Charlotte said, "I've got to think about this."

"Certainly. Thinking is the core of anarchy."

[157]

Over time, Charlotte questioned Chayim trying to find a weakness in the anarchy he envisioned. Finally, she thought she had him. "What if no one chooses to clean the streets? Soon the manure would be deep, and no one could cross the road."

He laughed. "I've never heard anyone ask that question. But the answer is quite simple. There will be no cities when there is anarchy. They will wither away. Small agricultural villages will take their place. If your horse leaves some manure, it is up to you to put it on the fertilizer heap."

"Do you mean everyone will live on a farm?"

"Something like that. Do you find the idea distasteful?"

"I don't know, I've never been to a farm."

"The one I am building is quite pleasant. You should come and see it. You will want to stay."

Charlotte looked at him in surprise. "Where is your farm?"

"In Russia, on the steppes. A group is planning a village based on anarchy. I am going to move there in a year or two."

"What about your piano career?"

"It has been fun, but the future is in anarchy, and I want to be a part of that future. I am serious about you coming to Russia. I want you to be a part of my future as well."

***

"Are you going to leave? Is that what you are saying?" I looked at her incredulously.

"I don't know. He wants me to go back to Russia with him, but I don't know if I should. My family is here, my music is here, my friends are here.....and of course, you are here. How can I throw all that away for Russian winters, even if Chayim is there to keep me warm, and yet...."

I was panicked. "Is he going to marry you?"

"I'm sure that's what he has in mind."

[158]

"Don't you think you should find out before you move to the Russian steppes a thousand kilometers from the nearest town?"

"We'll discuss that when the time comes."

I continued, "I'm afraid….I'm afraid of losing all we are, what we have. I can't force you to stay, and I wouldn't if I could, but we have built a special relationship. I don't want to see you walk out the door, never to see you again. I'm being selfish, I know that. I don't care."

"Well, come to Russia with us. You can write stories there."

"No. He wants you, not us. I would just be in the way. Besides, I could never live the way he intends to. For that matter, I don't think you can either. Let's face it. You are used to the finer things in life. How are you going to survive hoeing beets?"

Charlotte laughed, "You have a point. I'll have to drive the tractor."

"You can't even drive a bicycle built for two. Remember when you steered us into that light pole. How are you going to drive a tractor? And if you do learn, how are you going to be able to play the cello in the evening? Or are you going to give that up too?"

"I could never stop playing the cello."

"Oh, you're going to drag it from one commune to another, from one shack to another. Someday when you're starving, you'll sell it for two loaves of bread."

I tried a different tack. "Charlotte, you have a wonderful future here. If you go to Russia, you'll disappear. No one will ever hear of Charlotte Levy again. No one will even think of you again."

"I'm not going to be famous, here or anywhere else. Don't be silly. I don't have what it takes to be a top cellist."

"And another thing, you have talked often about the places you want to visit, the things you want to do. Because you want them, those ideas are important. For the first time in history, what a woman wants is becoming as important as what a man wants. Now you're going to throw your dreams aside

[159]

because someone wearing pants says, 'come to Russia?' Is that all those things are worth?"

"Catherine, stop. Just stop. I know what you want me to do. Now let me decide what I want me to do." She turned and went into her bedroom. A few minutes later I heard the sounds of her cello.

***

The better part of month went by without any word regarding Charlotte's decision. In fact, the atmosphere had been rather chilly. Finally, one morning she stopped at my desk and invited me to a cup of tea. It was the first one since our argument.

She had laid out our best set of linen serviettes, and what would pass for our best set of china. There were two pastries on a plate, and two roses in a vase.

"My, my. Did we win the lottery?"

"No," she glanced at me. "It has been a difficult time for us, and I wanted to tell you how important you are to me."

This didn't sound good, but I kept my mouth shut, although I did manage a tight-lipped smile.

Charlotte continued. "Last night I told Chayim that I am going to stay in Paris. I told him he is stimulating, he is intriguing. I told him I love his music. I love his ideas. I love to be around him. I told him that I loved him, but I have things I want to do, and I cannot do them in Russia, at least not the Russian steppes. I told him if he decided to live in Moscow I would come and meet him. He said he doubted that would happen. So, we said goodbye." I started to say something, but she stopped me. "Let me finish. I think what you said that night was unfair, and almost cruel. It was also true. I hope if you are ever in my position, I can find a better way of helping you."

I sat still, looking at my teacup. I was deflated. After a minute, my head cleared enough to speak. "I'm sorry to have hurt you. That was not my intention. I was being selfish, I know. I said what I believed, and still believe to be true, but

[160]

you're right. I should have been more considerate of your feelings. Please forgive me."

She looked at me for a few seconds with those dark brown eyes, "Consider yourself forgiven," she said quietly.

"Thank you. May I ask an intrusive question?"

"You are a reporter at heart. What other kind of question do you know?"

"How did Chayim take the news?"

I think he did not expect it. There was a little moisture in his eyes. I'm being honest. If he writes and says he has moved to Moscow, I'm going to him. I know that, and I want you to know that too."

She finished her tea and looked at the roses. "These are wilted, and it is your turn to buy new flowers." She smiled and cleared the dishes.

Chayim never wrote to her.

Chapter Seventeen

While Charlotte was considering living in Moscow, Sam was on his way to an equally remote place. At that time Albuquerque was a small city of about 3800 people. The territory of New Mexico was still sixteen years away from statehood. So, this was one of the few remnants of the western frontier.

July 1, 1896

Dear Cate,

The train is somewhere in Kansas as I write this. I have had breakfast, washed up and changed my shirt. Now it is time to write.

First, I visited the farm and had a good visit with the family. Everyone is fine although Cyrus and Hiram are looking older. The boys do a lot of the heavy work now. Aunt Margaret is also good. Like her brothers, Cousin Laura sees to much of the housework. Apparently, she has a beau. The men are taking bets on how long she will be single.

I went to Dr. Salisbury's office and turned in my keys to the museum. This was particularly difficult because I always felt the collections area as mine. Even though I am sure Rebecca, my replacement, will do fine, I am sad to leave it.

Dr. Salisbury wished me well and said his door was always open should I find my way back to Chicago. He said I did a fine job in both the museum and in my classes, and he felt I would

[162]

make the University and him proud in my future endeavors.

After final exams on Friday, the three musketeers met for our last supper. Ambrose and I met Eli at Bergoff's. We promised to stay in touch even though we will be, literally, a world apart. Eli will serve as a clearing house until Ambrose and I have permanent addresses.

Graduation on Sunday was a bit anticlimactic. After you have worked toward it for four years, the real thing cannot measure up. Ambrose and I walked leisurely back to the rooming house smoking cigars.

Monday, I shipped my books, *et al* by freight to New Mexico. Tuesday, Ambrose's train left early in the morning for New York, while mine was not leaving till 6 p.m. I packed my suitcase and went with him to the station. We stood around saying nothing, waiting for the train. There was just nothing left to say. We both knew the chances of seeing each other again were small since he would be in England and I would be in the Southwest, but it was nice just to share each other's company one last time. When it was time, we gave each other hugs and slaps on the back, and he left.

After his train departed, I had all day to wait with nothing to do. I had said all my goodbyes. So, I found a bench in the shade and pulled out a dime novel. I think it was quite fitting. On my first day in Chicago I was alone, and it should be so on my last.
Love,
Sam

Journal Entries
1896

[163]

<u>July 1-2</u>

On a railroad train the land close to you passes by your window in a blur, at speeds beyond that which your brain can comprehend. Objects such as a tree, or a wagon appear and disappear before you get a chance to look at them carefully.

On the other hand, the land at the horizon seems to crawl like a snail. These two landforms, the near and the far, appear to be separate entities yet they are the same. What a strange way to see the world.

It is easy to see that this area was at the bottom of an inland sea. I recall it was during the Mesozoic Time. Now it is very flat with only slight undulations. There should be fossils of fish and other water life throughout this area.

The food in dining car is over-priced, but convenient. I eat light. The waiters are certainly professional. I enjoy watching them carry a bowl of hot soup down the aisle while the train rocks and bounces along. They never spill a drop.

Stopped at Dodge City, Kansas. No gun fights in our ten-minute layover, just a heavy, unpleasant smell of cattle. It reminds me of the Chicago Stock Yards. I wonder how far west we have to go before seeing the snowcapped peaks.

I woke at the La Junta, Colorado stop where there was a ten-minute layover. It was 3:50 in the morning and quite dark except for the moonlight. I got off the train to stretch my legs, and to the west there were some looming shapes that had to be the mountains. That is exciting. Even though it is July, the night air is cool. I don't know how high we are now.

Reached Trinidad, Colorado where we had a fifteen-minute layover while they added an engine to the end of the train. Then proceeded to Raton, New Mexico where we stopped again while they detached the pusher. Got off the train and had a fried egg sandwich at a Harvey House lunchroom to celebrate my arrival in New Mexico.

A man got on in Raton, sat next to me, and talked incessantly all the way to Las Vegas, about two hours. When we arrived at Las Vegas, he left us. I asked the well suntanned man across the aisle if everyone in New Mexico talked as much as he did. *"No hablo inglés, Señor"* was his reply.

[164]

The mountains are much lower here. At some spots they are more like foothills. Although looking to the far-off northwest there are a few snowcapped mountains. Near Las Vegas I saw my first mesa. The terrain nearby is rugged with deep gullies and steep plateaus. It is much dryer, and small cacti are common along with large woody plants. Trees are found along stream beds.

We stopped at Lamy for a short time, so we should be in Albuquerque about 6:30 or so.

***

After receiving the July 1 letter, I didn't anticipate another one for a while. So, I was surprised when, two weeks later, I received another one from New Mexico, especially when I noticed it was someone else's handwriting,

July 7, 1896

Dear Cate,

I am sorry to have to send this letter, actually a nurse is writing it for me. My introduction to Albuquerque has been god-awful to say the least.

I arrived as scheduled in the early evening of July 2. My books and other things had not arrived. All I had with me was my suitcase. I looked for a rooming house near the train station. This is a laborers' neighborhood, nothing fancy and perhaps a little rowdy, but it is cheap. I figured I could get a room in this area and take my time to find a nicer place.

I found such a room on the second floor of an unpainted clapboard two-story house crammed in among a stretch of row houses.

The next day I went to the university to start my job. Two days later the crate with my books arrived at the station, and I had it delivered to the rooming house. After supper I managed to

[165]

pull out my journals and a few reference books which I put on the desk. Then I turned in.

Sometime during the night, I am told it was 2:30 or so, there was a pounding on my door along with calls for me to get up, there was a fire. It took me a few seconds to remember where I was, and a few more to light the oil lamp. I noticed the acrid smell of smoke, but it did not seem that strong. In my half sleep, it did not seem like an emergency. There was pounding on my door again. I yelled, "I am coming." Not particularly hurrying, I got dressed and started for the door. On the way I passed my desk. I debated and took my journals and a couple of the books just in case.

I opened the door. A wall of smoke was like a hot pillow. It actually pushed me back into the room. All of a sudden, I realized this was serious. Then I thought maybe I had waited too long. It is funny though, I do not remember being scared.

The stairs. I could not remember where the stairs were. Finally, I realized they should be on my right. I moved along the wall feeling my way as quickly as I could. My eyes burned badly I could barely see. I could barely breath. My asthma kicked in because of the smoke. I thought I would suffocate. I covered my mouth with my sleeve. That did not really help. I recall I almost fell down the stairs. I could not see them because it was too dark and smoky. I remember standing at the top and looking down the stairs to regain my equilibrium. Toward the bottom, I could see the smoky glow of several oil lamps for which I was most grateful. I started down the steps.

The stair railings were cast iron and quite sturdy. About halfway down I stumbled. I seized the railing to steady myself. As soon as I did, I remember screaming in pain because the iron was as hot as a fry pan. Then I realized those were no

[166]

oil lamps. The light was coming from open flames burning the side of the stairs. The flames were cooking the railing. Something told me that I had only seconds to get out of the house. The memory of the doomed firemen at the World's Fair flashed in my mind. So, like them, I jumped.

The base of the stairs was not burning yet so that area was safe when I hit, but my right foot caught the bottom step. A pain shot up my leg and I groaned. By falling I was laying on the floor where there was less smoke. I could not see very far, but I heard shouts to my left. I squirmed along as best I could and tried to yell. Someone grabbed and pulled me into the night air. I could not breath. I could not see. The pains from my right hand and right leg beat on my brain. Someone put a wet towel on my face and that helped, but I still could not breath. I must have passed out.

When I awoke my brain was a little clearer, but my pains were sharp. My head, my right hand, my left arm, my back, and my right leg. I still could not see. And my breathing...I know an asthma attack when I am having one.

I recall yelling for help. A voice told me to stop moving, that I was okay. It said to drink some water and relax. I did. The voice asked if I could talk? My voice sounded strange, old and strained when I answered "yes". "What's your name?" it asked. I told it. I asked where I was.

"In a hospital. Do you remember what happened?"

"A fire."

"That's right."

"My things. Okay?"

"The journals and some books you were carrying are a little singed, but they are okay. I'm sorry to say everything else is lost. It's time for you to sleep."

"Am I blind?"

[167]

"The smoke was hard on your eyes. Doctor bandaged them in case there is damage. We'll see tomorrow. By the way, do you have asthma?"

"Yes."

"We thought so. Here, drink this. It will help you sleep."

"What?"

"Laudanum."

"Tell the university where I am," was the last thing I can remember saying.

I do not have eye damage, but I do have a broken ankle, a badly burned right hand, a nasty scrape on my right arm and a wrenched back from jumping down the steps. Do not panic. I am going to be fine. Two other men were not as lucky. They were in the attic and never made it to the door. I only knew them from when we ate together, but they seemed like nice chaps.

Apparently, the fire was started next door. They think someone tipped over an oil lamp, but they were too drunk to put the fire out. Three men died in that house.

The nurse, who is writing this, says I've got to stop for now, and get some rest. I will write again soon.
Sam

This is Doctor Rice. His nurse, Sister Rosa, asked me to write a note. I want you to understand Sam is going to be fine although it may take a number of months. His right ankle had a simple fracture. It should heal nicely although it may be a little stiff from time to time, but that shouldn't interfere with normal usage. He is a very lucky young man.

I was frantic with worry, but there was no way to contact him. Everyone said he would be fine, but I had heard that before.

***

[168]

August 10, 1896

Dear Cate,

Before you ask, I am doing much better, thank you. As you see by the scratching on the paper, I am back to writing my own letters. My hand is still hurts but it is healing. My ankle is in splints, so I am hobbling around on a crutch for a while till it finishes mending. The rest of me is fine. I wish I could say as much for my belongings. Everything is gone. The lap desk Father made for me, my prized rock hammer, my books, and clothes, all are gone. I am very depressed.

I found a new boarding house on Gold Avenue. I hope this is a good omen because my previous boarding house was on Coal Ave. My new place is perfectly located for me. The landlady, an older Spanish-speaking lady, gave me a room on the first floor, and I do not have to climb stairs, thank goodness. She makes me breakfast, dinner, and a nice lunch I can take with me. My diet is almost all Mexican. Unfortunately, the main dish of my first dinner was full of hot chilies and I could not eat it. Mrs. Romero laughed and fixed me something else. Since then, some things have been warm, but edible. It is quite good.

My first day back to work was Monday of this week. I sent a telegram to Vice President Hadley last week telling him when I would return to work.

When I entered the building I found the entire faculty, all nine of them, gathered in the museum room. Vice President Hadley welcomed me back. He said everyone was shocked to hear what had happened. To help me get reestablished he said everyone took up a collection to help purchase necessary clothing, supplies and books. It was most touching. I thanked them profusely,

[169]

shaking hands with each of them (with my left hand). I assured them I would be back on two feet very soon and I would do all I could to build a museum they would be proud of.

Let me describe the "museum" as it is now. The room is the size of a regular classroom. When I arrived, it was filled with school furniture which I had to move to the basement. Now there are just boxes of things piled in one end of the room along with a small table that serves as my desk.

The helter-skelter artifact collection is terribly disorganized, but I think the material will form the good basis for a university museum

Other news. I received a note from Cora that she sent to the university. She is going to have a baby. Their two-year grant is about over, and they will return soon. I assume they will move back to Milwaukee so Charles can return to teaching.

Since leaving Chicago, I have sent a couple notes to Eli, but I have not heard back from him.

I will stop for now. My hand is beginning to pain me.
I Miss You,
Sam

***

September 10, 1896

Dear Cate,

I am getting very tired of moving around with a crutch. Everything else is fine. One day I tripped over a crate of rocks and fell. A dancer I will never be.

The museum organization continues. I have not opened all the boxes, but so far there are historical objects, biological mounts, skins, botanical specimens, geological specimens, and a

[170]

lot of archaeological artifacts including pottery. Some of the ceramic pieces are almost whole, but most are fragments or shards. I have been able to do some reading about old pottery. While I am not an expert, yet I can look at a piece and usually tell what type of pot it was and maybe begin to date it.

Of course, I am interested in the geological specimens. There is a lot of duplication, especially sandstone. I am anxious to get out into the countryside and see what other types can be found.

Autumn classes started this week. It is strange to walk, or rather hobble, down the hall. The students greet me, "Good morning, Professor Jeppe," and step aside giving me the respect due a faculty member. They little realize I was in their ranks just a few months ago. Still, it does wonders for my self-esteem.

Love,
Sam

***

October 24, 1896
Dear Cate,

I can walk! No longer am I tied to a wooden stick. I have traded the crutch for a cane. Now I do not look like an invalid, I try to look debonair, although, in reality I think I look like Father.

I am enjoying exploring Albuquerque. There are really two towns. The "Old Town" is the original community and is centered around a large rectangular plaza. It has a beautiful church, the usual frame buildings, and also many adobe shops and homes.

The east side, where I live, is "New Town." It has grown up around the railroad and is only now becoming settled. The two-story storefronts, the wood frame houses mingled with an occasional

[171]

brick structure make it look very much like Milwaukee or Englewood. Old Town is much more interesting.

Many of the people in Old Town are descendants of the original Spanish settlers. I learned they think of themselves as H*ispano*. I think their primary concern is raising their families and maintaining a cohesive community. As the Chinese in Chicago were, these people are often suspicious of the whites and with good reason. Their heritage and rights are often disregarded when changes in the town are made.
Love,
Sam

***

December 9, 1896

….I'm not sure this will get to you by Christmas. Merry Christmas anyway.

I have discarded my cane, for the most part. I notice a slight limp toward the end of the day when I get tired. There was a nice sixty-degree day a week ago, and I hoofed it to the university. I probably should not have done that because my ankle hurt the rest of the day.

The documentation of the museum collection is about half done. I am hoping to have it completed by the end of May.

I finally heard from Eli. I was beginning to think something had happened to him, and it had. His note said his father died of apoplexy. As a result, Eli has moved back to the family home to take care of his mother and sister.

Cora sent a note. She and Charles are headed back to Milwaukee....

***

[172]

February 19, 1897

....I received two pieces of very good news this week. President Stover has announced his retirement. Rumor has it that Vice President Hadley will be hired as the next president. He told me that if he becomes president, he will not only give me a new contract for next year, but he anticipates increasing the museum's budget some.

The second bit of good news is that Cora had her baby. It seems they made it to Milwaukee just in time. It is a boy and they have named him Charles Mutis II. Cora has resigned from the museum. I remember the wonderful hours we spent in the basement those years ago. It is sad for me, but not unexpected. I am sure Mildred will be hired as her permanent replacement.

I am planning my first serious expedition to find geologic samples. I will go into the Sandia Mountains. But first I have to get my legs in shape, so I'm doing lots of walking in my spare time. I also have to gather hiking and camping equipment....

***

March 25, 1897

....A short time after learning that Cora resigned from the museum, I received a letter from Mildred. She has been hired by the Field Columbian Museum in Chicago. She encouraged me to apply for her spot at the Milwaukee Public Museum. She said the head curator will be retiring soon and I could easily end up in that position.

Talk about a quandary! Do I want to be a small cog in a large museum or the driving force in a small one? In the end, I decided I wanted the

[173]

challenge more than the security. So, I wrote back to Mildred that I am happy here.

I received the box you sent. I can never thank you enough. There are so many things I lost in the fire. Yes, I am sorry to report Father's lap desk was destroyed. It saddens me whenever I think of the wonderful things people have given me that I no long have. I certainly appreciate the replacement copies of your two previous books and am excited to read your newest one. Also, thank you for the new rock hammer. You must have read my mind because I was just about to order one.

I have tramped the mesa and parts of the Sandia Mountains, so now I am going to explore the Rio Grande River bed....

April 30, 1897

....A great injustice has been done. The Board of Regents have hired someone other than Hiram Hadley. As Vice President, he had literally run the university since its inception, but they wanted someone more adept at seeking territorial support for the university. Personally, his support for the museum was an important reason I came. Now I don't know what is in store....

May 31, 1897,

....Since my last letter I have worked hard to make the museum the best I can to impress the new president. I do not know what his feelings are toward the project, but I do not want to give him any negative impressions. If he closes the museum, it will not be because of anything I have done or not done....

June 22, 1897

....Friday afternoon the faculty gathered to meet the new President, Dr. Clarence Herrick.

[174]

Come to find out, he holds a doctorate in natural history and is well respected in the fields of geology, and biology. He only came to the Southwest because he came down with consumption. Later in the day he spoke to me about how much he values the museum, and he is looking forward to helping it grow in the next decade. What a big relief....

July 21, 1897

Dear Sister,

I do not know just how to say this, but I have been let go. I am at a loss for words to show my indignation and anger.

It started the First of July. President Herrick called me into his office. I thought he would give me a new contract to sign. Instead, he told me the state legislature had frozen the funds for all the universities along with some other state departments. Operating expenses were cut by 25%, everyone's salary had been cut, and my position, along with others, was cut.

He spoke quietly, "Sam, please believe me. I knew nothing about this before July 1. Since then I've been working day and night to save your position, but there are some influential people in the state government that feel education is not important and should not be funded. They picked on you because you are the newest and you do not have tenure.

I was not quiet when I replied. "I came down to this godforsaken place because I was promised I could build a museum. I gave up a well-paying, secure position in the Milwaukee Public Museum because I believed what people said was true."

I went on, "What am I supposed to do now? I do not even have enough money to go back to civilization. And I have no prospects for a job around here. I have invested a year in that museum. To be told that some nameless people whom I have never met have said I do not deserve to continue is unconscionable."

"Sam, it is not my decision. If it were, you would have your contract. Your work has been exemplary. As far as alternative employment, will you let me ask some acquaintances of mine and see if I can get you a position with one of them? I realize it may not be what you came down here for, but it should tide you over until you can find something on your own." He placed his hand on my shoulder, saying "I'm sorry. I did not take this job to have this conversation."

I nodded and left his office. I bagged up my belongings and left the building without saying anything to the other faculty.

I got a note from Herrick. He heard of a man who owns a mining supply business in Los Cerrillos, a small mining town north of here. He said he does not know him. His name is Ursinus Taws, and he wants me to help around the shop. He cannot pay much, but my room and board will be included. What with the hospital and doctor bills from the fire, my savings have been drained. I desperately need a job, but the only one I can find around here is in a drug store. Just what a graduate of the University of Chicago would dream about as a life's goal.
Sam

[176]

Chapter Eighteen

The following year began as a difficult time for Sam. Since he was young, he always seemed to have a plan, an objective, that he was working toward. All of a sudden, his life had no real purpose. He was adrift.

A dying nineteenth century mining town was not a good place to redraw his life's blueprint, especially when working for Ursinus Taws.

August 15, 1897

Dear Cate,

Well, here I am in the thriving town of Los Cerrillos. The train stops here, and there is a stage to Santa Fe. I cannot wait to be on one of them leaving this place. Once upon a time, the town was an important community. Twenty years ago, prospectors found silver, followed by ore deposits, coal, turquoise, even a little gold. Speculators, engineers, shop keepers, saloons and churches quickly appeared. When the railroad was established, everyone figured the town's future was secure. But fifteen years later the minerals began to dry up and people began to pack up. There is still some silver being mined, but nothing like it was.

When I got off the train, I was struck by both the odor and the noise of the place. There was an old man standing outside the station. I asked, rather yelled at him, asking where I could

[177]

find Ursinus Taw's store. He motioned off to his left.

"Ol' Taw's store is down there a couple doors. But if you're gonna buy somethin', be sure to pin your money in your union suit or else he'll have it in his pocket quicker than ya can say boo, an ya ain't gonna get it back."

"No, I am going there to work."

He looked at me. "Ya don't say," then he spit tobacco juice on the ground and walked away.

As I wandered down the dirt street, I could see about half the buildings in the town are adobe in various states of decay, while the other half are wood frame, most of which are also in need of help. I almost walked by Taw's store because the sign is badly faded that you can barely read it. The windows have bars on them, and the place looks like the sheriff's office.

I opened the door and a bell, just like Mr. Diersdörfer's, announced my entrance. I entered into a dark, dusty room crammed with just about anything a miner would need. I could see shovels and picks in one corner, rubber boots on a rack, dynamite on the other side of the counter. On this side of the counter were rows of tables each with smaller items neatly lined up, anything and everything. Toward the back of the store were shelves of equipment necessary for assaying. Just below the ceiling and extending around the room was a shelf on which there were hundreds of pieces of old Indian pottery.

A gnarled stick of an old man appeared immediately from a door behind the counter. Some of his long, stringy, gray hair mixed with his uncut beard and together they framed a gaunt, cadaver-like face. His tight lips and clinched jaw gave him an expression of suspicion waiting for a fight. There was no greeting, no degree of friendliness as he asked, "What da ya need?"

[178]

I ignored his question and announced, "My name is Sam Jeppe, and I am here for the job you told Vice President Hadley about."

"You took your time in getting here, I'll say that. I have no use for someone who's got the slows."

I made no reply. I got that sinking feeling in my stomach like when you find you are overdrawn at the bank. I almost wished he would fire me on the spot because I immediately knew I did not want to work for him.

When it became apparent I was not going to respond, he muttered "Well you're here now. You might as well stay. I don't trust people, so I've got my eye on you. If you are planning to rob me, just remember I've got a gun. Come on, I'll show you where your bed is. Then we'll get started." He turned back through the door from which he entered. I stopped to retrieve my luggage. When he discovered I was not in his shadow, he came back.

"Well, I'm waiting and I don't have all day."

This has to be the strangest store I have ever been in. It is as much like the women's' department store in Chicago as night is to day. If a customer comes in, I am to follow him around making sure he does not steal anything. I was told to never stop watching customers because they are all thieves. The miner will walk around the room and point to items he wants to buy. I am to keep track of the desired objects and when he is finished I bring them up to the counter. The customer and Taws will then set to bargaining.

It was not until after lunch, which consisted of beans, just beans, that a customer came in. I noticed he was carrying a couple of paper-wrapped items with him. These he placed on the counter where Taws immediately unwrapped and began

[179]

examining them. I could not see what the objects were because I was busy following and watching the miner. After laying his desired items on the counter, I went to the attic to get replacement pieces. When I returned, the miner had placed his purchases in his haversack, and Taws had a piece of Indian pottery beside him. Once the man left, Taws took the pottery, climbed up a ladder and placed the artifact on the high shelf.

There are no other mining supply stores because Taws either drove them out of business or they went broke on their own. There are a number of such stores in Santa Fe, but that is a day away.

It is about 8:30 now and Taws will not waste oil. He insists on turning out his only lamp then, so I have to stop writing.
Sam

**

September 20, 1897

Dear Cate,

Los Cerrillos is not Chicago or even Albuquerque. Here, things happen in dribs and drabs. In our humble little burg, life creeps at a petty pace from day to day. Nothing is as it should be, it is only as it was yesterday.

There was a gun fight Friday night in one of the saloons. Neither shootist was seriously hurt because they both were so drunk they could not aim straight. After the shooting one of the duelists passed out while the other was tied to a chair till the sheriff arrived. They are both in the lock-up till the circuit judge comes to town. It turns out they are partners in a placer operation. They were arguing over half a few grains of silver. In case you are wondering, a placer claim is a spot in a creek where men pan for gold or silver.

[180]

Over the past weeks I have discovered Taws not only sells things, he barters. If someone has a pick and needs a shovel, they can do business providing the customer has something else to sweeten the pot. There is no such thing as an even trade. Taws can tell when a man is eager to make a trade and then he really piles on the demands. This happens most often when a man is down on his luck and needs the basics for survival.

Hungry men are his best customers. He may end up making a dollar on a can of beans that cost him $.08. Not bad for a day's work, I'll say that.

One time I pointed out the trade was not good for the miners. He glared at me, a deep anger rising to the surface. "What about the miners? They take their chances. Most of them flounder, but that's the luck of the draw. They knew the rules of the game when they came here. You think they would give me a nod on the street if they struck it rich? They would not."

It occurred to me that he is no different from the miners. Everyone wants the biggest piece of the pie. While miners deal with the vagaries of treasure hunting, Taws deals with the whims of people. I do not think he needs to be as miserly as he is, but perhaps he will end up with the biggest slice after all.

I admire most shop owners. Like the spider, somehow they have learned the art of patience. They wait until the fly, the customer, wanders in. Still, they cannot pounce for that would frighten off the prey. No, they must tease the prospect, pretending to be a friendly spider, not a dangerous one. When the unwary customer is at ease, then the web is gently woven around them. That is the technique used by most shop owners, but not Ursinus Taws. He makes no bones about it. If you

[181]

want to buy something, abandon all hope, ye who enter here.
Your Brother,
Cerrillos Sam

***

October 17, 1897

Dear Cate,

There are rivalries in Los Cerrillos between individuals and between groups, resulting in bickering, arguments, and outright fighting. There is no concern for the other fellow. Oh, there is still enough humanity left in most that they will not deny a plate of beans to a starving man, but if that same man is injured, no one will help him do his job.

Few men, besides the owners, are financially successful here. In fact, most men fail miserably. The vast majority of prospectors and miners gain nothing and leave town with just enough money to go home or travel to some new bonanza that, like all the rest, promises incalculable riches. Of course, some men are residents of unmarked graves in the Los Cerrillos cemetery.

All this is not to say there is no social consciousness here. Some people have built churches, a school, and a community house. The wives of company executives and some business owners try to create a social circle, and to an extent they are successful. Fancy dress balls with midnight dinners mark the changing seasons, picnics are sponsored, church bazaars are held, a baseball team was even formed, all for the entertainment of the upper class, of course. The rest of the citizens, the working classes who, if they are fortunate, own two sets of worn dungarees,

[182]

gather at one of the bars, visit a soiled dove, or stay in their camps for their entertainment.

The duality reminds me of both the slum landlord back in Milwaukee, and Eli's father. It is the principal cause for the constant unrest among the laborers.

I do not socialize, so I am lonely. Yours are the only letters I have to look forward to, because I have to admit, I am embarrassed to write to my friends back east, consequently they do not even know I am here. I do not want to be seen as a failure, yet that is what I am. While Eli will be an architect, Ambrose a lawyer, and Mildred an assistant curator, I am a stock boy. This may be a temporary situation, still it can be viewed as fitting end for a mediocre student who could not cut it.

In some evenings after the store is closed and on Sundays, I have begun to hike the area. Originally, I just wanted some exercise for my ankle, but soon I began looking at the area's geology. If you look past the filth and destruction brought on by thousands of men searching for buried treasure, there are some interesting aspects to the place.

Farmers caress the land, treating it as if it is a living thing, but here, men dig only to destroy. Their intention is to get through the soil and worthless rock as quickly as possible. When they sink a shaft, they throw the dirt and rock, the tailings, anywhere they can. If the resulting pit is dry, that is, nothing of interest in it, they just pick up their belongings and move a little further on. They never refill the hole they dug. The result is skeletons of trees and bushes, discarded lumber, human refuse and waste, and hundreds of deep pits, all creating a scene that can be mistaken for a battlefield which, in a sense, it is.
Closing for now,
Sam

[183]

***

November 3, 1897

Dear Cate,

There is a mill and smelter just outside Cerrillos, and oh how it stinks up the place. Its smoke and soot descend upon the town when the wind blows just right, which it does frequently. When it does, I start wheezing. If it happens at night, I cannot sleep.

Fortunately, Taws' store is right next door to Richards' drug store. I can slip over and buy some asthma cigarettes. They usually help calm my lungs. Everyone calls the owner "Doc" even though he is a druggist by trade. He has the title because he has been known to bandage up cuts, medicate sprains, and offer unprescribed medicines for various aches and pains.

Doc is middle aged, and married to a very nice woman, Jane. He is one of a hand full of residents with whom I have become friends. I began to stop by the store a couple of times a week just to pass the time. When she hears our laughter, Jane will often bring some pie or cake from their residence on the second floor, and then stay to join in the merriment. As a couple, they offer me a quiet cove in which to rest from the constant storm going on next door.

There is another man with whom I have gotten to know. I began eating at a restaurant on Wednesdays and Saturdays because I am thoroughly sick of Taws' beans which we have almost every meal. It gives me something to look forward to.

In the beginning I tried most of the establishments in town, and while they range from

[184]

acceptable to good, I settled on a Mexican restaurant a few blocks from the store.

The first time I went to there it was fairly busy and the owner was quite brusque. The menu was limited to beans (yes, more beans), rice, tortillas, and a puffy deep-fried bread called *sopapilla*. Besides those things there was the *comida del día*, the meat dish of the day (I like *carne adovada* the best). All the food was kept in large pots on a wood stove. The customers called out what they wanted when they entered, the food was dished up and presented at a counter. Everyone paid when they got their food. When the customer was finished eating, he put his dishes in a pan by the door. This way there was no need for a waiter or a cook. When the food was gone, the door was locked.

I was not thrilled with the restaurant itself. It was the proverbial small hole-in-the-wall with only a couple religious prints to brighten the dirty plaster walls. None of the dishes seemed to match, nor did the chairs at the three tables. But the place was clean, and the food was good. I returned a second time. This time I was the only customer since it was after the usual lunch time. The owner was still quite formal, but friendly enough that I tried striking up a conversation with him. He seemed hesitant, however I persisted, and he opened up a little.

His name is Amarante Luis Oñate Martín. He is short, like many of those with a Mexican heritage, and he looks like a farmer, lean and strong with a complexion that comes from years in the sun. He speaks English much better than I speak Spanish, so during our visit I asked him to help me learn some Spanish words. He grudgingly agreed to do so. Since then, I have gone there without fail. I get a good meal for $.15 and a Spanish lesson for $.10. I do not think he would

[185]

charge me anymore, but I always pay him. He does not seem to mind me being there in the afternoon since all he has to do is wash dishes. I help dry them which he appreciates.

Amarante started the restaurant based on the idea of the street vendors down in Mexico. He lives nearby with his wife and family, and they help prepare the food at home. He then brings it to the restaurant in a wagon. Coffee is the only thing he makes during the day.

The other day I told him about my experiences back in Chicago at the Chinese restaurant. I asked if he enjoyed being in the restaurant business. This brought on a sudden chilling.

He stared at me for a minute and replied sternly, "I am not a *peon*, I own land, the *Mesita de Nuestra Señora del Sagrado Corazón,* (which translates to 'Ranch of Our Lady of the Sacred Heart'). *Un anillo de saqueadores publicos* (a ring of public looters) paid the government to take the land away from our family in 1893. They said our grant was not legal, but it is legal, and we have the papers to prove it. They thought there might be copper on our land, and they wanted it. Why they thought so I do not know because the *bastardo* miners have swarmed in and destroyed my land looking for minerals for the past twenty years. They still come and they pay no attention to boundary markers and signs. They go where they want to go and dig where they want to dig." He turned and walked away but then turned back with another thought. "Anglos like to say they are builders, but they are not. They destroy everything and everyone they meet."

He continued, "I would shoot them, but there are too many, one of them would shoot me. Then there would be no one to provide for my family. My wife would have no land to farm. She

[186]

would have to go to a city and work as a servant. My children would have to work in the fields among the *suramatos* (Mexican migrants) so, I serve beans and rice to those same *gringos* who are laying waste to my property because it is the only way I can earn some money."

His voice was beginning to rise and become more strident. "But someday all of them...including you...will go away. Then all the *paisanos* will have a great fiesta. We will again live the way our ancestors intended. We will be surrounded by our wives and children. When we plant our fields, we will honor *San Ysidro*. We will work together to build our community, not someone else's. My *compadres* impatiently wait for that time."

I sat quietly for a moment. "Amarante, I have not harmed you in any way. I have always been honest and friendly. I respect you, but I feel you hate me."

"I do not hate you. I do not hate any Anglos...I do not like them either. Anglos are like the summer locusts. They come. They lay waste to our crops. They make our lives difficult. They go. They, and you, are not evil. You are just what you are. You cannot help being a locust. Are there good Anglos? Is there a good locust? Perhaps. But I cannot tell a good Anglo from a bad one, so I treat them the same as I treat locusts, with indifference. I'm sorry *amigo* if I offend you.

"You do not offend me Amarante. I am just bewildered. You may not like me, but I like you. I hope someday you will see me for what I am. I am not a locust."

"Maybe you are not a locust...perhaps a butterfly."

"I have been called many things, but never a butterfly."

[187]

"*Dime no con quien naces, sino con quien paces*. That means 'Birth is much, but breeding is more.'"

I couldn't help but be embarrassed at what I took as a compliment.

He continued, "Butterflies are always welcomed. Like the locusts, butterflies come and they go, but they do no harm. They only make you feel good as they glide past on the summer breeze. You probably do not remember the butterflies you see, but you would notice if they were not around. People remember evil and they forget the good. That is wrong, but that is what people do.

"I like butterflies because they carry messages to me. Like the little orange and black ones that come in the spring. They tell me warm weather is close. The big yellow ones in the summer seem to say rain is coming. Even the little white ones who seem to be here whenever there is warm weather, they tell me the plants are growing as they should. And when the big orange butterfly appears for a while in the late summer I know cool weather is coming. One time I saw hundreds of them in a big cloud. It was beautiful. The chamiza were covered with them and the yellow flowers and their orange wings made the bushes look like they were burning as in the Bible. Yes, perhaps you are a butterfly. You bring me a message. In all the hatred around us, you tell me there may be hope after all. Thank you."

Since then, he calls me '*mariposa*' (Butterfly), and I call him '*toro enojado*' which means 'Angry Bull'. Between Amarante, and Doc, my life in La Cerrillos is bearable, if not pleasant.
¡hasta luego!,
Sam

[188]

Chapter Nineteen

December 4, 1897

Dear Cate,

Merry Christmas from New Mexico. I hope you and Charlotte have a pleasant holiday. I am sorry that I cannot send a present. My funds do not allow it at this time.

Speaking of, if I am to ever leave this place I must build up my cache. I can never do that if I rely on the pittance Taws pays me. I must resort to building my own business. I am curious about the pottery that sits on the high shelf. There must be money in it or Taws would have nothing to do with it.

A week ago, I asked Taws about his collection. Of course, he was suspicious at first. I am sure he thought I was going to rob him. So, I spent some time raving about how wonderful the pieces were. Hadley's letters told him I ran the university museum, and he probably believed I knew what I was talking about. In a short time, he was quizzing me about various pieces, as I was pumping him.

As I figured, he sells the pieces in Santa Fe to curio shop owners. Scanning the collection, he said with a grin that he has gotten pretty good at making a profit.

Two days ago, Taws made a trip to Santa Fe to sell some of his pottery. As usual, he did not

[189]

want to leave me at the store so I had to go with him as I hoped I would.

On the way, Taws said there were a number of curio shops, but his favorite was Gold's Old Curiosity Shop on San Francisco Street. I saw that it was a small shop whose merchandise spilled out onto the wooden sidewalk. It had a cluttered look with interesting things wherever you looked. In a way it reminded me of the shops in Chinatown back in Chicago. The owner, Jake Gold, had a large selection of Indian objects on display mixed in with geologic specimens, old Spanish objects, nice paintings, and even some strange pieces of wood. I saw blankets, a variety of baskets, grinding stones, and of course pieces of pottery.

While Taws and Gold dickered over pieces, I listened in while I pretended to walk around and examine artifacts. I also checked the prices Gold was asking. It was not until they had finished their dealings that he made a comment that explained everything to me.

"Your timing is perfect, Taws. I need a few more pieces to top off a shipment to New York. Now I can send two barrels on Thursday," he said.

That is where a lot of the pottery goes. Other dealers back East will resell the pieces to individual buyers at inflated prices. If I could find outlets, I could pack pottery in barrels as well as Jake Gold. It was then that it occurred to me, I do have contacts. Museums.

On the way back to Los Cerrillos I silently made my plans. Once back I wrote to Mildred at the Milwaukee Museum and explained my situation and plan. I have not heard from her yet, but I have also written to several other large institutions.

Love,

Sam

[190]

***

Quite soon Sam received replies from three museums and a university. They were all interested in southwest pottery, but it had to have good background information. Otherwise, it would be worthless. He understood this because geological specimens are treated the same. If researchers didn't know where it came from, they couldn't use it.

The only way Sam could be sure about the documentation was to collect the pottery himself. Then he could take good notes. He had two problems. First find the pottery, then store the pieces where Taws couldn't find it.

Sam asked Doc if there was a small space he could borrow to keep any pieces he might find.

....Doc chuckled and readily agreed. He also had a lead for my search. He told me there is supposed to be an old, deserted pueblo, called San Marcos, northeast of town, but he was not sure exactly where it is. He thought there are also a couple of smaller pueblos to the east and southeast as well....

As soon as the winter weather cleared, Sam set out searching for this deserted pueblo. His search was in vain:

....Occasionally, I find small pieces of pottery perhaps an inch across, they are interesting, but not worth collecting. Each time I go out I travel a little further from town since that is the only clue I have to go on....

Journal Entries
1898

February 5

I have been thinking about patterns. I am going to have to think like an ancient Pueblo Indian if I want to find this village.

[191]

If I were an Indian, I would build my village on flat ground so its construction would be easier. I would also build my pueblo on high ground to make it easier to watch for enemies. And I would find a place near a reliable source of water. I am sure there are other factors in their decision, but maybe these three are enough to help solve the mystery.

February 8

The Galisteo Creek flows from an easterly direction through Los Cerrillos and then turns northwest. It is dry or nearly dry much of the year, although I have been told it flows in torrents after a heavy rain. There are several large arroyos coming out of the hills that feed the creek. One that flows in from the northeast is called San Marcos. The name has not escaped my attention although there are many things around this area that share that moniker.

The arroyo in question is dry this time of the year. Its channel is flat and covered with sand and small rocks. By the time it empties into Galisteo Creek, it is quite wide, so it must carry quite a bit of water during the wet season. I have decided to walk the arroyo this Sunday and see what I can find.

February 13

Soon after sunrise I began my journey. I made rapid progress at first since I rejected the early terrain because it does not fit my theory. Once past some volcanic flows however, the arroyo begins to branch off and each of these smaller channels subdivides not unlike tree limbs. The arroyo and its tributaries seem to originate in the open flat lands. The sides of the smaller channels have a gentler slope often not more than twenty feet high. Most of them are damp from the melting snow still left in the shade of rocks and trenches.

I decided to explore each of these smaller arroyos starting with the right hand one and progressing to my left. I climbed the sides of each one and examined the ground. Some spots seemed level but not suitable because there were large rocks. Others looked suitable but yielded no returns.

It was beginning to get late, and I still had to allow enough time to return to town, but I wanted to follow one last

[192]

branch. It twisted and turned and went further than the previous two. I was walking in the dry channel and as I came around a bend, I suddenly burst out laughing. I had walked through all this wilderness only to come to a ribbon of civilization. It had slipped my mind that the road between Los Cerrillos and Santa Fe had to be around here somewhere. The road came down the south slope, crossing a bridge above the channel, and up the north side.

I was about to start walking back to town when I figured I had better finish exploring this arroyo. I do hate leaving a job unfinished. I crossed under the bridge and continued up the arroyo. Its end was within view which was good because the sun was headed for the hills to the west. From the dry channel I could see nothing of interest and again almost turned around. The south side of the arroyo was rather hilly and rocky. I did not even climb up there to investigate. I did go up the north side and found a pleasantly flat area. I walked around for a few minutes and started back to the arroyo when I spotted what looked to be a series of low, straight dirt ridges no more than a foot high. They were partially hidden by some juniper trees, but I could see some were parallel while others were at right angles of others. I walked around and found some ridges were well formed while others had practically dissolved into the ground. When I finished my survey, I still was not sure what it all meant, but my imagination said that if the ridges were the remnants of walls then this was a pueblo. I stood looking back down the arroyo breathing with pride as if I had just discovered Troy.

I was not sure what to do at this point. I only had a small tablet for sketching, and I hastily drew a diagram of the ridges. Then I looked carefully in the gravel nearby and found small pieces of pottery. Most of it was a yellowish white with black lines and red shapes. None of it was large enough to sell to museums back East, but if I sent samples perhaps they could tell me about the site and whether it was worth pursuing. I filled a bag I had used for a sandwich.

By now the sun was starting to dip behind the hills so I had to leave. I headed back to the road. I decided to take it back to town since it was somewhat safer than walking in the

[193]

arroyo at night. I had gone only a short way when the late stage came along. I flagged it down. They said it was only a few miles and I could ride free. After climbing in beside the other two passengers, we were off.

I could not contain my excitement. I told the men what I found.

"You mean the San Marcos Pueblo," one of them asked?

"Well, I am not sure," I answered.

"The one on the top of the ridge maybe a half mile from where we picked you up?"

I had a sinking feeling. "Ya, I guess so."

"That's San Marcos, alright. Been there many times. People like to go there and look for pottery. There's plenty to be found."

"Is that so," I said. We got to Los Cerrillos, and I did not have to say anything more.

I am happy to have found a good source of pottery, but I am disappointed that I wasted time finding something that was common knowledge. I make this record to remind myself. In the future, ask the locals before charging off to find the Holy Grail.

***

Quickly he sent off samples of his pottery and copies of his rough notes to his prospective customers. With nothing else to do until he heard, Sam decided to begin excavation of the site. But before he could begin, he received a reply from the American Museum of Natural History in New York.

....They would like pottery from the site. They have some pottery similar to it, but nothing specifically from San Marcos Pueblo that they know of. They would like a diagram of the it including measurements along with anything else I can supply. Hooray! I feel like a real professional for the first time....

[194]

When he showed Doc the letter and described his plans, Doc stopped him. He pointed out to Sam that it would be impossible to run his business while he stayed at Taws. He encouraged Sam to quit his job and move over to the drug store.

...."There's a small storeroom in the back that we can clean up. Jane can throw another potato in the pot easy enough so you can eat with us. What do you say?"

I thought a second. "I do not have any money, and I cannot live here without paying you something, but thank you. It is a wonderful idea."

"Now just a minute," he said. Don't go shoot'n the horse because it loses a shoe. I will hire you to do some things around here that never get done because I'm always minding the store. Besides, I need someone who can take medicine to people who are too sick to come here. Can you do that?"

"Well sure, but..."

"Then it's a deal." He held out his hand. I shook it....

....One of my tasks I have set for myself is to write to my friends and let them know I am still alive. It is strange, but the promise of success is almost as good for the mind as the actual success itself....

Journal Entries
1898

March 14

During the days before returning to San Marcos, I imagined digging pottery and then drawing a map to show where the finds were found. After thinking about it for a while though, decided to make the map first and then dig. Made a trip to the hardware store. Funds just about gone, I hope this pays off. Bought supplies.

Once on the site, laid out north-south and east-west base lines. Made a grid with the string. Now the whole site was a series of squares. Now the ridges can be drawn without distortion. While map is not large, it is fairly accurate. That took all day, but well spent.

Back at Richards' that night I drew four duplicate maps, one for the American Museum of Natural History, and three more for other anticipated customers. They looked pretty good. Should impress buyers.

March 18

Had a nagging problem. It is about five miles from town to San Marcos. It takes about an hour and a half to travel that far, or three hours of every workday is spent in transit. I miss my bicycle. Decided to try camping. Thought I could get through the cold nights with the help of a campfire and a decent blanket roll. It could not be any worse than camping in the rain at Mazon Creek.

Packed up last Wednesday, let the Richards know what I was doing, and made the trek. Found the site as I left it, which was a great relief. Set up camp and started a small fire. Not sure where to dig and how deep to go. Chose some spots at random. Started to work like a coal heaver.

That was first mistake. Had taken several large shovel fulls of dirt when heard a dull thud. Cleared away dirt cover and discovered a beautiful, but smashed potsherd. It was in many pieces. Beyond hope of repair. My first treasure was ruined. Disgusted, I stopped and made a cup of tea. I am still annoyed.

That experience taught me to work slowly and carefully. Am not dealing with layers of rock, but layers of man-made artifacts. They break. Take thin layers of dirt, then look to see what was revealed. If I am going to be successful at this, I have to learn to be delicate.

Found several other pieces. Numbered each one, noted the finds on the map. Put them in the crate padded with straw. Took a sample of the dirt from several spots and put each in its

[196]

own cloth bag. Not sure if soil samples are important but taking no chance.

Had twelve good sized pieces and numerous smaller ones by end of the first day. The map was beginning to fill up. Decided to draw a larger edition when I got back to civilization. Tomorrow, dig deeper.

The night was tolerable if not comfortable. In the morning my ankle ached some, but soon a good fire and hot tea water helped warm things. When it got light enough first explored beyond the area I had mapped. The remains of the village extended far beyond my original guess. Just before sunrise I began digging. I worked in the first two of the holes I made yesterday but found nothing even though went down about a foot and a half.

The next hole I dug yielded another piece of pottery. Continued digging and found a second fragment only a few inches below the level of the first piece, but it was quite different. It was much cruder than the other shard. The maker had not bothered to smooth the surface very well because I could see where individual coils had been pressed together. In addition, there was no decoration that I could find. From the curve of the piece, I could tell it belonged to a smaller bowl than the flatter curved painted pieces.

Nothing succeeds like success. Invigorated. Continued digging. The original hole was about two feet across, but now I enlarged it to three and then four feet across. Two more painted pieces, very close together. From their gentle curves and pattern, it looks like they came from the same vessel. This is fun.

After enlarging the hole again, I found another piece matching the previous two. This made three pieces from the same pot. Dug down another foot with no success, although did notice a change in the soil. Yellowish clay. Took samples of it. This level was only a few inches thick. What is this? Manmade? If so, is it the floor of the room? Below this level was more soil, but not alluvial mixture. I was carefully removing this when I found yet another piece of pottery unlike any of the previous ones. This piece was almost half a bowl and was the largest piece I had yet uncovered. It was

[197]

yellowish like the previous painted pieces, but the design was not as well done. If the clay level is a floor, this piece means someone lived here before the pueblo, or at least before this series of rooms were built. It is just like layers of sandstone. The deeper you go the older the material. Stratigraphic evidence. How old? Were they the same people living here for a long time, or different people living in the same spot but at different times?

After stopping for a quick lunch, continued digging. Eventually hit alluvium. It seemed to be undisturbed, but I dug a little deeper. Eventually any more digging would be pointless.

I remembered the way miners left holes for people and animals to fall into. I decided I would not do that. Refilled the hole as best I could. Then moved to another spot close by and started the process over again.

My luck had run out. I dug several feet down, and while I found the same clay layer, there was no pottery. I did however find charcoal. Marked it on the map along with its depth. What does the charcoal mean?

By this time, it was midafternoon. Stopped to make a cup of tea and consider the next move. While sitting on one of the walls, (now I am sure that is what they are), Doc and Jane walked up from the road. They said they wanted to check to see if I had survived the night. Jane brought a picnic lunch just in case I was still alive. While devouring the sandwiches, I showed them each piece like a proud father presenting his children.

"If you want to load up your storage crate and send it back on the wagon, we'll be glad to carry it," Doc said.

I thought about it for a few seconds. "If you do not mind, I will break camp and return with you. I've got a good start here, and now that I think about it, I am tired."

"That's fine. I'll put things in the wagon while you finish up here."

I had a luxurious ride back to town.

March 21

[198]

Went to the butcher shop and got several pieces of wrapping paper for the enlarged maps. Did only two of them, but still, that took most of a day. I can still use the smaller maps for notes.

Washed the artifacts, wrapped them in newspaper and packed them in the shipping crate between layers of straw. Need half a dozen more pieces to fill the box. Then it can be shipped off. Will go back to San Marcos in a couple of days and try to get that much.

March 25

I have sent off my first shipment of artifacts to the American Museum of Natural History in New York City via Wells Fargo. I sent along a big map of the site, along with several pages of notes, and soil samples. I hope they are happy.

Now I will begin collecting for the Field Columbian Museum in Chicago and the University of Chicago. I wanted to complete one order to check for any snags in the process.

I received letters from Eli and Cora. Eli reports he has finished his classes at the Art Institute and has become a full-time assistant to Frank Lloyd Wright. He also said Ambrose is working his way through law school and anticipates finishing within a year or so.

All is well with Cora and Charles. The baby is standing and beginning to walk so she is kept busy. Charles was appointed as Acting Chair of the Biology Department for the year. They have talked about perhaps looking for a position in a larger university, maybe in a southern state.

I literally ran into Ursinus Taws the other day. He was coming out of the post office while I was going in. I tell you, if he was a rattlesnake, he would have bit me. As it was, he only hissed. Hopefully I will never see him again....

April 19, 1898

Dear Cate,

Great news! The American Museum likes the pottery I sent them. They were impressed with the map and notes I sent them. Not only are they

[199]

are sending a money order within the next thirty days for payment in full, they want more pottery.

I really enjoy going to San Marcos. It is so peaceful. Now that warm weather is here, I camp overnight quite often. I could live here.
Love,
Sam

By the end of May Sam was feeling much better about himself and his finances. He had money to leave Cerrillos, but he had his own little bonanza that he was not about to relinquish. During the next month he continued his explorations and excavations.

Because archaeologists comprise a tight knit family, it is not surprising that Sam's name became recognized among the small group of them working in the Southwest. While he was unknown as an individual, the American Museum of Natural History spoke highly of his work. Likewise, the archaeologists at the Field Columbian Museum casually mentioned his name as a professional of potential importance. Being isolated in Los Cerrillos, he had no idea he was seen as an up-and-comer by people he had never met. That is, until a gentleman walked into the drugstore.

Chapter Twenty

Late one Tuesday morning Sam was packing pottery to send east when Doc came in his little room to tell him he had a visitor. Sam never had visitors. Only a handful of people even knew him, so he was curious. The slight, tanned, well-dressed man introduced himself as Edgar Hewett.

> "I am by training an educator, but my avocation is that of an archaeologist. In my correspondence with professionals back east your name keeps popping up, so I decided to track you down and make your acquaintance. We serious archaeologists must stick together since there are so few of us."

With that he launched into an extended oration on his archaeological sites near Santa Fe. Some fifteen minutes later he finally got to the reason for visiting Sam.

> "I'm just not sure where the Basin pueblos that you deal with, fit into the scheme of things. I was hoping we could work together to try and solve this problem."

"Of course," replied Sam, only too happy to extend his own knowledge of the area's archaeology. Over lunch, Hewett probed Sam's background, and was very impressed with his knowledge of geology. Afterwards, they took a quick look at Sam's pottery collection. Hewett said he had to catch the Albuquerque train for a meeting. On his return trip, could they look at the San Marcos site? Sam responded that he would be happy to show what he had been working on.

Hewett reappeared late Friday morning just in time for lunch. This time the topic was geology. After lunch they took a wagon to the site and spent the afternoon discussing Sam's discoveries.

> ....All this time, I was feeling quite confident about my abilities. Thinking back to when I first met him, I never did feel my usual insecurity. Was it a matter of getting older or that I had met with success and that gave me the confidence to meet someone head on? During our stay at San Marcos our conversation became less of a one-sided field lecture and more of a give-and-take between professionals. On the way back to Los Cerrillos we agreed to meet in Santa Fe and he would show me his work at Pecos....

About a week later, Sam took the stage to Santa Fe and met Hewett at the appointed spot. Pecos is an abandoned pueblo about 25 miles east of Santa Fe, so much of the time was spent in travel.

> ....We spent the some of the afternoon looking at house structures, kivas, and an old mission church. By then it was time to return to Santa Fe so I could catch the stage back to Los Cerrillos....

On the way back to Santa Fe, Hewett sprung his trap.

> ...."Jeppe, I have had two problems hanging around my neck, but today I have solved them both."
>
> "Well, that must be a great relief to you. Problems do tend to weigh you down."
>
> "Let me explain the situation. I have known, for some time, that I needed a geologist to help me with my archaeological sites. I'm sure you

[202]

would be an excellent associate because you not only know geology but have archaeological experience as well. "

"However, like I said I am an educator by profession. What I didn't say was that I have been hired to be the president of a new college to prepare teachers. The normal school is in Las Vegas. It is opening this fall. I have hired all my teachers...except one. The gentleman I had hired to teach geology and geography was forced to back out due to some family illness. So, I need a replacement, and I think I have found one in you. That is, if you are willing.

"While I was in Albuquerque, I visited with the president at the university there and he heartily recommended you. He showed me your letters of recommendation from the University of Chicago. I must say I am very impressed. This is a full-time faculty position that can't be cut. The pay is not as much as you might receive at some eastern colleges, but you will find it is sufficient for a single gentleman in New Mexico. What say? Can I introduce you as Professor Jeppe...?

Sam was startled by the offer, but he had reservations.

....My little business is growing. The prospects are good. I am becoming known and respected back East. I also enjoy being able to set my own hours and schedule. It is not such a bad life, still....

***

July 4, 1898

Dear Cate,
Happy Independence Day from Las Vegas, New Mexico. I have a surprise. I have been hired to teach geology and geography at a teacher's

[203]

training college in Las Vegas, New Mexico. Because the offer was too good to turn down, I arrived ten days ago. I have been busy looking for a place to live and buying necessities.

It was more difficult leaving Los Cerrillos than I anticipated. When I first came there, I was an angry person. But eventually the little town gave me a chance to be more at peace with myself. Therefore, I have resolved that if I become dissatisfied with Las Vegas, I will return to Los Cerrillos, and build a cabin outside of town.

I said good-bye to my friends. It seems that I am always saying good-bye. Anyway, Doc and Jane were sad to see me go, but understood I have to try to grab the brass ring when it is within my reach. I told them I would be only a few hours away, so I would visit from time to time.

Amarate was not surprised at my departure. He foretold it sometime back. "Well Butterfly, the flower blossoms are as sweet in Las Vegas as they are here, so feast well. Should you find your way back, I will be happy to see you."

It was even harder to leave San Marcos. It became more than an archaeological site to me. I was as happy there as I was in the vacant lot back in Milwaukee. Even on the coldest of days, I could feel the presence, the warmth, of the people who used to live there. So, on my last day I did my best to make it look pristine. I picked up all the trash others had left. I removed my grid and smoothed the ground that I and others had invaded. When I left for the last time, the site was such that an unsuspecting hiker might miss it all together.

Las Vegas is a good-sized city. A mile or so to the west are the mountains while a mile or so to the east are the Great Plains.

It is a very modern town with electricity, city water, sewers, telephones, and a trolley system.

[204]

There are four different railroad lines that stop here every day.

Yet Las Vegas retains the feel of the ol' west. A decade ago, gun fights, murders, and hangings were a common occurrence. It is quieter now though. The town fathers are making an effort to build a positive image by building the teacher's college.

The college's building, Normal Hall, is a four-story brownstone that will never be finished on time. Hewett is hoping that the first floor will be completed.

Opening day is on October 3rd, and the closer that date comes the more nervous I become. My main concern is the classes I will teach. All my notes from college were burned, so I will have to depend on my memory and the books I have acquired since Albuquerque. My first quarter's class is physical geography with which I feel quite comfortable.

Hewett does not make great demands on my time as of yet. I do not think he has a lot of spare time to go to the field with the opening of classes only two months away.

July 7

I discovered there are actually two towns going by the same name. West Las Vegas is the original village and is the equivalent of Albuquerque's Old Town. It has narrow winding streets and small houses built on hill sides. Many of the original Spanish families live.

To the east, across a small river, is East Las Vegas. Like New Town in Albuquerque, it has been built in response to the railroads. The straight checkerboard streets lined with Victorian houses could be mistaken for any proper community in the Midwest.

On my third day in Las Vegas, Hewett took me to a bank where a vice president set up a small line of credit based on my position at the school and my "stellar character." This has allowed me to purchase some much-needed clothing and supplies. I think I will buy a cowboy hat. Once I get a haircut, I will be quite the man about town.
Write Soon,
Sam

***

July 27, 1898

Dear Cate,
        I had a room at Griswald's boarding house. Mrs. Griswald made good meals, the room was clean, and the other boarders were friendly. I should have had no complaint, yet I was dissatisfied.
        I spent some time thinking about my dissatisfaction, and I decided my time at San Marcos had changed me. All my life I have lived in noisy cities. At San Marcos however, silence and solitude were the norms. At first the absence of sound bothered me, but I learned to look forward to the quiet like a comfortable bed at the end of a hard day.
        I promised myself that if I returned to Los Cerrillos I would have a home in the country. But now I could not think of a good reason to wait. So, I began to look for a house outside of Las Vegas.
        I visited a business specializing in real estate and explained what I wanted. He mentioned a little house located east of town, a little off the dirt road. Because it had been vacant for some time, the owner was anxious to sell.
        I walked out to see the house for myself. The one-acre estate sits on the eastern edge of a

[206]

fairly deep arroyo which in turn serves as the eastern edge of town and western edge of the Great Plains. As I stood by the front door, I could look upon the rooftops of Las Vegas and the slopes of the Sangre de Cristo Mountains not far beyond. To the south of me are juniper trees, to the north, more grasslands. I am told the old Santa Fe Trail passed somewhere close by.

The walls and roof of the house are in need of some repair, but on the whole, they are in decent shape. All in all, the cabin meets my requirements, I can afford it, it is within walking distance of the school, and the nearest house is over a quarter mile away.

The owner and I agreed on the price of $150, a very reasonable price indeed. I will pay him in five monthly installments. So now I am the proud owner of real estate. Very exciting, to be sure.

My little house is a perfect size for me. It has two rooms. The larger one has a fireplace and will serve as kitchen, office, and parlor. The small room will be bedroom and storage. Windows open on each side of the house so it should be comfortable in the hottest weather. There is no well, but a nearby spring can supply all my needs.

I dare not over-extend my credit at the bank so shipping crate furniture and my trusty hammock will do till my first paycheck. I stopped at a pawn shop and purchased a set of dishes, silverware, a tea kettle, a skillet and pot.

The morning after my first night in the house seemed especially bright. I stepped smartly through the school's main door thirty minutes after I left home. An excellent time. I felt, how shall I describe it? I felt like I belong.

Love,
Sam

[207]

Journal Entries
1898

<u>July 30</u>

I have met my neighbors, if you can call someone living a quarter mile away a neighbor. They are nestled in a shallow depression to the east. One afternoon I walked over to introduce myself. As I approached, I could see their small house, several old corrals, one which had a horse in it, and a decent-sized barn. A single, large cottonwood was on the opposite side of the house. It offered the only shade for some distance. There was a stool and a chair beneath its sprawling branches. Just beyond the tree was a small cemetery surrounded by a crude fence with four crosses in it. Not too far from the front door of the house was a good-sized garden. Overall, the picture gave an impression of determined self-reliance.

As I walked toward the house, I saw an old woman was working in the garden. She spied me as soon as I became visible and continued to watch me. I could see her call into the barn. A moment later an equally ancient man hobbled out with a rifle and they stood together waiting for me to approach. They were a gray-haired Spanish American couple quite thin and short in stature. Their nut-brown faces looked as if they had been chiseled from rock, baked by the sun and weathered by the wind. They reminded me of Ah Kum.

I was a little concerned about the rifle so when I was within shouting distance I greeted them in my broken Spanish and asked if I might visit with them. The old man nodded but shifted the rifle to let me know I should careful.

Stopping about ten feet away, out of respect and some fear, I introduced myself and explained I had just moved into the house to their west. You would have thought I was a long lost relative because they broke into broad somewhat toothless grins, began chattering in Spanish, and motioned me over to the shade tree where I was given the chair. The woman disappeared and momentarily reappeared with a cup of water. The handle of the cup was broken, the rim was chipped in

[208]

several places, but the water was surprisingly cool and refreshing.

They apologized for the gun, but they had to be careful with strangers because there were still some bad men around. They had heard someone had finally moved into my little house. If there was anything I needed just ask, if they had it, it was mine. All this was spoken in rapid Spanish. It was not until I began speaking that they realized my poor handle on the language, so the man translated what they had just said in passable English. I apologized, and told them I was trying to learn Spanish, but was making slow progress. He translated to her, and they both laughed, he said "*si, si, no hay problema amigo.*"

I learned his name was Modesto Soto y Diaz and his wife was Consuelo De La Rosa. *Modesto y Consuelo* from now on. They have lived on their *rancho* for over thirty years. They used to have more horses and cattle, but they are too old now, so they just have one horse and keep a few head of beef to sell from time to time.

We visited for a respectable length of time before I took my leave. They are nice people. Once again, I felt that I was not an outsider, but a welcomed part of my very small community.

I have planted a vegetable garden. I figured if my uncles are farmers, I could grow something too. The soil is pretty rocky, and it takes a lot of water, so I am going to get some manure....

August 1

This evening Modesto brought me some tamales Consuelo had made. They were hot, but delicious. This old, mostly toothless man who is obviously pained by walking came trotting up bareback on his horse. I do not know how he got on the horse, but once there his years vanished in the breeze because he was no longer an old man, but a young man with white hair. When he spoke to me his voice was stronger than when we first met, more authority. His eyes twinkled too.

He declined to come and sit while we talked. Instead, he sat easily on the horse with his leg thrown over its back. I

[209]

gave him some apples I had bought at the grocery store for which he was grateful saying Consuelo would mash them to sauce and they would have them for their dinner. We visited for a while in mixed English and Spanish till it started to get dark. Then he said he needed to return home or Consuelo would worry, so we said goodbye. With that he sharply turned his horse and cantered off, sitting tall, straight, and proud, clearly saying without words, "Young man, I may be old, but I am still a horseman." I watched him with growing respect till he disappeared over the hill. I sense this couple is anxious to form a friendship. I may be the only person close by that they associate with. I have decided to stop once a week to check on them.

August 20
It has been quiet so far. We are in the midst of a drought and a hot spell, so during the day it gets pretty stifling. Everything in my garden has died. I will try again next year. There was a forest fire north of Las Vegas, but quick work by the farmers contained it. People are nervous about the prospect of other fires.
The road running past my house has several steep hills which were difficult for wagons to go up and down. So, the city fathers decided the hills should be graded. Dynamite made short work of the shale overburden, but there were tons of debris to clear. Prisoners from the state penitentiary were brought in to do the job. It was very hard work in the heat. One of the prisoners died. Nether the guards, nor the other prisoners, seemed to care much.

September 3
Things have cooled off a little, but still no rain. One month before school begins. I think I am ready for my classes.

September 6
The people of Las Vegas remind me of two streams coming together. One stream, the Spanish, is unhurried, staying within its banks, maintaining a polite disregard for whatever obstacle is in its bed. The other stream, the Anglos,

[210]

is filled with surging water tumbling over anything that it meets, cutting a new channel wherever and whenever it finds a weakness. When the two streams meet, sometimes the result is a swirling confusion of contention, while in other places they blend together with few ripples.

Along the sides of the frenzied confrontation there are little backwaters where everything is quiet. If I wander into one of these eddies like a leaf in the brook, I can stay there for hours watching life going on around me.

For instance, I like to rest on one of the weather-worn benches along main street and watch the stream of people go by. It brings back memories of the walk to Mr. Diersdörfer's.

I am inspired by the books Cate writes. I agree that while it is the star of the show, the hero of the team, the celebrity, that usually gets the attention, those of us in the background also have stories worth telling.

For instance, there is a painter in town who is actually quite good. I have never met him, actually I do not know anyone who has since his Spanish wife peddles his art. She is attractive, about my age, but she is a real odd duck. Some of the people refer to her as *loca*, the crazy lady. Dressed in men's clothing, wearing an old cowboy hat, she smokes cigarettes in public, and can cuss with the best of 'em. Her gallery is anywhere she chooses. If that is in front of a store, she will prop the paintings against one of the store windows and she is open for business, at least until the store owner comes out and chases her away. However, while there, she proceeds to badger any passersby. If they stop to look at the paintings, she will usually get pushy till she makes a sale. Like I said, the paintings are quite good, and the price is always very low. While she is always polite to women, she has no time for men and has no fear of offending them, in fact it seems that she tries to. But strangely enough, she always has a coin and a kind word for any pauper who walks past. Animosity toward those with power, benevolence toward those who are down and out. Striking.

I wanted to buy a painting myself, but I had no money at the time. My home looks a little barren these days and

[211]

needs some art on the walls. So, soon I will buy a landscape or maybe a still life.

Chapter Twenty-One

While Sam was settling down in Las Vegas, Paris was anything but settled. A civil war of sorts was taking place throughout the country. On one side were liberals, or republicans comprised of many Parisians, Protestants, socialists, and Freemasons. Opposing them were traditionalists, or anti-republicans which included the rural landowners, the Roman Catholic Church, a smattering of royalists, and the army.

Since the Franco-Prussian War in 1870 the two sides had traded control of the central government with the usual back-and-forth banter that one finds in any two-party system of government. But in 1889 various right-wing newspapers began to carrying articles about Jewish conspiracies that included corruption, fraud, and bribery.

Soon after that, the articles became absolutely inflammatory. These pieces said France was controlled by Jews. Fabricated stories portrayed all Jews as dishonest and deceitful. The stories claimed that now Jews controlled the French economy so non-Jewish Frenchmen were slaves to this small group of all-powerful foreigners.

For centuries, there had been an anti-Semitic undercurrent in parts of the population, and the newspaper articles, by appealing to these attitudes, began to disrupt the social stability that had been prevalent since the beginning of the nineteenth century. Back then, the French government passed laws giving Jewish citizens full and equal rights. Efforts were also made to assimilate them into society which resulted in Jews taking an active, productive role in many

[213]

facets of French life. But now, most French Jews, quiet working members of the Parisian community, were caught off guard by these attacks. There was little they could do to refute the accusations.

The army was one area of the government that obsessed the Traditionists. Even though hundreds of Jews had faithfully served as officers for many years, conservatives attacked this minority claiming they were a threat to national security.

However, these attacks were not having the effect hoped for by the radicals, but that was about to change. In late 1894 an anonymous letter was sent to the conservative newspaper *La Libre* proclaiming a Jewish army officer, Alfred Dreyfus, had been arrested and charged with espionage, along with the sale of secrets to Germany. The traditionalist papers sensationalized the case, and the public reacted accordingly.

His court martial lasted four days. Dreyfus was found guilty and sentenced to life on Devil's Island off the coast of French Guiana. First, he was stripped of his rank and insignias during which thousands of people demonstrated outside shouting *"Mort aux Juifs, Àmort le Traître, Àmort Judas!"*, "Death to the Jews, Death to the traitor, Death Judas!" He was beaten by more demonstrators on his way to the ship that would take him to Devil's Island. However, once he was safely locked away that should have been the end of it. But it was not. The traditionalists kept up their printed attacks. Dreyfus came to represent all Jews, and Jews came to represent all foreigners. The cry "France for the French," became their rallying cry as they sought to inflame the French populace.

While this was going on, a small group of Dreyfus supporters were gathering evidence to prove his innocence. Their findings showed conclusively that the army's General Staff had colluded to create forged documents, they had lied under oath, they had withheld evidence, and had done what was necessary to make it impossible for Dreyfus to have a fair trial.

The public knew little of the Dreyfus supporters' findings until Émile Zola began to publish articles in liberal newspapers. Zola was an immensely popular French novelist

[214]

and journalist at that time. His articles strongly criticized both the court martial and the public reaction.

In response, the conservative papers published even more outrageous accusations. Soon it became impossible for people to even stop in a cafe for a cup of tea without being drawn into an argument over the state of affairs.

Such was the situation in January 1898 when Zola published his article *J'accuse* in which he exposed the illegal and immoral actions of numerous military officers, and as he said, "the wild investigations, the monstrous fantasies, the whole torturous insanity."

The reaction was immediate. The day the letter was published, several thousand university students gathered to protest the letter, shouting "Down with Zola." Police did their best to blockade the mob to no avail. The next several days saw more of the same. On a personal level people yelled obscenities at their Jewish neighbors, previously congenial co-workers came to blows, families divided as members took opposing sides.

It was at this time I received a telegram from the New York Herald asking me to do a series of columns on the Dreyfus affair. I replied that I would with the usual stipulation that the subject matter was to be my choice.

I decided interviewing the military in the case would be a waste of time because they would not offer anything different than what was already in print, so I first wanted to talk to the demonstrators.

It was not difficult to find Parisian protesters. I just followed the chanting. They were almost always university students. Consequently, they started to gather in the afternoon when classes were over for the day. They tended to group themselves according to their area of study. One cluster might be law students, the next engineers. To a man, as there were few if any women, their enthusiasm was focused on maintaining a team-like message be it *"vive l'armée,"* "long live the army," or "Zola à la potence," "Zola to the gallows" or whatever their leader seemed to fancy. However, students frequently chatted or laughed with one another giving the appearance of a procession to a sporting event instead of a

[215]

political protest. While within a larger mass these groups often competed with others close by, seeing who could be the loudest.

No one had any interest in talking to me until I mouthed the magic words, "American reporter", then I had their complete attention. Their original goal of altering current events was quickly thrown over, and replaced by the highlight of their young lives, that of being quoted in a foreign newspaper. However, I heard little worth repeating.

I did find there were two types of people involved in the demonstrations. One type of protester had rationalized his actions by believing he was saving the country from a dangerous threat. This was the "France for the French" player. To this individual anyone who did not agree with the traditionalist philosophy was part of the dangerous threat. These people had no interest in alternative ideas. Some expressed a true hatred of the Jews most likely resulting from indoctrination, but often Jews were only a symbol of things impeding society's return to the way things used to be.

The other type of protester I called tag-alongs. These individuals participated in the activities but had little knowledge of or little concern for the purpose of the demonstration. These young men joined because everyone else was there. They looked to the leaders for directions not particularly caring what those directions might accomplish. When I asked them why they were there most couldn't be precise. They often refused to explain their reasons, instead they spewed such phrases as "the Jews are evil and should be shot", or "Dreyfus is a spy and should be shot," or "Zola is the devil and should be shot," as if the answer was self-evident.

I found only one individual who even knew a Jewish family, and he was protesting because he thought Dreyfus was really guilty of spying. The rest were responding to what they had been told, or by what they had read in conservative newspapers, not because of any personal experience. If this was the case, then perhaps I should talk to the newspapers.

My first stop was the office of *La Libre Parole*, or Free Speech. It was the leading anti-Semitic newspaper and was owned by Édouard Drumont who some called the pope of anti-

Semitism. I expected to find a big man who is used to dominating large audiences with a loud voice, so I was surprised when I was ushered into his office only to find a rather short, quiet, demure man who seemed to be hiding behind a full bushy beard.

"How may I help you, Miss Jeppe?"

"I would like to talk to you about the demonstrations that have been organized in response to Zola's letter *"J'accuse ."*

"What is there to say. The people of France are expressing their contempt for the despicable accusations made by a foreigner who should not even be allowed in the country. Zola is merely parroting the words and thoughts of his masters. I can tell from your manner that you are not French by birth, but surely even you can see that Zola is attacking our army, and our courts for no other reason than to help secure the conquest of France by the Jews."

I was irritated by his condescending attitude, but I was determined to continue. "Zola is only pointing out the failure of the courts to correct the illegalities perpetrated on an innocent man by the General Staff of the army. Are you not concerned about the protection of the blameless?"

"By the "innocent", I assume you are referring to Alfred Dreyfus. He was found guilty by a court martial. There is nothing left to say regarding that. Except the court martial failed in their responsibility to the country by not executing him. The later courts also have failed in their responsibility by not executing the rest of the Jewish criminals."

"M. Drumont, you seem very sure of yourself when you call all Jewish men and women criminals. Do you have proof supporting that statement?"

"Have you read my book, *"La France juive?"*

"No," I lied. I had read his little book and found it full of garbage.

"Please read it before you come here again to waste my time. Now if you will excuse me, I have important matters to attend to."

I kept my seat, and asked "What about other foreigners, are they to be executed as well?" He stared intently at the

[217]

article he was editing and ignored me. When I gave him enough time to reply and I knew he was not going to, I stood up and walked out.

I've been thrown out of offices by better men than M. Drumont, but I was discouraged that I didn't get anything new. As with the students, there was not one good quote. This was becoming a problem. I wanted the traditionalists to tell their own story, but no one seemed able to. I asked myself, how can you demand a whole segment of society be expelled or exterminated without a well-developed rationale.

There was one other place to visit to find the answer. Since the demonstrators seemed to be all students and they appeared after classes, I wanted to talk to their instructors to see what part they played in this drama.

I went to one of the universities and waited till the students left for their afternoon protest. One student noticed me and ducked back in the building. When the crowd had cleared, I walked down the hall looking for a professeur in the classrooms, but they were all empty. I found the floor where the offices were. All the doors were shut, and no one answered my knocks. So instead of Daniel in the lions' den, it was just Catherine in an empty building.

It was beginning to look like this was going to be a failed assignment. I had very few of those over the years, and I had a reputation to maintain so I didn't want to quit. A cafe across the street gave me an idea. I could wait in there till I spotted someone leaving. Then I would corner them and get my interview.

I settled in at a table by the window and began to organize my notes that I had made. About fifteen minutes later a little white-haired man with a handlebar mustache approached me. He had a cup of tea in one hand and a cane in his other.

"Are you the reporter who was trespassing in the university building a while ago?"

"Well, I was there, yes."

"I have volunteered to talk with you."

"How did you know I'm a reporter, and what do you mean?"

[218]

"You talked to a student yesterday and he warned us. We felt it would be better this way because a number of us are uncomfortable speaking in public about the demonstrations. I am retiring this year so I don't care, but others have years to go, and there are some people who could make things difficult for us, so I offered to act as a representative."

"In what way could instructors be hurt?"

"They could get fired. Rumors can get spread and students refuse to take their classes. Things like that."

"I'm sorry. I do not want anyone to suffer because I ask them questions."

"That's why I am here. What are your questions?"

"Well, Professeur, Professeur...what is your name?"

"That is unimportant."

"I see. Professeur, do you or other instructors help to set up the demonstrations?"

"No, but there are others in the university that do help organize events."

"Can you give me some names?"

"Next question."

"Do these people coordinate the demonstrations with others such as M. Drumont?"

"Probably, but I don't know."

"Do the students know what this is all about?"

"Our students come from the best families. These are not the riffraff you can find on any street corner. They must pass difficult examinations before being admitted. I'm sure most, but not all of them are well aware of the current events. Because they come from business and professional families, they share the ideas of their parents."

"Do you share those same conservative ideas?"

"Next question. You are asking good questions, but not the important ones."

"Why are the Jews being attacked?"

"Good. Now we get to the crux. During the past fifteen to twenty years some very important people in government and out have made some very bad decisions. Those decisions have cost the citizens of France untold millions of francs. A lot of that money has ended up in the

[219]

pockets of those same important people. If the public were to find out about...ah, certain events, these important, now very rich people would most likely go to jail. What is worse though, the republic might crumble, and that would be very bad for everyone. They need someone to blame for all the troubles. The Jews are a natural target because they are not very well liked anyway."

"Why are they not liked?"

"Because they choose to be different, that's all. Humans are funny that way. If you are different, you are considered suspicious."

"People told me Jews own all the banks."

"Posh. That's a lie. A few banks are controlled by Jews, but many more are run by non-Jews. A few Jews are wealthy, but many more struggle to put food on the table. No, Jews are condemned because they are convenient. Next question."

"Are you Jewish?"

"Next question."

"Is that why people like M. Drumont hate the Jews? Because they are convenient?"

"You have to ask him."

"I did. He won't tell me."

"Let me ask you a question. How do you know Drumont hates Jews?

"Because of the things he writes."

"Drumont is a mediocre writer who has found his niche. He does what he must do to keep his followers' attention and devotion."

"Do you mean he's a fraud?"

"He has no love for Jews, but that is not the reason behind what he writes." The gentleman was looking out the window and apparently saw something. He continued, "My time is up. I told the others I would help you, but I must leave now." I looked out the window but saw nothing unusual.

He stood and adjusted his cane. "Perhaps I will read your article. The library subscribes to some American papers. Which one do you write for?"

"The New York Herald."

[220]

"I think the library receives that one. I will look for it. I have enjoyed our conversation. Good day." The Professeur smiled down at me and walked out the door.

***

Local governmental officials all over France eventually succeeded in controlling the mobs, and restored order. As a result, the anti-Semitic rage of 1898 gradually burned itself out. Alfred Dreyfus was eventually declared innocent in 1906. He was restored to his rank in the army. Some of the officers who had been instrumental in his conviction had retired by that time, but the ones still in active service remained convinced of his guilt. Émile Zola died in 1902. Even though he was condemned by many people for writing "*J'accuse,*" he remains one of France's greatest and most respected authors. Édouard Drumont left the *La Libre Parole* in 1898 to enter politics. He served as an official for Algers, Morocco until 1902 after which he gradually faded into relative obscurity. He died in 1917. I never had any further contact with the old professeur, nor did I ever find out his name.

***

I must admit the columns I sent to the Herald were not my best work. The situation in France was so complex I found it difficult to write about. To make the relationships between the people and events clear would take a book or two, and I had no desire to undertake such a chore.

However, the way people's emotions were manipulated by some of the press during the Dreyfus affair left an indelible impression on me. Since then, I have seen the same exploitation occur again and again. Groups with ulterior motives have become very good at spreading propaganda. People have a responsibility to question what they read or are told. If they don't and they accept things as fact without checking, then they are apt to be misled, misinformed, and misused.

[221]

Chapter Twenty-Two

Sam was enjoying his little house. There were a few minor problems, but that was to be expected. One of the problems was the mice. Prairie mice were prolific, and they were difficult to control.

September 8, 1898

....I got a cat, named Patches. It was supposed to live outside but decided early on that it prefers to live inside. That is alright with me as long as he understands who the owner is and who is the tenant. Actually, it is nice to have him as company. I talk to him, and he talks back in cat language. Our conversations are fairly simple since his needs are few. I have not tried discussing geology or archaeology with him, but the weather and the quality of dinner are fair game.

When I moved here, I sought seclusion, however, over the past few months I have found silence is nice, but I do find that too much of it weighs on me....

September 12

....On Saturday last, I had some shopping to do. As it was a pleasant day I went to town bright and early. While walking toward the

[222]

hardware store, I saw *la loca,* the crazy lady, setting up shop in a vacant lot next to one of the diners. I decided it was time to buy a painting from her. I casually strolled over to examine the three paintings she had displayed. As I expected, the badgering began immediately.

"Ah, a rich Gringo coming to get a cheap painting as a gift for his *señora* to make up for a worthless time last evening. Well, choose quickly. There are others who are waiting, and they have more money. It doesn't matter which you pick, it will not make her forget the terrible mistake she made in marrying you."

I quickly looked around and snapped, "There are no others waiting and I am not married. The painting is for me."

"Oh, an art collector. Forgive me. I didn't recognize your artistic taste in those peasant clothes. Next time you must wear your gold chain and calf skin gloves. Please take all the time you need."

Her barbed comment was having its effect. I was tempted to grab the closest painting, stick some money in her hand and leave as fast as I could. Then I made up my mind not to let her ruin my day so easily. I was going to give her tit-for-tat. "Hush. How am I to make such an important choice when you are standing there clucking like a chicken?"

She laughed. "I doubt you are capable of choosing between salt and pepper, let alone choosing which painting to buy. You couldn't choose between good art and the pile of ca-ca your dog leaves on your bed."

"I do not have a dog, but I see you have taught yours to paint."

She laughed again, and then replied, "You have no wife, no dog and no painting. You probably have no money either. What do you do on

[223]

all those lonely evenings besides stare at blank walls?"

"I enjoy the silence. Something your husband has never known."

"My husband...is a great artist. He creates beautiful paintings while I must deal with the likes of you. For that he worships the ground I walk on. He waits impatiently to see me return because he knows what a courageous feat I perform each time I come into this den of thieves."

"Not nearly as daring as when I come to suffer insults in order to buy one of these mediocre paintings."

"Mediocre! I...he does the best he can to paint something for ungrateful people like you. Go away. I would sooner burn all these paintings than sell one to you."

She was no longer engaged in verbal jousting. I could see I had over-stepped the bounds of friendly combat and hurt her. I stood silently for a few moments, not sure of what to say or do.

"I am sorry. That was a mean thing to say. I got carried away and forgot myself. "You are right. I do not know much about art, but I think these are very good. Please forgive me."

"You really think so? Which do you like best?" Paying her a sincere compliment seemed to make up for my blundering comment. I looked at each one carefully.

"I like this landscape." The colors in the foreground were muted, and they darkened as they receded toward the horizon. There were dark silhouettes of juniper bushes and pine trees throughout. The sky at the horizon was peach-like with lavender clouds. As it faded to a light blue higher up the clouds turned gray. Venus shown bright on the right side. The name Velez was carefully inscribed at the bottom. "It makes me

[224]

think of the few minutes just before sunrise. That is one of my favorite times of the day."

"Mine too. I guess you do know about art. That one took a long time to do. I...he worked hard to get the colors just right."

"That is twice you said I instead of he. Did you paint these?"

She straightened her back and glared at me. "Don't be silly, women can't paint. They can't do much of anything other than bear children. My husband painted these."

"Why do you say that? I know women who are scientists, teachers, and musicians. My sister is a writer. How can you say women cannot do anything but bear children? You are a fine artist. Why do you hide behind your husband?"

She advanced toward me aiming her finger toward my chest as if it were a knife. "I have to sell these to survive, and men will not buy paintings done by women. They think only other men are good artists. You may know women who are fortunate, but they don't live here. Now, if you want to buy the painting, it's three dollars. If you don't, move on, and keep your mouth shut, Gringo."

"Do not take your anger out on me. I mean you no harm. Take a compliment where you can get one. I like the painting regardless of who painted it and I will buy it. I do not have a lot of money, but I will give you five dollars for it. Take it or leave it."

She looked at me for a moment. Then she quickly turned her back, picked up the painting, and presented it to me.

"Thank you, she murmured. "I do appreciate the compliment and the money. Enjoy the painting." She turned her back to me again to move the remaining paintings together. Our conversation was over....

[225]

Journal Entries
1898

<u>September 25</u>

I have not seen *la loca* for several weeks, but I think about her, more out of curiosity than anything else. Eventually, I made a trip to town yesterday, this time on the pretense of needing a pair of shoelaces. I found her next to the bank on the plaza with three more paintings.

I greeted her. "I just stopped by to tell you how much I am enjoying your...ah...husband's painting. It does more than cover up my blank wall, I look at it often."

"Then you need another painting to keep it company. Paintings get lonely too." she said with what I think was an honest smile.

"Perhaps you are right," and I pretended to peruse her work. "Which one do you suggest?"

Looking at the paintings, she replied thoughtfully, "None of these. They are not my best work. I will bring a good one next week for you."

"That is very kind, thank you. Señora Velez. I will wait in anticipation."

"It is Señorita, and my name is Delores, but everyone calls me Lola."

"How do you do, Lola. My name is Sam, Sam Jeppe." I extended my hand which she looked at for a moment, and then shook with a firm grip.

I felt I should not press the matter further, and since there was a lady approaching, I withdrew making a slight bow.

"Till next week then. It is a pleasure."

<u>October 2</u>

With the start of school only a week away, the following days have been busy. Saturday morning, I almost forgot my appointment. I quickly finished my chores, and with mounting nervousness I carefully combed my hair, brushed my suit and, instead of my usual bowler, my splendid cowboy hat.

It was closing in on noon by the time I found her again by the bank. She must have done a good business because she only had one painting left plus one turned away from view.

"I thought you forgot."

"No," I fibbed. "I had a number of chores I had to do first."

She looked at my hat and giggled. "I didn't know you are a cowboy. You don't look like one."

"I am not. I only wear this on special occasions. Do you like it?"

"It looks very nice on you," she replied coyly. There was somewhat of a strained pause which she broke by picking up the canvas that was turned away from the public.

"I looked at all my other paintings and decided to paint a new one. I think it goes with the one you bought."

The scene was exactly like mine except it was in the evening. The sun setting behind the viewer made the trees and brush glow in golden light. The creamy clouds still retained some white accents, but their shadows were gray with a hint of lavender.

I stared at it for a long time. "Lola, it is beautiful. How can I ever thank you?"

"You can pay me three dollars and buy me lunch. I didn't have time for breakfast. I'm starved."

We walked over to the Plaza Hotel and entered the dining room. With Lola in men's clothing and me dressed to the nines and each carrying a painting, we must have made quite a pair because every face turned our way. I was somewhat embarrassed, but I noticed Lola had an almost haughty expression. We had a pleasant lunch during which, to my frustration, we chatted about everything except her. She wanted to know how I came to be in Las Vegas and what I do at the college. Then she wanted to know everything about Cate, and how she ended up in Paris. By the time we finished our apple pie, I felt I had given her my whole history. She, however, was still a question mark.

I tried to do everything just right. Outside, she turned to me, "Thank you for lunch. I really enjoyed myself for the first time in a long time."

[227]

"You are most welcomed. I had a good time too. I owe you for the painting, but I need to go to the bank and withdraw some funds." Just then a vagabond walked by. His haggard face, dirty, torn clothing, rough beard, and bed roll gave him away. Lola reached out and stopped him.

"It looks like you could do with a cup of coffee and a sandwich, sir."

"Ya, I could."

"Then go right through the doors behind us." She opened her change purse and pulled out a dollar. "Give them this and they will take care of you."

"Thank you, ma'am. I surely do appreciate it," and in he went.

Lola turned back to me, "No hurry, Sam. Next week is soon enough. I must try to sell this last painting now. I make it a practice never to carry a painting back home. Till I see you again." With that she turned and walked back toward the bank.

I feel pretty good. Things have gone well, and her interest is unmistakable.

***

October 11, 1898

Dear Cate,

This has been a hectic time for me here in Las Vegas. The college officially opened. The first time I stood in front of the class my stomach was churning even though I had my lecture notes all ready. When I finished them and looked at my pocket watch I discovered I had fifteen minutes left in the hour and nothing to say. I told the class it was my first-time teaching and begged their forgiveness.

In my last letter I mentioned my curiosity about Lola Velez. Well, I found out about her, but not the way I had hoped to. I made my usual Saturday morning trip to town with a short shopping list, and the intention of taking Lola to

[228]

lunch. As I approached the plaza, I heard a commotion and hurried toward its source. The source was Lola. But this was not the Lola I was used to seeing.

She was dressed in a skirt and blouse looking ever so much like a typical woman of Las Vegas. Originally her hair probably had been carefully combed and covered with a stylish hat complete with feathers. Now, it was messed, her hat was cockeyed, her skirt and blouse were dusty, and her face red and tear streaked. She was shouting obscenities at three cowboys who were laughing at her. A couple of ladies were trying to hold Lola from hitting one of the men with a painting while some bankers were trying to push the cowboys away. A sheriff's deputy was attempting, unsuccessfully, to restore order.

I made my way through the small crowd to Lola's side. "What happened?"

"Get out of my way, *hijo de tú puta madre.*"

"No, I will not. Do you want to go to jail for assault? Now put the painting down and stop shouting."

"Not till they apologize to me for their rude remarks."

Turning to the three men, I asked them what in hell they said that set her off?

One of replied laughingly, "We was just fun'n her. She's all dressed up like a normal person. We didn't mean no harm." At this point the deputy finally saw his opening and stepped in.

"You boys go on about your business and leave this lady alone. You've had enough fun for one morning. *Fuera de aquí.*"

Grumbling, they moved away, but not before making some loud additional comments about Lola. The rest of the people dispersed as well leaving us alone on the boardwalk, Lola

[229]

shaking with anger. I did not know what to say so I said nothing. I picked up a painting that had a deep dent about the size of a head.

I smiled, "Looks like you got at least one of them."

"Oh, shut up. Look at my skirt and my hair."

"Your skirt will wash, and your hair will comb. They should not have done what they did, but you should not have lost your temper. By the way, you still look awfully nice."

"I wanted to look nice for you and those *hijos* ruined everything. Why can't people just leave me alone?"

"Why do you get so angry? Besides those three characters, I have never seen anyone mistreat you, in fact people go out of their way to be nice to you. In return you insult them, belittle them, do everything but spit in their faces. Is that fair?"

"Fair? You ask me to be fair, Gringo? You want to know why I'm angry? I'll tell you, then you decide if I should be fair." She told me her story.

The Velez family, father, mother, two brothers and Lola owned a sheep ranch in the northern part of the county. They were successful but were by no means rich. The father reinvested most of their money in sheep. The sons were partners in the operation.

Lola, the youngest, was serious-minded and mature for her age. She showed an avid interest in painting, so her parents paid a local artist to give her lessons. After six months he told them she should be giving him lessons. He encouraged them to give her formal training even though that was very unusual. Her mother rebelled at the idea. Lola should get married like any self-respecting Hispanic girl. Her father was adamant. She should learn to paint. Therefore, when she was

[230]

eighteen, she was enrolled in the University of Denver's art program even though it was a Protestant college.

During her third year, a gang of desperadoes, having heard a false rumor that the Velez family kept a large amount of cash on hand, descended upon the ranch during the night. They tortured the parents and sons, but they got only twenty dollars. In a fit of anger, they killed everyone, and burned the house and its belongings.

When Lola was told what happened, prostrated by grief she left school and returned to Las Vegas. But she was unprepared to run the sheep ranch so eventually she decided to sell it. She spent the better part of a year trying to find a buyer.

Only one man made an offer. The man who owned the ranch next to them had disliked the Velez family since an argument over water rights was settled by the court in their favor. He called her *una Bruja,* a witch, he told others about ghosts haunting the land, he said there were still bandits nearby along with large wolf packs attacking the sheep, anything that would drive potential buyers away. Because he knew no one else was interested, his offer was far below the ranch's true value. In the end, Lola was forced to accept his bid. Some women suggested she join a convent and become a nun. She rejected this idea.

During that time, nothing was done to find the killers. Consequently, Lola employed a so-called private investigator to solve the crime. He did not try very hard to find any evidence but continued to bill Lola large amounts for his time. As a result, she lost almost all the money she had received from the ranch sale.

In the end Lola, now an orphan, and just about penniless, found a small cabin for rent outside Las Vegas. There, as she nursed her

[231]

depression and hatred for just about all men. She evolved the persona of a *loca,* a crazy woman for her safety and the needed isolation while she painted pictures as a means of escape.

By the time she finished, my eyes were watering.

"Lola, I am so sorry. I had no idea what you have been through. You have every right to be angry."

"Thanks, *Señor,* for being so understanding. Now go away. Here, take these paintings with you. Go hang them in your empty house."

"Go hang them in your own empty house," I said indignantly. "If we cannot be friends, I do not want to look at them."

"I never carry a painting back home." She picked them up, put them in a nearby trash can, and walked away.

I am frustrated and angry at myself for caring about yet another woman, and this time a *loca.* I should stick to rocks and pottery. They are not crazy.

Love,
Sam the Bachelor

[232]

Chapter Twenty-Three

In one of his letters, Sam said October is one of the best times to be in New Mexico. The heat of the summer has given way to comfortable, dry temperatures. But this year, Sam was not enjoying much of anything.

Journal Entries
1898

October 14

My classes are going well enough although I am still struggling with the length of my lectures. The problem is that thoughts of Lola keep popping up at the most inappropriate times. I was talking the Hewett, and her angry face appeared. When I lost track of what I was saying Hewett got a strange look on his face.

October 15

I am confused about the situation. On one hand I think it would be best if we go our separate directions because our personalities did not mesh. On the other hand, I think I should go and apologize to her for how I bungled the situation last Saturday, because I really like her.

It does not help that I have no idea where she lives so if I were to apologize, I would have to wait till Saturday and the take the chance of being rejected and embarrassed in public. I think it is best to do nothing, and just let the situation ride.

October 16

This afternoon I had just dismissed my last class and was occupied in putting away maps and the globe when I heard a voice behind me.

"Professor Jeppe, may I speak to you?"

"Certainly," I replied turning around expecting to see one of the students.

Lola was standing in the door. She again had her skirt and blouse on, so she looked like a student.

"Lola, this is a surprise." I admit to being suspicious and being in a college classroom where anyone can see me, I was a bit formal. The last thing I wanted was to get into an argument.

"Come in, please. Rules forbid me from closing the door when I am alone with a female, but the rules say nothing about you having to stand in the hall. What can I do for you?"

I could see she was nervous, but once bitten, twice shy. I recall she looked at the floor.

"I want to apologize for the way I acted last Saturday," she said. "I have a terrible temper. Usually I control it, but those men just brought back all the bad memories. I'm sorry."

I had two ways of reacting. I could formally accept her apology and change the subject, thus signaling an end to things. Or....I melted.

I drew her further from the door and spoke in a low voice. "Lola, I am so glad you came. I did not know where to find you. I am sorry for the way I treated you Saturday. Can we get out of here? I cannot even hold your hand. If anyone sees us, I would be fired."

"Really? I was hoping you would sweep me off my feet."

"I would like to, but not here. There is a little restaurant over by the railroad depot. We can go there."

"Good. I'm starved."

"You are always hungry."

"See what you do to me."

We slipped out and were several blocks east of the campus when I took her hand. The rest of the afternoon was most enjoyable.

[234]

***

November 7, 1898
Dear Cate,

The only thing I can compare the last few weeks to is a railroad trip. It seems each day I wake to a different situation.

Lola and I have come to an understanding. It is no longer necessary to display our courtship plumage. We have succeeded in attracting each other.

I have been seeing Lola quite often lately. One evening she and I went to the concert. Coming from her good family, Lola is well-versed in the social graces, something one would not expect from a woman who dresses in men's clothing. Anyhow, we got all dressed up, and had a nice dinner before going to the opera house. Did I mention Las Vegas has an opera house? It does. There are some local groups that perform there, but mostly it books traveling shows. An orchestra came through and played an evening of Mozart. Neither of us are experts, but they sounded pretty good to us.

Another day a circus came to town. She rode a camel. The following week I rented a buggy and on Sunday we drove to the Pecos Pueblo where I showed her Hewett's excavations. On the way I gave her a running commentary on the geology of the area. I would like to take her to Cerrillos and San Marcos, but they are too far.

A fourth time we took some paper and charcoal to a rock outcropping near the Hot Springs Hotel, and she gave me a lesson in art. I made more of a mess than a picture. She said I did fine though, and we enjoyed the time immensely.

I am learning what to do and what not to do. She is used to being in charge of herself, and I must beware of being directive.

[235]

I finally got to see her cabin. It is actually on the very outskirts of town in the low foothills. An older lady owns it and lives just a step away. There is just one small room. Paints, brushes, finished and unfinished canvases are everywhere leaving little room to move. On the table is a plate with four candles which she lit as soon as she entered. She said it is a memorial to her parents and brothers who give her the light and strength to paint. All in all, it has served Lola's needs in the past, but perhaps it may not work so well for possible future situations.

In return, I took her to my little house. The trip was planned ahead of time, so I had a chance to clean. She likes everything about my castle especially the view and the trees. She also approved of my placement of her paintings.

We walked over to Modesto y Consuelo's where I introduced Lola to them. If they thought there was anything improper in our being together, they did not show it. Modesto cut open a watermelon which was enjoyed by all. We had a good visit.

I have begun working on my notes for my geology class next term. It will require a number of different rock samples, so I have been exploring the area for suitable specimens. A number of times Lola has accompanied me on my expedition

You may be curious about Lola's sometime problem with citizens when she sells her art which she still does every Saturday. She no longer abuses her potential customers, although she has sharp retorts to anyone making unjustified comments. So far, she has controlled her temper, although sometimes I catch a glimpse of it if she relates an episode that occurred. She continues to wear men's clothing since she feels it draws attention to her thereby helping to improve sales. I suggested she raise her prices a little, but she is hesitant.

I noticed something in her work. In her previous landscapes there were never any signs of people, barren of humanity. However, the last couple of scenes contain a distant figure. Most interesting.

Love,
Sam

Journal Entries
1898

November 18

Lola and I decided to cook a Thanksgiving meal at the house. There will be just the two of us, so a chicken will take the place of a turkey. I insisted on mashed potatoes which she agreed to as long as we have beans. We will have fresh vegetables, fruit, and tortillas. I am splurging by buying a pumpkin pie at the bakery. I am looking forward to the holiday for the first time in a long time.

November 26

What a great Thanksgiving. We made dinner together, and it turned out very well. The weather was a bit cool and rainy so afterwards we just sat by the fireplace visiting and enjoying each other's company. This was the first time we had just been ourselves around the other. I read a little while she sketched in her notebook. Toward evening the rain let up so I walked her back to her cabin. Upon returning, my home seemed very empty and far too quiet. This surprised me because until then I always prized my solitude. Now, without Lola the place seems empty. Before I met Lola, I did not mind being alone. Now it does not seem quite right.

***

December 14, 1898

[237]

Dear Cate,

The end of the semester is fast approaching. My class is doing well, and I expect smooth sailing from now to when I give the final exam. Because the school will be closed for Christmas, Lola and I are going to do something outrageous. We are going to take the train to Albuquerque for the holiday.

We have it all planned out. If anyone we know sees us at the train station, we will say we are going to spend Christmas with Lola's imaginary aunt. Perfectly proper. Once we are on the train, since she chooses not to wear gloves, Lola will slip on a ring her grandmother gave her and we will look just like any married couple traveling for the holidays. This will solve all sorts of problems, but frankly I am exasperated at having to sneak around pretending to be so proper when in fact it is no one's business. I will continue the charade for Lola's sake though.

Although the question has not been broached, I believe marriage has been an unspoken destination for some time. However, neither of us is likely to engage in a flight of fancy. We are both pretty level-headed, so we are both being careful. I think that we have come to trust another. Because of that trust we are comfortable being together.

While I know Lola has a temper, I can live with that. For instance, I noticed that when I lit up a cigar in the cabin, a slight look of repulsion crossed her face. She did not say anything, but I now know that cigar smoking is an outdoor activity.

I have been lacking focus for a while now. At home I wander around unable to concentrate on much of anything. I see things that need to be repaired, and I will do them when I get inspired,

[238]

but not now. I have thought about building an addition that would be Lola's studio. I am assuming she will continue her artwork, at least I hope she does. I must ask her about that at the appropriate time.

I certainly am not interested in becoming the patriarch of a family. I have seen the animosity caused by Eli's father assuming such a position, and I do not want that. Women cannot be thought of as a possession. I have seen too many instances of women being treated as inferior to men when if fact they are just as capable as any male. And yes, it is a travesty that women cannot vote. I want and need a wife that is my equal. Her opinion is just as important as mine. I do not think that will be a problem since Lola does not hesitate to express her thoughts. That is one thing I like about her. I always know exactly where she stands.

December 27

We are back. This was the best Christmas I am sure I have ever had.

We got a very nice room in one of the more expensive hotels and had a fine dinner. We watched one of the *posades* or Christmas processions. The next day Lola wanted to see where the house fire was. Even though I did not really want to, I showed her the still vacant lots. She could tell I was uncomfortable being there, so she urged us to leave after a couple of minutes.

We then went to the old section of Albuquerque and thoroughly enjoyed ourselves just wandering the narrow streets. It was chilly in the morning, but the sun helped warm things up in the afternoon. I saw a broach in a jewelry store and bought it for Lola. Later on, she bought me some calf skin gloves. In the evening people displayed *farolitos* near the cathedral. They are

[239]

little bags containing sand and a burning candle. Very beautiful.

We were walking down one of the streets when a vagabond came by. Without being asked, Lola stopped the man, opened her purse and gave him money enough for lunch. He thanked her, wished her a Merry Christmas, and went on. I asked her why she is always giving money to the down-and-out.

She said, "There was a period of time I was where they are. Some people helped me then and I'm helping others now."

"That is a wonderful attitude, but may I suggest you avoid opening your purse in front of them. Someone might not be satisfied with lunch money." She laughed and we went on.

Christmas day we walked past the upper-class residences in New Town. They were all decked out as if they were in Milwaukee instead of Albuquerque. Families were either visiting or receiving visitors. Frequently they greeted or waved to us, and we returned the salutations. It was all very festive.

Late in the afternoon we returned to the hotel and looked for a restaurant. Alas, everything was closed, and for a while we thought we would have to go hungry. Then I remembered. Sure enough, on a side street we found a Chinese restaurant. Of course, it was open. We had a fine dinner of duckling. It brought back warm memories of the times I had with Chung, Xue Mei, and Au Kum. I spent most of the meal relating my adventures to Lola.

The next day we had to return to Las Vegas. I must admit we dozed off and on. I guess we were both tired. I escorted Lola back to her cabin where with some reluctance she removed her mother's ring. I stayed for a cup of tea since neither of us were anxious to separate.

[240]

Actually, it was Lola who brought the subject up, although I must make it perfectly clear she did not propose to me. But she did state she was ready and willing to enter into matrimony. She went on to say she had made up her mind ever since she painted the evening landscape. I noted, with perhaps only a little exaggeration, that I arrived at the same conclusion about the same time.

Neither of us could see any reason to wait since there are no families involved, except you. I assured her you would have no objection. We set December 30 as the date to visit the justice of the peace. We will proceed with that plan, unless you say you are coming, in which case we will wait, however long it takes.

So, the next time you hear from me...from us, we will be
Sincerely Yours,
Mr. and Mrs. Samuel Jeppe

Chapter Twenty-Four

January 9, 1899

To My Dear Sister Catherine,

I have wanted to write to you for some time. I thought I should wait until Sam and I were married. He has told me so much about you. Sam loaned me several of your books which I enjoyed very much. I think you are a great writer. I hope to meet you sometime in the near future.

Since we were married I have moved my things from my little cabin to Sam's home. My paintings and supplies are stacked against one wall. I need to sell some and get them out of the house. Sam said he is going to build another room that I can work in. That will be wonderful.

Things are very pleasant here even though it is cold. Sam goes to work every day while I stay here and paint.

With Love,
Your Sister-in-law,
Lola

Dear Cate,

Happy New Year from the Jeppe family. I am sure Lola's short note is the first of many, but she is unaccustomed to the written word, and nervous about writing to such a famous person!

[242]

Things have settled down a little. I have found being married to an artist is different than what I would have guessed. I thought painting was like any other job, pick up the brush in the morning, and put it down in late afternoon. Not so. Lola must paint when she is in the right frame of mind. Often that seems to be during the afternoon and evening. So, we have to visit and do our planning in the morning because she gets irritable if I break her train of thought while she is painting.

We are still trying to make room for two in a space that was cramped for one. I think that in addition to Lola's workroom we need to enlarge the main room. When I was by myself it was convenient to have food supplies, dishes and pots close to the fireplace. Now there is a constant clutter.

Classes have resumed at the college. My geology course is going to be fun. Right now, it is too cold and snowy to take the students outside, but toward the end of the term we should be able to get our hands dirty.

Hewett wants me to help him write an article on the geology and archaeology of Pecos Pueblo. My part, the geology, should not be too difficult. We have also talked about co-authoring an article on Pecos and San Marcos. If we do that, it should be more challenging. I'll close for now.
Love,
Sam and Lola

***

February 2, 1899
....We have settled into a routine. Lola continues to paint while I continue to teach. We have come to respect each other's interests. The success of one becomes the success for both. We have become a team without a leader. It reminds

[243]

me of Lin Chung and Xue Mei. Decisions are made by both of us.

We have decided to add on two rooms to our little house. There will be a kitchen off the main room. It will have a stove and a little pantry. Maybe someday we can see about an indoor water pump. Off the kitchen will be Lola's studio. Because it is a ways from the fireplace, we will put in a small heating stove, so there will be heating in every room except of course the bedroom.

An additional purchase is a gun. I have never fired one much less owned one, but Lola said she would feel safer with a weapon close by because I am gone so much. It only makes sense especially after what happened to her family and since there are still a number of roughnecks in town....

February 5

....Friday I happened to stop at Modesto y Consuelo's to see if they needed any supplies from town. I was surprised to find their daughter, Isabella, and her family had come over from Santa Fe. She, her husband Manuel Rodarte, and their children are staying several weeks to help get ready for winter. We had a nice visit and they invited Lola and me to supper.

That evening after the meal was finished the men went outside to do the chores. Manuel and I split some kindling and piled firewood near the door. Since it was not terribly cold, we took the opportunity to smoke cigars. He told me the story of Modesto y Consuelo.

After the Civil War, the U.S. Government for no good reason, decided to round up members of the Apache and the Navajo Nations and herd them from their traditional lands in Arizona to a plot of desiccated semi-desert on the eastern border of New Mexico called the Bosque Redondo

[244]

Reservation near Fort Sumner. It soon became obvious that someone had forgotten that over 8,000 people need food. The Indians tried to gather enough to eat on their own, but it was not long before they began to starve. Rather than admit their mistake, the government offered top dollar for Texas ranchers to drive cattle to Fort Sumner. The problem lay between Texas and the fort. The *Llano Estacado,* a huge, waterless plateau about a hundred miles across and covered with very high bluffs made it impossible to cross with a herd of cattle. So, no one took the offer until Oliver Loving and Charles Goodnight decided to try driving their herd around the southern end of the plateau, and up the western side of it. They organized the drive at Fort Belknap, Texas before heading southwest with 2,000 cattle and 18 men.

When he first heard of the drive, Modesto did not want to spend a couple of months driving cattle to New Mexico because he had just proposed to Consuelo. But she, being the practical half of the couple, pointed out the $100 he would get would allow them to buy acreage for a *rancho.* He signed on as horse wrangler to be responsible for the care and herding of 80 or 90 horses the drovers would use during the drive.

During the drive, they had experienced Indian attacks, a stampede, storms, and dry spells, but Modesto did not lose a single horse. Upon reaching Fort Sumner they found the Army only wanted some of the cattle. Being left with hundreds of cattle, Loving and Goodnight decided to drive the rest to Denver where there was a good market. On their way north they stopped at Las Vegas, Raton, and some towns in Colorado.

It was in Las Vegas that Modesto saw the land he wanted. He completed the drive, collected his wages and headed back south. When he reached Las Vegas he bought the land, built a one

[245]

room cabin, and headed back to Texas to marry Consuelo. After the ceremony, they packed up their few belongings, and left Texas for good.

For more than thirty years, Modesto y Consuelo raised horses, cattle, and children. Tragically, they lost one daughter in still birth, and three sons to cholera. Isabella is their only child to reach adulthood. These are some of the nicest and most interesting people I have ever met.
From New Mexico,
Sam & Lola

***

March 16, 1899
Dear Cate,

It is starting to get warmer here, and we have started the addition. We have a couple of good men working on it. While I am at the school Lola watches over them. She is quite particular.

She also wants to buy some wallpaper for the parlor. It sounds like a good idea. This primitive little cabin is starting to look like a town house.

As far as school is concerned, Hewett wants to publish our report on Pecos in the Annual Report of the Smithsonian Institution. A year ago I would have considered the opportunity to write for such an august publication a great honor. Now, while it is a challenge I enjoy, it is also interfering with my projects at home. I guess that means I am an old married man now.

In addition to the articles, I have taken on another project. I have organized a geology club for the students. There are only a half dozen members, all of whom are quite enthusiastic about hiking so we may include that in our future activities.

[246]

I also got a letter from Dr. Salisbury. His summer field school this year is out to the Grand Canyon. Since Las Vegas is a scheduled train stop, he would like to stop over a day and visit. He wants me to show them the area and lecture on the local geology. He also invited me to accompany the group on the remainder of the field school. Of course, I invited them to stay as long as they cared to, but I would not be able to go with them.
With Love,
Sam & Lola

***

May 17, 1899
Dear Cate,

Wonderful news! Lola is pretty sure she is expecting. We don't know exactly when it is due, but it should arrive November or December. I want to move into town, but she will not hear of it. There is a midwife in town, but Lola says she and Consuelo can handle it.

We have already started selecting a name. If it is a boy, we are leaning toward José Samuel. José was her father's name. If it is a girl, we like Francis María.

I will write more soon.
With Love,
Lola & Sam

Journal Entries
1899

May 23

I insisted we buy a horse and buggy. We have to be able to get to town and back again quickly and safely. But first we need a small barn, and a corral. Then I have to get a horse, the harness, and a buggy. I can ask Modesto to help me pick

[247]

out a good horse, because while I can tell a live horse from a dead one, that is about it.

May 29
        Modesto says he can find a good horse without too much trouble. I can order a new buggy from Sears Roebuck & Co.

June 10
        We picked out the buggy we want and sent the order yesterday. It will be shipped direct to Las Vegas in 10 days or so. Modern times are just wonderful. Tuesday, Modesto and I went to town to look for a horse. I liked a brown one, but Modesto said it was too young and would be too hard to handle. Eventually we found an old, docile, roan Morgan that passed muster. It should be easy for us to handle and is in good condition. The rancher will keep it there till the barn is finished.

June 15
        Professor Salisbury and eight students arrived on the 12th. Previously I had asked if I might invite some of my students to join the group. I felt it would be a good experience for them to meet and mingle with some of the nation's outstanding students. The response was an enthusiastic yes. My four students and I met the travelers at the station. After a late lunch we took the first of two walking tours. On this one we covered the Great Plains geology east of town.
        Early the next morning I met the combined field school again and we went on a walking tour of the Sangre de Cristo Mountain geology west of town. Back at the station, I presented Dr. Salisbury with a representative collection of geologic specimens of the area for the museum. He in turn praised the Highland students and encouraged them to never fear to make their mark in whatever area they go into. He sincerely thanked me, and only wished all his students would be as successful as I am. As they resumed their trip to the Grand Canyon, I admit that part of me wanted to go with them,

[248]

but the days of being a student are behind me. My future adventures must take a different form.

***

June 27, 1899

Dear Cate,

Just a quick note to let you know Lola is doing fine. At least Consuelo says she is. If you ask Lola, you might get a different answer. Her stomach has been upset a lot, but Consuelo says that is normal. She also seems tired and is often grumpy. If this is normal, I wonder why there are so many children. I try to do things for Lola like washing dishes, getting her wildflowers, and doing some of the cooking.

The buggy came right on schedule. The crate was put on a freight wagon and taken to a harness shop where the owner said he could assemble it. Three days later I found a most beautiful little buggy waiting for me.

The barn and corral have not been built yet, thus I still have no place for the horse. I bought a little book on harnessing and was studying it when Lola noticed it.

"I can show you how to harness and hitch the horse when it gets here," she said with more than a little disdain.

"You can?"

"I have done it for many years. Do you think men are the only ones who know anything about horses?"

"I wish you had said something before I bought this book," I responded irritably.

"You didn't ask."

"I suppose you can drive the buggy as well."

"Of course. Like any self-respecting woman."

"Well, this self-respecting man has walked his whole life, and he needs to learn how."

"I'm sorry, I didn't mean to snap at you. Of course, you need to know about these things sooner or later," she said with a smile.

With Love,
Sam & Lola

[249]

***

July 16, 1899

Dear Cate,

All is good here. Lola continues to paint, but of course she no longer sets up her displays in town. She found a drug store that hangs the pictures and do it for only ten percent of the price. She has already sold two small pieces.

It never occurred to me before, but Lola is going to need some new clothes soon. She bought some Butterick patterns and cloth. In the evening she works on cutting and sewing. Do not tell her, but I am going to buy her a sewing machine for Christmas.

Three sides of the corral are finished. The barn which is the fourth side is underway. It is made of adobe so it will be warmer in the winter. I am anxious to get the horse.

I have finished my section of the Smithsonian report. Now it is up to Hewett to finish his. It gives me a lot more time at home for the next month.

I am including Lola's separate note.
Yours,
Sam

Dear Catherine,

Just a short note. Everything is fine with me. I'm not uncomfortable yet. It is warm during these July days. Often, we get an afternoon rainstorm and that cools things off for a while.

Sam is being really good to me. Every few days he brings a pitcher of milk from town. He tries to make me as comfortable as he can. You have a good brother.
Love,
Lola

***

August 14, 1899

Dear Cate,

Everything continues to be as it should be. During the hottest part of the day, which is early to mid-afternoon, Lola sits under the tree where she can usually catch a cooling breeze. It is a good thing she sewed some new clothes for herself, because she needs something loose. She has begun doing charcoal drawings, more for herself than to sell.

As for me, because school is not in session now, I do the housework and some of the cooking. I am feeling like a regular rancher. The barn is finished, and we are proud owners of a horse. The mare, Rosie, is very gentle and patient with me. I do not know who enjoys the daily brushing more, her or me.

With Love,
Sam, Lola & ?

Charlotte and I wanted to send a gift to Sam's baby, but were unsure of what to get. It was Charlotte, of course, who suggested a painting. I wrote to the future parents asking if they thought a picture would be appropriate.

August 24

….Yesterday we received your letter of August 8. We would be thrilled to have a picture by a French artist. It is something he or she will treasure. Lola likes Impressionism while I do not have enough experience to have an opinion, and we will rely on your judgment. Thank you and Charlotte from both of us....

***

[251]

September 20, 1899

Dear Cate,
Lola has trouble sleeping and complains about back pains and stomach nausea and pains along with other things. Consuelo suggested Lola should see a doctor.
There is a lady doctor who specializes in women and children. When the doctor finished her examination, she explained that Lola was fine, but there was a chance the baby might arrive a little early.
The doctor said there is a new invention called an incubator that we might need. I have to buy six hot water bottles, a thermometer and some glass. She drew a picture of what it is supposed to look like. I will go to the local cabinet maker and have him do it.
I keep asking Lola if she needs anything. She keeps saying no. I need to have to do something to do. Rosie has never been so well groomed in her life. I also have school to take my mind off Lola and the baby for a few hours. Normally I would walk to work, but now I take the buggy in case I have to come home quickly. This is one time I wish we lived in town. If we did Lola could just call on the telephone if there was a problem.
If anything happens, I will send a telegram.
Sam

Telegram From Sam:

October 12, 1899
To: Catherine Jeppe
Paris, France
Lola gave birth to girl. Both are doing well. Letter to follow.
Sam

[252]

***

October 13, 1899

Dear Cate,

It is 3:00 in the morning. Lola and Francis Maria are both asleep. They are coming along fine. Francis is 5 pounds and is 17 ½ inches long. A little small, but the doctor says she will grow. Her black hair and little turned-up nose, and bowed mouth are perfect. No one has ever had a more beautiful daughter.

The doctor said it is vitally important to keep Francis warm for a while. The days are in the seventies, but at night it gets close to freezing. Even if we keep the wood stove going it is still too cool for her. That is what the incubator is for. Lola has to feed her every three to four hours. Consequently, Lola needs to sleep when she can. It is my job to watch the thermometer and heat water to put in the hot water bottles every two to three hours.

As far as school is concerned, I have taken a short leave of absence. Thank goodness Hewett is well-versed in geology. He offered to substitute for me during this time.

October 20

All continues to improve. Lola has regained her strength and except for a lack of sleep, she is her normal self. Francis is gaining weight. The doctor came by yesterday and said she can be out of the incubator during the day. It is still too cold for her at night, but I do not have to keep her quite as warm.

October 26

The incubator is a thing of the past. I gave it to the doctor so she could loan it to other families. To keep Francis warm at night we bundle her in a blanket and nest her between us. She still fusses, but Lola takes care of that. During the day Frannie lives in a cradle which we keep by the wood stove. She does not cry much as long as someone pays attention to her.

I am back to work. I am looking forward to Thanksgiving this year more than any other time. We have a lot to be thankful for.
Take Care,
Sam, Lola, and Frannie

When we received this letter Charlotte and I felt comfortable picking out our gift for "Frannie". We found a beautiful pastel picture by Berthe Morisot of two children playing in a grassy field while nearby their mother carries a butterfly net. We had it framed and shipped.

November 30, 1899

Dear Cate & Charlotte,

We received your gift. The picture is beautiful. We had some glass cut to fit and now it hangs over her crib. I am sure she will treasure it forever. We glued a note to the back of the frame. She will always know who gave it to her. Thank you so much.
Love,
Lola, Sam and Francis

December 16, 1899

Dear Cate,

Not a very long letter today.

We had a wonderful Thanksgiving. We all went to Modesto y Consuelo's in the afternoon.

[254]

Isabella and Manuel and their children were visiting from Santa Fe, and it was a house full. It reminded me of the Thanksgivings with Hiram and Cyrus.

It was the first trip out for Francis, and she was a hit with everyone. I did not hold her once because she was passed between the others all day. She loved it and except for feeding time she never whimpered once. She seems to love being around people.

Since then, it has been busy for me. I mentioned that I was going to buy Lola a sewing machine for Christmas. It was hard sneaking it into the barn without her seeing it. Francis is getting some stuffed animals and a bright star for over her crib.

I am buying myself a present too. A tobacco shop in town has begun rolling cigars. I am buying a box. I look forward to being in the barn brushing Rosie and enjoying a hand-rolled cigar after dinner. Could a king have anything better.

School is just about finished. Final exams were yesterday. I have to grade them and turn the final grades by Wednesday. I have received a letter from Dr. Salisbury asking me to write a short summary of northern New Mexico geology for the University of Chicago geology bulletin. I will work on that over Christmas.

After Christmas I am also going to take some of the geology club members up Hermit Peak just outside of town. A bunch of the boys have been after me to do it for some time and I cannot put it off any longer. I have never been all the way to the top. It will be an interesting experience for me too.

Other than that, things are settling in rather nicely. Family life in Las Vegas agrees with me.

[255]

I hope you and Charlotte have a wonderful Christmas.
Yours,
Sam

Charlotte and I decided to take a short vacation over Christmas. Paris had been especially dull and drizzly for the better part of a month. We felt like rewarding ourselves with the sun and warmth of Italy. We enjoyed ourselves in Rome and Venice. However, upon returning I found a telegram waiting for me:

December 29, 1899
To: Catherine Jeppe
Paris, France
It is with great sadness I must inform you that your brother, Samuel, has died. He suffered an asthmatic attack while climbing a mountain.
Edgar Lee Hewett
President
New Mexico Highland Normal School

Chapter Twenty-Five

"He suffered an asthmatic attack while climbing a mountain." I couldn't believe Sam could be that stupid. I was not shocked, I was not grieved, I was overflowing with anger. In a fit of rage, I threw Mother's cut glass vase across the room. Sam had to have known he was taking a foolish chance by climbing a mountain any time, certainly in the middle of winter. He knew his limitations and chose to disregard them as he had done many times before. He needed to consider Lola and Francis and act responsibly, and yet he did not. I knew I shouldn't be angry, but I was. It was only later that I cried for him.

Several weeks later I received a note from Lola and a letter from President Hewett.

January 10, 1900

Dear Catherine,

You know by now Sam has died. I still cannot write about it. I do not know how. I have asked Dr. Hewett to write for me. I am all right for now. Modesto y Consuelo are looking after the baby and me. I will write more in a while.

Lola

Dear Miss Jeppe,

I have never had to write a more difficult letter than this. If I am clumsy with my words,

[257]

please forgive me. Sam told me you were a newspaper reporter at one time. Perhaps it would be best if I just describe the events.

Sam may have told you about the geology club he formed for the students. He loved to organize field activities for them. They frequently went to different geologic sites to explore the local rocks.

One of the sites both he and the students were excited about was Hermit Peak. It is a rather unique mountain about 10,000 feet high located just outside Las Vegas. It would have been better if they had waited till warm weather to climb it, but a couple of the students are graduating at the end of spring quarter and they wanted to be included. So, as students will do, they teased Sam till he relented. The weather was not bad here in Las Vegas for December, but Sam failed to consider the altitude. It was quite cold near the summit.

Apparently, Lola tried to talk him out of going, but I'm sure you know better than anyone how Sam couldn't resist a challenge. Anyway, they borrowed a farm wagon from a rancher close to the mountain's base because a fairly good road goes about half-way up. At the end of the road, they left the horse and wagon and proceeded on foot from there, about a five-mile hike.

From what the boys tell me, Sam was a good sport and kept pace with the most enthusiastic hikers even though they noticed his breathing was raspy. As they reached an open slope to the highest point which overlooks Las Vegas and the plains to the east, the boys began to race each other to the top. They called for Sam to join them. He began to run but had a sudden acute asthmatic attack. He was out of breath, coughing

[258]

and wheezing and stopped to catch his breath, but began gasping for breath. It was apparent he was in trouble because he was on his knees clutching at his chest. He could barely get a single word out. The boys gathered around him not really knowing what to do. One of the older boys took charge and they began carrying him down the mountain to get to a doctor. Later they all agreed that after a while Sam's face and fingers began turning blue. He was unconscious, and his breathing was labored. They went as fast as they could, but in places snow drifts slowed them down. Somewhere along the line Sam's breathing stopped. They couldn't find a pulse or a heartbeat.

They got to the buggy and raced ten miles back to town. The first place they came to was the sanitarium. There, the doctors pronounce Sam dead. While waiting the boys telephoned me. I hurried right over.

It would be natural to blame the boys for their seemingly callous behavior, but none of them knew of Sam's health problem. He never told any of us. They were, to a man, brought to tears over the events. I told them that none of them were to blame for Sam's death. Once I talked to the doctors, I had the dreaded responsibility of telling Lola.

I have to admit, Lola never shed a tear while I was there. Her face was like it was carved from stone.

Miss Jeppe, I can't tell you how sorry I am this happened. Sam was not only an important member of our faculty, he was a dear friend of mine. I shall always miss him. It is not often you run into someone who is both highly capable and unassuming at the same time. Sam was one of those people. He will be missed. If there is any

[259]

way I can assist you, please do not hesitate to call on me.

With Very Sincere Regrets,

Edgar Hewett

I didn't hear anything more from anyone for over a month. I didn't know what to expect though. It was like everyone had forgotten me, again. Then I did get a short note from Lola.

February 23, 1900

Dear Catherine,
      Francis and I are doing alright. It is not a real cold winter but we have had a lot of snow. Modesto y Consuelo have helped me since Sam died. He brought me enough firewood to last till warm weather. I give him money and he buys supplies in town once a week. Consuelo brings me food she has made.
      Frances is growing fast. She has a loud voice. Perhaps she will be a singer.
      I have not done any painting. I should because our savings is about gone. Still, I do not care to yet.
      People from the school stop by to visit and give us money. I hate to take the money but I have to. Modesto y Consuelo have asked me to come and live with them. I do not want to.
Your Sister in law,
Lola

I immediately sent Lola a large check to help her with the expenses. I asked her to keep in touch, and if there was anything else, I could help with she should let me know. I did not hear back from her for some time. It wasn't surprising though that Lola just wanted to be left alone. After all she had

[260]

first lost her entire family and now she had lost her husband. I'm sure she felt cursed.

When I had not heard from her in four months, I wrote a note to her, hoping she would respond. The note and other letters I sent were returned as being "undeliverable". I didn't know what that meant other than perhaps she had moved.

In August she did send a very short note.

August 4, 1900

Dear Catherine,
    Thank you for the money. I do not want to be a burden. Please do not send any more.
    Francis is doing fine. We have moved over to Modesto y Consuelo's for the summer. Soon we will move to Santa Fe where I hope I can sell my paintings.
    Thank you for all you have done for Francis and me. I will always tell her about her wonderful aunt that lives in Paris.
I love you so much.
    Lola and Francis

Over a year passed and I had given up hope of ever hearing from her again. Then one day a box arrived from Santa Fe. With excitement and trepidation, I opened it. Inside were some of Sam's journals and original papers he had written. There was also a short note from Lola.

November 8, 1901
Dear Catherine,
I am sending you what is left of Sam's writings. Other things have been destroyed. I am sorry. I have remarried. Francis is doing very well.
Lola

That was the last time I heard from Lola.

***

During this time, I came to terms with my brother. I was no longer angry at him for dying the way he did. Sam was never a confident person. He saw everything as a challenge, and he was always afraid he would fail. His many successes meant little to him. To him, they were the result of luck or because someone else had helped him. He tried to climb that mountain because he had to prove to himself that he could do it.

My anger turned to sadness. It is a shame he never could see in himself what others saw in him. He was bright, creative, insightful, and happy. He was someone people liked to be around. I envy him and I shall always miss him.

Except for Charlotte, now I was alone in the world. Eventually I realized that all those years ago in Milwaukee I had readily left my family in exchange for the adventure of living surrounded by excitement and rubbing shoulders with the great and those who would be great. These were the very things I had dreamed of doing when I wrote those essays for my mother. I rejected the very things I now longed for. It was suddenly too late, and I had to live with my choices.

Chapter Twenty-Six

I had a difficult time of it for the next few years. I never realized how much Sam meant to me until he was gone. Because he was always my little brother, of course I retained some feeling of responsibility for him even though we were half the world apart. But there was more than that. He and I had always been close since Mother's death. While we never saw each other, our letters took the place of in-person conversations. They became an important part of our lives. Through our letters we told each other of our feelings, plans, experiences, successes, and failures. We trusted each other because each knew the other would not be judgmental. Our love for each other was shown through our interest, encouragement, and pride in the other's accomplishments. For me, opening the mail now became a sad responsibility since those letters stopped appearing every month or so.

My writing lacked the spark it had previously. I had a difficult time finding interesting subjects to write about. I even talked to Charlotte about seeking a position in a department store or café until I wanted to return to writing full-time.

In another part of the city, a wealthy American by the name of Gertrude Stein moved to Paris in 1903. She and her brother started collecting modern art which at that time was quite inexpensive. Soon word spread about the paintings, and they started having Saturday night receptions or salons so people could enjoy the Stein paintings. As will happen, regular attendees began inviting some of their friends, and those people invited other people which is how I got invited.

Sometime later Charlotte was asked to play in a series of concerts. The *premier violon* or concertmaster invited her to accompany him to one of the Stein salons. She was interested, but insisted I be invited as well. Since he could see no reason to go to the salon alone when he could go in the company of two women, he agreed. I had heard of these salons and while I was still not interested in going to social gatherings, I agreed as well.

Once you attended a salon, you were welcomed to continue coming unless you committed a *faux pas* by splashing wine on a painting or arguing with Gertrude who had a ferocious temper.

Once inside the house, Charlotte and I wandered throughout the studio at will. The room was quite large, and its walls were decorated from floor to ceiling with paintings. At one end was a wood stove and a lounge chair where Gertrude held court when she wasn't circulating among her guests.

Charlotte did not fair very well during the evening because she is somewhat timid at taking charge of the scene. On the other hand, I had no problem. Years of being a reporter taught me how to insert myself into any conversation. Soon I had made the acquaintance of several people.

Over a period of years, I began to attend the Stein salons frequently, Charlotte not as often. While there, I met people like F. Scott Fitzgerald, Sinclair Lewis, Ernest Hemingway, Ezra Pound, Thornton Wilder, Sherwood Anderson, and many others.

One lady I met, Mable Dodge, played an important role in my life years later. I didn't meet her till 1913 when she and her current boyfriend came to Paris. Sometime after that she and Gertrude got into an argument over something and she stopped attending Stein's salons, but not before Mable and I became friends. Over time we have kept up a casual pen pal relationship, but I'll talk more about that later.

***

Charlotte and I didn't know that August 3, 1914 was not only going down in French history but was going to change our lives as well. For us it began like many other days. It was

[264]

Monday and my turn to buy the flower bouquet. I went down to Marie Gravois's flower stand and I distinctly remember choosing some red dahlias. I didn't realize the color was an omen of things to come.

We spent the morning straightening the apartment in preparation for a small party we planned for that evening. It was nothing major, just two couples we often met with. It wasn't until our guests arrived that we learned Germany had declared war on France.

This is not to say conflict with Germany came as a shock. The relations between Germany and France had been antagonistic ever since 1871 when France was defeated in the Franco-Prussian War.

The European pot had been simmering for some time. All that was needed to bring things to a boil was a spark. That spark came on June 28, 1914, when Archduke Ferdinand, the heir to the throne of Austria-Hungary, and his wife were shot and killed while visiting Bosnia. Things quickly went out of control. Austria-Hungary declared war on Serbia. Russia hastened to the aid of Serbia. Germany declared war on Russia, and that's where things stood on August 3. Most French thought our country could remain apart from the Balkin conflict, but suddenly most of the countries in Europe were declaring war on someone. This was more than a disagreement between two governments, it had the possibility of involving most of the world.

During the following few weeks Charlotte and I spent much time talking to other friends, shop owners, and strangers on the street about what they knew, or thought they knew about events. When a new edition of a newspaper came out it was quickly snatched up, but it rarely had much new to say.

There actually was not much difference between the stories passed among individuals and the official press releases. Since many people preferred to remain ignorant of facts, the government and some of the press worked together to print only positive news whether it was true or not.

***

[265]

Almost immediately after war was declared the call went out for men from the age of eighteen to forty-five to report for military duty. As you might expect, millions enlisted. Marie Gravois's son was one of them. Charlotte's brother was another.

Charlotte and her brother, Maurice, were very close. When he joined the army, she too wanted to do her part. Of course, she could not join the military, although I think she would have if women could do such an outrageous thing. She did the next best thing. She volunteered to be a nurse.

She was accepted at the Fondation Ophtalmologique Adolphe de Rothschild. Originally this institution was designed for the study and treatment of optical diseases, but soon after the war began it was transformed into a hospital for wounded.

The first day Charlotte found there were different ranks of nurses. The *la vraie,* the true nurses, the professionals, were the authorities who were to be obeyed without question. Below them, far below, were the volunteer nurses.

The *la vraie* generally resented volunteer nurses, often with good reason. Some volunteers saw the opportunity only as a means of raising their social standing. They would appear, when their schedule allowed, with cigarettes, flowers or candy and no intention of getting their clothing soiled with blood. The falseness of their declaration of concern and sympathy was obvious to the soldiers and anyone else nearby. These women tarnished the efforts of well-meaning individuals like Charlotte.

From the very beginning, life as a nurse was difficult for Charlotte. She is, by nature, very empathetic to anything in distress. A lame bird or stray cat always requires her immediate attention and she attends to it regardless of how pressing other matters are. At the hospital, when changing a bandage she was so careful to avoid inflicting any pain it would take her twice as long as it should have. As a result, the head nurse reassigned her to the feeding of soldiers. Mant of these men had no hands or were so severely wounded they could not use their arms. Charlotte finished the job but went in another room and cried for fifteen minutes. She sought out the supervisor saying, "I can't do this." The head nurse was very

[266]

understanding. "Very well. I understand. Not everyone can do this work. The patient in bed 41 is dying. Go sit with him until he does. He won't ask anything of you."

The man was not really conscious, his breathing was labored, and he would groan quietly. She laid her hand upon his shoulder or placed it on the back of his hand. When she did, he seemed to relax. Half an hour later his breathing stopped. Charlotte did not cry over his death. She was there with him to help him meet the inevitable. The next day she was told to sit with another dying patient. The third day she was walking down the ward when she heard one patient say to his neighbor, "there goes the Angel of Death. If she sits with you, you know you're a goner.

Again, she went to the supervisor and relayed what she heard. She told the supervisor she wanted to help but must be placed in a job that required no contact with patients.

"The only job that needs to be filled is that of washing the bed linens. It is most disgusting, and I don't think you would last long."

"I'll do it," was Charlotte's response.

The supervisor was right. It was disgusting, but Charlotte did it anyway. After five days her hands were rough and raw from the lye solution in which the linens were soaked. A few days later they started to bleed.

She could no longer play the cello because her fingers were so raw she couldn't press the strings. One day the supervisor took pity on her and gave her a pair of rubber gloves reserved for surgeons. They were a treasure. Her skin healed, but the sensitivity that is required by serious cello players never did completely return. To this day, she cannot play some demanding pieces. Some people might resent the loss of a promising career, but Charlotte said, "At least I still have my hands."

One day the same head nurse came to Charlotte to say they had a different job for her. "You know the hospital always writes a letter of condolence to the family of a soldier who has died while with us. I have always done it, but now I have too many demands on my time, and I'm falling behind.

[267]

Would you take on that duty? It requires the very compassion that made it impossible for you to deal with their injuries."

"Of course, I will try. May I talk to the soldiers who knew the deceased? My housemate is a writer and may be able to offer some suggestions."

"Charlotte, please do whatever you need in order to write the letters. I will greatly appreciate you taking this weight from my shoulders. Thank you."

For those soldiers who made it to a hospital and then died, a personal letter was often written by a nurse giving what amounted to sanitized details of his hospital stay and then impressing upon the family the contribution the soldier had made to the cause. There was quite a long list of families for Charlotte to write to. It was clear the head nurse had been avoiding writing them for some time.

Charlotte, however, took her new job very seriously. For her it was not enough to write some maudlin paragraphs and move on to the next name on the list. She made every attempt to find compatriots of the deceased, get some actual accounting of his life in the military and what he meant to his company. If that was impossible, she talked to soldiers who took part in the action where the soldier suffered his wounds.

In the evenings Charlotte would tell me about the men who died. She also heard good stories about life on the front line. Sometimes she asked for advice from me on how to deal with a particular matter or condition. I suggested she keep a journal of her experiences. Later she could refer to them. That journal eventually led to our co-authored book, "Little Brown Birds".

***

It had been some time since I had written any newspaper articles. In late September I was surprised by a telegram from my old boss Gordon Bennett at the New York Herald. He wanted me to start writing regular articles about the French at war.

The idea concerned me because now I was used to writing books, not newspaper articles. However, we could use

[268]

the money. I wrote back that I would try, but only on my terms. The topics would be my choice, and I would pull no punches. In addition, my work would not be edited without my permission. He agreed and made a reasonable offer for twelve columns.

In France during the war the press was heavily censored, so their stories were usually fictionalized. Exaggerations based on governmental reports which were scarcely accurate.

Besides the censoring, the war was almost always told from the standpoint of men. Granted, there were only men on the front lines, thus they were suffering the deaths and dismembering. Still, wives faced their own set of serious problems. Up to this point they had the same legal status as minors. They were expected to be quiet and follow the husbands' orders. Now on a farm, women had to be both the farmer and the housewife. If they lived in a city, she had to find employment while raising a family. So, I decided half the columns would deal with women.

***

The other half of the columns would deal with the common soldiers. I'd leave the great battles and heroics to someone else. I recalled Charlotte's tales and decided to interview some of the wounded. One of them gave me the material for my first column:

"I'm a farmer. When two emperors have an argument, that's not important to me, but when Germany attacks France, that is important. So, I joined the army. I don't know much about war. All I know is what I see in front of me. I still don't know why we invaded Belgium. Have you ever been there? No? Well, it is flat, good farmland.

About a week ago my buddies and I knew it was going to be a bad day because we were told we were to attack Germans who were in the village just ahead of us. I don't even know its name. It's not a big town, but it looks, or at least it looked like a pretty one. It was clear to us that the Germans

[269]

were nestled in the buildings while we had no cover to speak of. They would have clear shots at us and we couldn't even see them. To make things worse, it rained a lot the day before. Everything was mud. Artillery might have helped, but there wasn't any. They must have been off shooting at something else.

Our commanding officers must have known what was going to happen because we soldiers knew. We knew and we talked about it. Some wanted to run away. Others said it was our duty to serve France. I wondered how taking a little village in Belgium is going to keep France safe, but the generals must have their reasons.

We were given our orders and words of encouragement just before the command to "avancer". No one listened to much the officers said because anything other than "advance" really didn't matter. We knew most of us were going to die as soon as we stepped out from the grove of trees we were in. And that's what happened. Four or five men went before me and a machine gun killed them all right away. It was impossible for me to get past them without stepping on them. I wanted to apologize to the bodies of my friends I had just shared a cigarette with, but I didn't have time.

I and a few others got into the mud just beyond the bodies and most of us were mowed down by the same machine gun fire like so much wheat being harvested. That's where I got it. A bullet went through a man in front of me. It must have hit the stock of my rifle and ricocheted into my leg. I fell into some muddy water and someone fell on top of me. No one could help me without getting shot, and I laid there all day which seemed like an eternity. The water became more and more bloody from the bodies laying about, including mine. How I wished I was back feeding the chickens because what a terrible mess I was in now. There was a dead body on top of me that kept pressing me deeper into the water. I had to keep my head raised or I would have drowned, my leg was all shot up, and there were a thousand Germans trying to kill me, my leg hurt terribly, but at times I couldn't help laughing. If I had only held my rifle at just a slightly different angle the ricochet would have missed me. If the man ahead had only been a few

[270]

inches to the right I would be dead. I didn't care which had happened, just not this.

From my vantage point I could see the advance was a total failure. No French soldier got to within fifty meters of a building. Most were killed or wounded. Those that were not shot ran back into the trees.

It was dark before I pushed aside the body of the man lying on top of me and dragged myself back to the French line. During the advance I had only gotten maybe ten meters before I was shot so it didn't take long to get back to safety. Soldiers got me to the medical tent, but they couldn't do much for my leg. It was a mess from laying in the bloody, muddy water all day. They sent me to the field hospital and finally the next morning they chopped it off. Then I was sent here.

I wish I could have shot the captain who ordered us to advance. It would have saved a lot of my friends. Well, he was only following orders from the Colonel who was following the General's orders. I guess I would have had to shoot them all. It wouldn't have been as bad if the advance had mattered, but it didn't. Those men who survived the day ended up hiding behind the same trees they woke behind that morning.

***

I recall that on a warm day during June 1917 we played hooky and went to the Louvre for the day. In the afternoon we wandered down the rue de Rivoli and stopped for our daily cup of tea. We became aware of a distant, dull sound like very big trucks several blocks away but coming toward us. It kept getting louder till it began to separate into a pattern, a rhythm. We realized it was thousands of marching feet coming our way. Then suddenly we saw them. The Americans were here.

We instinctively arose and along with everyone else we moved to the side of the street to cheer the rows of young men as they marched smartly past. People in the buildings raised their windows and joined in the cheering. I looked at the soldiers' faces and knew that had Sam been alive he would have been among them. I suddenly missed him more than ever.

[271]

Tears began welling up in my eyes. They were tears of sorrow, not tears of pride.

***

That signaled a turning point in the war. But the following year was one of mixed emotions for Parisians. While the French, British, Americans, and Italians began pushing the Germans back from their trenches, and victory became inevitable, the Germans refused to give up. Their airplanes and zeppelins had dropped bombs on Paris for some time, but now explosions increased. In addition, by 1918 they had installed huge canons that shot projectiles from fifty or sixty miles away. During that forty-four day bombardment, a round would land somewhere in the city every hour and a half or so. The wait to hear the whistle of the incoming shell caused great stress and tension among its citizens. Charlotte and I became irritable toward each other for one of the few times in our relationship.

***

The war ended November 11, 1918. There was great joy in our apartment when Charlotte's brother, Maurice, came home, just as there had been great sadness when Marie Gravois received the letter saying her son, Vincent, had been killed. While some people danced in the streets to celebrate the end of the war, others cried when they counted up the deaths and destruction endured by the country over the past four years. All in all, France was a country of ambivalence.

***

The rejoicing was muted because people all over the world were engaged in a battle with yet another enemy. People called it the Spanish Flu, the Great Flu, the grippe, the War Plague, and half a dozen other names. Early in 1918 Charlotte saw it in the hospital when soldiers started being admitted with a racking cough, labored breathing, and a

[272]

rasping sound from the lungs. Its progress was very rapid, often soldiers came down with it one day and died the next. While many recovered, over fifty men a week died in her hospital alone. Yet the government refused to admit the seriousness of the disease. Thus, it didn't take long for it to spread to the general population. There were so many deaths in Paris that burials were conducted throughout much of the night.

Charlotte caught it from the first soldiers to come into the hospital early in the spring. I caught it from her. We were two very unhappy women for about two weeks although it seemed longer than that. We were lucky because people who caught it later were much worse off. By the middle of 1919 the flu disappeared for the most part, although I heard of people getting it for some time.

***

During this time Paris was a city of contrasts for me. The war had shredded many French families, the economy was ruined, a way of life was gone. Yet when I walked through the city the trees in the parks looked the same, the trains once again ran on schedule, children played in the streets again. I kept asking myself, which is the real Paris? This quandary formed the basis for *Ici et Lè*, "Here and There", a love story set in Paris during and after the war. It sold pretty well.

The quiet, hidden Montmartre remained much the same during this time, except most of the artists who made it their home for thirty years now moved to the cheaper area of Paris called the Left Bank. It was a little sad to see Picasso's workshop standing empty and the cafés that previously held nightly debates and revelry return to being just quiet little coffee shops. Still, our apartment was on a side street part way up the mountain where little change took place. Early on we did talk at length about moving, but we decided we were happy where we were. So, our little apartment became an island where Charlotte could practice her cello and I could write in solitude late into the night.

[273]

Chapter Twenty-Seven

In the late 1920s and early 1930s the anti-Semitic platform of Adolf Hitler was gaining influence in Germany. As the despicable acts of his followers became more outrageous, they were reflected in the increased activity in France and other European countries as well.

While there had been a reappearance of antisemitism in France since the end of World War I, it had been restricted to the sentiments and attitudes of a minority of the population. Now acts of violence began to occur. Demonstrations, vandalism, and physical attacks took place, not only in Paris, but throughout all of France. The whole situation frightened French Jews including Charlotte's family. The lack of any action by the French government only added to Charlotte's concern.

By late 1937 it was apparent to anyone who lived through the Great War that the situation was only getting worse. Another war was coming, and neither Charlotte nor I wanted anything to do with it. We knew we would have to leave France before something terrible happened. Her family agreed, and together we all quietly started to pack our most important belongings and sell the rest.

The two of us debated where our destination should be. We were both familiar with England. The Levy family was able to move there, at least for a while, and we both knew people who would help us get settled. If war did come however, England would be in the thick of it, and who knew what challenges the country was going to face. The alternative was the United States. Because I had been away for forty-eight years, there were only a few people I knew. It would be a new country for both of us. However, we both felt it would be safest there.

In September, Charlotte and I visited our friends and our favorite spots to say good-bye. It was hard because we both loved Paris and its people. It had been my home since that trip to see the World's Fair long ago, and I wanted to make it my home for the rest of my life. I think I kept the hope of returning alive in my heart, but in my mind, I knew it was probably an impossibility. The world Charlotte and I lived in for all those years was being shattered and swept away. Our seemingly peaceful, gentle way of life was quickly becoming a memory locked away in the past. It could not be revisited by me any more than could my times in Milwaukee. The best hope for us was to start a new life that hopefully had some of the same feel to it.

Once in England, Charlotte and I stayed a month with her family helping them get settled in their new country. Then we booked passage for the United States. We landed in New York, and surprisingly, were met by none other than Mabel Dodge. It was Mabel Dodge Luhan by now. I had written to her a month before explaining that we were emigrating and would appreciate any help in finding an apartment. I had not expected her to greet us, and it was even more of a surprise when she insisted that we stay at her house in Greenwich Village till we found something.

Mabel had a reputation for taking charge of a situation, and she lived up to her billing. She demanded we stay in her house for several weeks. After the second week I began to feel like Mabel's pet.

Charlotte and I agreed we needed to take matters into our own hands. On a Monday we pretended we wanted to get some fresh air. We liked the feel of Greenwich Village and wanted to stay in the area. It had no skyscrapers to interfere with the sun, and its architecture reminded us a little of Montmartre. We looked at three or four places and then found one on Bethune St.

It was a four-room apartment on the third floor, plenty big enough for the two of us. It was very well kept with the superintendent on location.

[275]

I saw a notice advertising the local newspaper's need for a part-time editor. With my background as an "internationally known reporter" at the Herald and a published author besides, I had little trouble getting the position. This and Charlotte's modest inheritance from her grandparents allowed us to rent the apartment.

***

Because of the damage to her hands during World War One, Charlotte found it difficult to become accepted as part of the classical music culture of New York. As a result, she began volunteering to teach cello at the nearby Greenwich Music School. Several times a week she would meet with groups of youngsters and some adults to give free lessons. These were not trained musicians. Instead, they wanted to learn to play an instrument for their own well-being. Eventually Charlotte began giving individual lessons much like Mother had done long ago in Milwaukee.

After we had been in the apartment a couple of months Charlotte also began attending synagogue more frequently than she had in France. She said she was missing her family and friends, and she enjoyed being around other Jews even though most of them were German. In addition, the news from Germany was frightening. She asked me if I would mind if she celebrated *Shabbat* occasionally to which I replied "Of course not. I'd like to participate if I'm allowed."

***

Since moving back to the United States I found myself missing Sam more than usual. Little things that would normally go unnoticed reminded me of him. When I looked through the mail, sometimes I thought I saw a letter from him, but of course that wasn't possible. Every day, when the weather allowed, I would take a walk. One time I found a little vacant lot where a building was torn down. It has been empty for some time because weeds were growing. I liked to walk by there because it reminded me of Sam. When I did pass by, I

[276]

always hoped to see a young boy studying the flowers, insects, or pebbles. I never did.

After dwelling on it for quite a while I decided after all these years I had to bring some sort of closure to Sam's death. It had always bothered me that I had had no contact with Lola after his death except for those few letters in the months immediately following. Then there was an extended period of silence. There was the package containing most of Sam's journals and her last letter saying she had remarried and moved to Santa Fe. I never heard from her again.

I also wanted to find Sam's grave, that was for sure. But I wanted to find Lola too. She was my only link with Sam, and I wanted to reestablish our friendship with her. We could visit in person and afterwards exchange letters. Together with Charlotte, she could be the family I missed all those many years.

During this time Mabel Dodge divided her year between New York City and the village of Taos, New Mexico. In the spring she would pack up and make the trip west to her home in the Sangre de Cristo Mountains near the old Taos Pueblo. Then when the weather started to get cold, she would pack her things and move back to her home in Greenwich Village.

Soon after we got settled, she began inviting us to Taos for a visit. She was quite insistent in her persuasive manner. Charlotte had no interest in going out to the wilds. Besides, she felt she was obligated to meet with her students. However, I saw it as an opportunity to visit Santa Fe and Sam's hometown of Las Vegas which are close to Taos. Such a trip would give me the chance to complete my plan. For the first few years, finances kept me from accepting her invitation, but in 1940 I felt I could make the trip.

***

On the train I reread Sam's journal entries about his impression of the same trip forty-four years before. The train was very different, but the landscape had not changed. After a bus trip from the train stop at Lamy to Taos I managed to find

[277]

Mabel's house. The first week was nonstop entertaining and visiting. I must have been introduced to every artist, writer, and musician in northern New Mexico. The following week was the one I had been looking forward to although of course I didn't say that to Mabel. She lent me a car along and driver who knew the area and spoke both English and Spanish. Rather than drive back and forth to Taos, the driver and I stayed at a hotel in Las Vegas.

My first stop was the New Mexico Normal School or New Mexico Normal University as it was now called. The college librarian sent me to Alfonzo Chavez. He was a jeweler, and the self-appointed town historian. "If anyone would know about your brother, he would." I found him in the phone book, called and asked to visit with him.

A cheerful voice replied, "Of course, come now if you would like. I am never too busy to talk history. Come down to the Chavez Jewelry store on Bridge Street. You cannot miss it because there is a big clock on the front."

Alfonzo was a short, rotund, balding man with wire-rimmed glasses and a dark apron. "I am sorry, I do not personally remember your brother. I was only a little child then. Anglos come and go. Unless they own a business or shoot someone, we don't keep track of them." He checked the cemetery records with no success.

This concerned me. "I want to find his grave. It is important to me. Where else could he be buried?"

"I am sorry, that is hard to say. He could be anywhere. Here in the west people do not go by the same rules as you in the east. Are you able to tell me anything about him? Where did he live?"

"He lived east of town within walking distance. He was married to a local girl named Lola Velez."

"I do not remember her name either." He checked the cemetery records and found nothing. "There is only one road going east of town, but there are no houses within easy walking distance. A couple of ranches, but no houses. I have walked that whole area many times. There was an old cabin just beyond the cut, but it burned many years ago."

[278]

"I remember he mentioned a cut when some prisoners worked on it. Maybe that's his house."

"I will be happy to take you there if you would like."

"Well, I'm only here today."

"Then let us go now. Business is slow, and I have nothing to do. Come."

We drove the short distance to the cut and parked the car. He led the way to the top of a low hill where we quickly found the rock foundation and a few burned remnants of a small wooden house, along with the melted walls of a small adobe building close by.

I wandered around trying to prod my memory for his descriptions. "Do you know why it burned," I asked?

"Probably squatters. They find an empty house, but they are careless. They start a fire to keep warm and then get drunk."

"I think this is his place. Now I'm beginning to remember things he wrote about. He said there were some nice people living over the next hill."

"That was probably Modesto and Consuelo Diaz. They are both gone of course, but their grandson Tomas Rodate runs the ranch now. Let us go and talk to him. Maybe he knows something."

***

It was just a short drive down the road. A house, two barns, a garage, some horses in a corral with a few more in the field beyond, and a big tree off to the side made up the ranch. Alfonzo introduced me and explained what I was after.

"Of course, I remember your brother. He was a good man. He is buried over there under the cottonwood along with my parents, aunt and uncles."

I cried out, "What!"

"Yes. Come, I'll show you."

Three rows of graves were carefully placed in the shade of the huge tree. Cobblestones outlined the graves, and all were surrounded with a small black wooden fence. Each had a neat white cross at its head with a name painted on it. The first

[279]

row had two crosses with the names "Modesto Soto y Diaz", and "Consuelo de la Rosa". The second row had four names I didn't recognize, children of Modesto and Consuelo no doubt. The first cross in the third row was the one I was looking for, "Samuel Jeppe." I had been looking for his grave, still I felt a wave of sadness when I saw it. His name carefully painted on a cross was final, nothing could change it. No Ghost of Christmas Future was going to give Sam a second chance. I stared at it for a long time. Then I happened to glance at the grave next to it and gasped. On that cross was painted "Lola Velez Jeppe." I started to quietly cry. The two men quietly, quickly withdrew back to the barn.

I had prepared myself to find Sam's grave. I wanted to find his grave. But when I saw Lola's name my selfish side came to the surface, I felt deflated, cheated, because my hopes of meeting her were utterly destroyed. Now I would have no chance to know her. I had looked forward to becoming reacquainted with her after all these years. She was to be the sister I never had. Now all that was snatched from me, and in its place was a simple wooden cross.

I remember staring first at one cross and then the other. I didn't know what I should do now. I looked around for some help, but I was utterly alone. The men had gone somewhere. The two horses in the pasture beyond were ignoring me. I looked at the rolling, fractured landscape surrounding the ranch. The sky, the rocks, and the plants didn't even know I was there. I realized those things had not even noticed the forty years since Sam, Lola, and little Francis had walked here.

Suddenly, I felt like an intruder, a trespasser. I had no business being here. The boy to whom I had said good-bye so long ago in Milwaukee had been transformed. He had become someone else. Somewhere there must have been an empty cocoon from which this man had emerged. Then he migrated all the way here to live out his life.

Now both Sam and Lola had transformed again. No longer did they have any interest in me or my time. Their spirits belonged to this ageless land, and I was only disturbing them. I took some quick snapshots for no particular reason, turned, and hurried back to the barn.

[280]

Once back in the present my reporter instinct clicked in. Tomas got me a glass of cold water while I composed myself.

I looked at him. "Can you tell me why Sam and Lola are here? I'm sorry, I don't mean to say they shouldn't be, but..."

"I understand," he said. "Lola knew how much Sam liked being away from town. She said he would never rest if he was buried among a bunch of strangers. So, she asked my grandparents if he could stay here. Of course, they said they would be proud to care for him. Before Lola died, she asked to be close to him. They brought her back to take her rightful place.

"I didn't know she had died. When did that happen?"

"It was during the flu epidemic. About 1918, I think. You will need to check with my parents, Manuel and Isabella Rodarte, to be sure."

"So many people in New Mexico died then," inserted Mr. Chavez.

Ignoring the comment, I asked, "Where do your parents live?"

"Santa Fe. I can give you their address. They will be very happy to see you, I am sure."

"Will they be able to tell me what happened to Francis?"

"You mean Francisca? She is fine. She also lives in Santa Fe. I can give you her address too, but she is usually at the store, Estrada's Dry Goods on Don Gaspar."

"I know where that is," injected Mr. Chavez. "I have gotten very nice hats there."

"Ah, sí, and at good prices too," responded Tomas.

"You seem to know all about Francis," I observed.

"She is my sister," Tomas said smiling.

I was silent. I must have had a questioning look on my face because he continued.

"After Lola died Francis came to live with mom and dad, and they adopted her. They will explain it all to you. I wish I could be there. They can tell you things I never knew, but I have much to do here.

[281]

"I won't keep you from your work, Mr. Rodarte. Thank you for showing me where Sam and Lola are. I have always wondered where he was. Now I know."

"You are welcomed to visit with him anytime."

"No, I won't be back. I got the strange feeling they are happy, and I'm only interfering. He was my brother, but that is no longer important. He belongs here."

"I know what you mean. I get the same feeling when I take care of the graves. We are not part of their world, and they are not part of ours. Let me write down my parent's address and telephone number. Oh, and Francisca's too."

Ten minutes later Mr. Chavez and I were headed back to town.

"I am happy you found what you were looking for, Miss Jeppe."

"Well, I'm not sure I found what I wanted to find, but I found answers, nonetheless. And thank you."

***

The next day I called Isabella Rodarte and explained who I was and asked to come to visit them. A couple of hours later, Angelo dropped me off.

The neat little tan stucco had large rose bushes on either side of the front door. I rang and was promptly greeted by a stout woman about my age with salt-and-pepper hair.

"Please come in, Miss Jeppe. Since you called Manuel and I have done nothing but talk about Sam and Lola. We will be happy to tell you anything you want."

For the next three hours Isabella and Manuel told me all about the events of thirty to forty years ago. My questions were merely starting points for their memories.

However, by the end of my visit I learned that, like she said in her note, Lola and Francis stayed with Modesto y Consuelo for a while. While she had a little cash, Lola had no real way to care for Francis. Isabella and Manuel learned of her trouble and suggested she move to Santa Fe and live with them till she found work. With eight mouths to feed, what are two more. Lola was adamant, she did not want to leave her

[282]

home. But in a short time, Modesto y Consuelo convinced her it was the only thing for her to do.

Once in Santa Fe, Lola got a part time job and began painting again. She persuaded a small art gallery to hang some of her work, and it sold fairly well. From time to time a man by the name of Barrett Davidson would buy a piece. He was a well-to-do lawyer in town known to be active in politics.

A year after Sam died, Davidson made contact with her. Romance was the last thing on Lola's mind. As it turned out it wasn't on Davidson's either. He was aiming to be elected governor of the territory and he needed a wife who could relate to the Hispanic community. He was very self-assured, sophisticated, and he was not used to being rejected. He said Francis would be well taken care of, and as the daughter of a governor many doors would be open to her. At first Lola refused the idea, but after a while she decided she wanted Sam's daughter to have every chance to succeed. After a year Lola accepted his proposal of marriage. Soon after the ceremony he insisted Francis's last name be changed to Davidson. After that he said Lola could not paint anymore because it was not socially acceptable. She had to act her role.

During the summer months Lola would occasionally return to the cabin in Las Vegas for a few weeks. To Davidson she claimed it was to regain her strength from the active social life he forced on her. But those who knew her understood she was not happy and used the time to commune with Sam. A few years later the cabin suspiciously burned. Most people thought squatters had broken in, gotten drunk and accidentally started the fire. But Modesto y Consuelo were sure the fire had been set on purpose. Lola lost all the things she had left at the cabin when she moved to Santa Fe. She never went back to Las Vegas after that.

In due time Lola had another child, Cavanaugh Barrett Davidson. It was immediately apparent Cavanaugh was the pride of his father's eye, while Francis held no place of importance. There were frequent arguments between Davidson and Lola about anything that might give her some freedom. Things reached a climax when he went through her belongings and found Sam's scientific papers, and my letters to

[283]

Sam which Davidson burned. Lola was lucky to save most of Sam's journals which she mailed to me in 1903.

Shortly after that Lola moved out of the Davidson house taking Francis and Cavanaugh with her. Davidson took her to court to gain custody of Cavanaugh after which he filed for divorce in 1905. Shortly after that Davidson was accused of fraud and left the territory never to be heard of again.

Once again Lola and Francis moved into the Rodarte home. Her brief absence from the art scene was not enough to damage her growing reputation. Art was beginning to be an important part of Santa Fe society. Because well-known painters were starting to settle in both Santa Fe and Taos, it was a good time for art sales. While not a large amount, the money from her art gave her enough of an income to allow her to buy a small house near Rodarte's.

Lola never remarried. She remained in her little house with Francis. In 1918 she came down with the Spanish flu. Francis cared for her as best she could, but Lola died within three days.

After her mother's death, Francis moved in with the Rodarte's. She began using the Rodarte last name because she hated the Davidson name. After a while everyone agreed that Isabella and Manuel should legally adopt her. She took the name Francisca Maria Rodarte thus dropping all reference to her Anglo heritage.

Francisca was a strikingly beautiful, and intelligent young lady. She was much sought after by the young men of Santa Fe, but she was in no hurry to be married. She was an excellent seamstress, but her real talent came in playing the guitar. She was a member of a mariachi group. In her traditionally braided, black hair, Mexican bolero jacket and matching floor length skirt, she was not only the principal guitarist, but also sang solos and duets. The group was always featured in fiestas. There was some talk of them turning professional, but Francis would have nothing to do with that. She played merely for the joy of performing for her community.

In 1923 she married Antonio Estrada. They had been courting for a number of years, but she would not consent to

[284]

his proposal until his dry goods store was well established. The next year, a son, Samuél, was born. When the depression hit, Francis began sewing traditional fiesta wear for sale in the store. In 1925 their daughter, Maria,was born. Another son, Carlos, was born in 1927, a daughter, Isabella in 1928, a third daughter, Gabriel, in 1931. The store survived the depression and became a mainstay for the Hispanic community.

***

After a light lunch, photos, and a tearful good-bye, Angelo drove me to Estrada's Dry Goods store. Isabella offered to call the store to tell Francisca I was coming, but I asked her not to. If, for some reason she did not want to see me, I could at least see Francisca for a few minutes. When I entered the store there were a few customers one of whom was talking to beautiful middle-aged woman behind the counter. When she noticed me, she smiled thus telling me I was in line to be helped. I walked around the large sales area looking at clothing, but keeping an eye on Francisca. She worked her way through the customers in a professional, yet friendly way till I was the last one in the store.

She came over apologizing. "I'm sorry it took so long. Usually it's not this busy, but there is a fiesta coming up and everyone wants something new. How may I help you?"

"I flashed a friendly smile and asked, "Are you Francisca Estrada?"

A look of concern crossed her face. "Yes, how may I help you?"

"Francisca, I am your Aunt Jeppe."

"What?"

"Samuel Jeppe, your father, was my brother."

"Aunt Catherine?"

"You know who I am?" I said in complete surprise.

"Are you really Aunt Catherine?

"Yes!"

"My mother talked about you many times. You live in Paris and write books."

[285]

"I did live in Paris, but I moved back the United States just recently. How did you know about my books?"

"I've read them all, or most of them." Tears began running down her cheeks. She was almost jumping up and down in excitement. Her tears were contagious, and I started tearing up as well. "Aunt Catherine, I can't believe you are standing here. I wanted to write to you, but I never knew how to reach you. How did you find me? I can't believe you are here."

We hugged, and laughed, and cried, and hugged some more.

"Your brother in Las Vegas told me where to find you and Isabella and Manuel. I moved to New York City, and I had to find you."

"You've been to the ranch, and talked to Tomas? You know about Isabella and Manuel?"

"I've been talking to them for several hours, and they told me all about you."

"Then you know about mother."

"Yes, I am sorry. I was looking forward to visiting with her."

"She would have loved that. She talked about you ever since I can remember. She said you were famous, and she was so proud to be your sister-in-law." She wiped her eyes and dried her tears. "Oh, I apologize, I want you to meet my husband. Antonio." Turning toward a back room, she called out, "Antonio, come here."

A distinguished looking man with a square face, and graying mustache quickly came out of the backroom. He wore a red plaid shirt, bluejeans, and cowboy boots. He glanced around the room looking for customers. Seeing none he then walked over to us.

"Aunt Catherine, I'd like you to meet my husband, Antonio Estrada. Antonio, this is my Aunt Catherine, Papi's sister. She is the one who lived in Paris, but now she lives in New York City. Remember, she is the one I told you about who writes those wonderful books."

"Yes, of course. My goodness. It is my pleasure Aunt Catherine. What a wonderful surprise."

[286]

"She came to find me. Can you believe it? All that way, just to find me."

He gently placed an arm around her waist. "Francisca, you can't waste the time you have standing around in the store. I can watch it. Go home where you can be comfortable and visit all you want. Don't worry about dinner, I'll bring something."

"Yes, let's do that," Francisca said. Turning to me she said, "there is so much I want to ask you about Papi. And I also have something to show you. Have you had lunch?"

"Yes, but I can always have a cup of tea. Before we leave, I want to ask about those two paintings above the counter. Did your mother paint those?"

"Yes, she told me she gave them to Papi before they were married. They used to hang in their house in Las Vegas. She kept them with her wherever she moved. She said they always reminded her of him. After mother died, I brought them here."

"They are wonderful."

We walked to their home four blocks away. As soon as we entered the two-story stucco, Francisca took my arm and lead me over to a picture of two children and their mother in a grassy field.

"Mom made sure I knew who gave me this. It is special to me. In my mind I have played in that field for years and years. Thank you so much."

"Honestly, I had forgotten about it. You are more than welcome. I recall now when we picked it we hoped it would speak to you. It goes very nicely where you have placed it."

The rest of the afternoon and much of the next day we spent talking and sharing our memories. I met her five wonderful children. The seed for this book was planted during that time.

Since that trip, Francisca and I have kept in close contact through our letters and occasional phone calls. She isn't the sister I longed for, but a loving niece instead. Two years ago, she and two of her children traveled to New York City to spend some time with me. It is wonderful to have a

[287]

family again after all those years. One sad note, in 1945 Tomas Rodarte, a corporal in Patton's Third Army, was killed during a counterattack in the Battle of the Bulge. His brother, Santiago, runs the ranch now.

***

I have lost track of many of the people Sam knew. I do know that Ambrose Arbuthnott was elected to Parliament sometime back. I think Eli Redding became a successful architect. A few years ago, I heard Cora Loomis died, but the others have gone their various ways be they happy or sad.

I am an old woman now. It has been forty-five years since Sam died. I can't believe the time has passed so quickly. This book is my last effort, and frankly, I look forward to relaxing in my rocking chair in the sunny front room which is so much like the one back in Milwaukee. I will sit, and rock, and think about the past.

My memories are about all that I have because neither Sam, nor I have made any lasting contributions to humanity. Already my work is largely forgotten, and his testimonials are some reports that geologists and archaeologists no longer read. But a life is not measured only by its prominence. As with an alcoholic in Wisconsin, a lost soul sitting on apartment steps in Milwaukee, a malcontent selling flowers in Paris, a tormented Chinese family in Chicago, a philosopher running a small restaurant in New Mexico, and many others, our lives have been only as important as those of butterflies passing by on a summer breeze, and that's all right because really, can you ask for more.

Afterword

Catherine Jeppe finished this book in 1948, but it was never published. She died two years later. Her lifelong friend

[288]

and companion, Charlotte Levy sent the manuscript to my grandmother Francisca. It has remained in our family for these many years and has been passed from one generation to the next so everyone could learn about all these uncelebrated, yet exceptional people.

Dr. Michael Estrada
Denver, Colorado
2020